Published by Arrangement with J. C. Phelps

First Printing, August, 2004

NEWPUB Books are published by
Phelps Publishing
16202 Spring Valley Road, Piedmont, South Dakota, 57769
ISBN 978-0-9817690-0-4

For:
Alexandra
Edy
Jim
Rick
Robert
&
Robert

Special thanks to:
Lynn
Rachel
Robert

Chapter One

My name is Alexis Stanton, but I always introduce myself as Alex.
Most everyone calls me Lexi though. I always thought Lexi sounded like a silly
girl's name. Lexi just doesn't reflect my personality. I can be silly, but
generally I'm pretty serious.

I can get silly when I'm with my childhood friend, Colin. He's a few
years older than me but we grew up together. Our dads worked together in the
service and we spent quite a lot of time at each other's houses.

My dad is pretty picky about who I associate with. One of his favorite
sayings is, "You are who you run with." I didn't understand that until I got out
of the house and started college. Then I started to run with the wrong crowd. I
eventually started the party thing and got myself a boyfriend; my very first
boyfriend at twenty, pretty sad, but the truth.

I didn't just get any boyfriend; I got one of *those* boyfriends. You
know the kind. I was in love with him and so was he, in love with himself. His
name was Anthony. That's a different story though.

My parents have money and could have paid for any type of education I
wanted. I was home schooled and then, of course, I attended college. College
was my only formal education. At first I worked hard and did great. Then I got
involved with the wrong crowd. Eventually my brains returned. I dumped my
boyfriend and managed to graduate at the top of my class and can pretty much
do anything with a computer.

Going from home schooling to college was fairly difficult. It wasn't
that it was too much work, it wasn't enough and I didn't know my way around
people. I had too much time on my hands and didn't know how to make friends.
I was usually found with a bong in one hand and alcohol of some kind in the
other trying to be accepted.

When I was little I used to ask my mom and dad why I couldn't go to
school with the rest of the kids. Dad would say, "Most of the teachers out there
aren't as smart as you. You can't learn much from a dumb teacher." I found
that he was pretty much right.

My education started at a very early age. I think I was three when Mom and
Dad brought in my first teacher/nanny. Consequently, I could read and write at
the age of three and a half. I think I went through two grades a year until I
reached nine. Then at nine I was somewhat allowed to choose what I wanted to

Color Me Grey

learn. The subjects I picked were like extra curricular activities to my parents. I would pick karate and Mom would pick literature and Dad would pick history and I would have to continue to do well in the subjects they chose or they would make me stop the one I had chosen until I started doing well again. I always wanted to try something new, so I was always busy with learning one thing or another.

I grew up wanting to be a boy, so I chose boy pursuits. I wanted to be strong. I wanted to be a part of the A-Team. I wanted to learn self-defense, karate, rock climbing, and mechanics, that kind of thing.

Thanks to Mom and Dad and their money, I tried my hand at many things. Mom didn't want me to be such a tomboy so she made me take etiquette classes. But Dad liked the idea that I wanted to be tough so he paid to have a Special Forces drill instructor teach me to infiltrate and take over a small country. I've been schooled in everything from how to be a lady to the basics of dressing a wound with some covert maneuvers and chef skills sprinkled over the whole education casserole.

I've since decided that being a boy instead of a girl has it's advantages, but being a woman is *much* better than being a man. I actually like the way I look and as far as I can tell, so do most men. I'm 5'4", fairly petite but not breakable. My hair is a light brown, straight and long. I like it long. I can put it up if I want it out of the way or I can leave it down if I want to make an impression. I have blue eyes and pretty straight teeth.

I can do what any man can do for the most part. Of course I'm not as strong as I'd like to be but I know tricks that make me seem stronger. I've never been in any real trouble in my life because I don't get caught. Then again, I don't do bad things often either, unless provoked.

When a girl turns twenty-one she must celebrate for at least a year or so. I did my share of celebrating and found that I don't like to get stupid. I can still hold my own when I'm drunk, but I can't seem to keep myself out of trouble. If I drink vodka, gin or rum I either get much too talkative or turn into a blubbering baby. If I drink bourbon I get nasty and mean. Beer and wine make me that silly, giggly girl I don't want to be so, I stick with the whiskey. The only problem with the whiskey is that it makes me feel invincible and that's what gets me into trouble. I've always been the type of person to speak my mind when it's necessary, but give me whiskey and I speak my mind despite necessity. Many people get offended when you tell them what you really think of them and some of them take action.

Mom and Dad live on an eighty-acre estate and I'm lucky enough to have their love and support in whatever I choose to do. I live in the guesthouse rent-free. It has it's own private drive for my puke green 1967 Mustang. I love that car. I bought it with my own money a few years ago and have been able to hang onto it and keep it in pretty good shape.

J.C. Phelps

I was doing all right with a career in computers but compared to my younger years, there just wasn't any excitement. For a few years now I had not been enrolled in any of Mom or Dad's educational experiences, no sky diving lessons, and too much time on my hands. I decided today would be a good day to look for a different job. Hopefully I could find some adventure.

I picked up my phone, called in to my job and quit. I knew it was irresponsible, but it felt so good. If I couldn't find a new job I would go to Mommy and Daddy and ask for some money to set up some private classes for something more interesting. I could always learn to fly a plane or helicopter.

I walked the mile or so to the local convenience store and got a paper. On the same block was a really nice coffee shop called Express Espresso. I went there often to read. Reading is a habit of mine, not a hobby but a habit. It seems I just can't get enough. I will read anything.

I got myself an espresso with cream and sugar. I like the kick but black espressos are a little too strong for my tastes. Every once in a while I feel like being rough and tough and drink a straight espresso, but mostly I chose coffee with French vanilla creamer. Today, I felt kind of tough, but not quite 'Ramboish'.

There was an empty table in the back of the store. I sat with my back to the wall so I could see what was going on around me and see who came in the door. This also was a habit of mine. I was taught well by my private drill instructor. Not that I really needed that training with being a data processor and on the computer everyday. It was just ingrained in me from my several years of having Chief Slade screaming at me and also because I practiced being a spy often.

Dad had hired Chief Slade to teach me self-defense as well as covert ops. Dad liked the idea that someday I could be a spy if I wanted to. Heck I still don't know exactly what my dad does. All I know is that he works for the government and makes damn good money. Maybe *he's* a spy. Probably he is a spy except he doesn't go out of the country very often.

I opened the paper and took a sip of the weenie espresso. Data processor, I could do that job, but that would be the same thing I'm doing now. Waitress, been there, done that and DO NOT like it. Bartender at the Skylight.

The Skylight was a semi preppy bar downtown. I went there regularly and so did the Navy men in the area. I had some friends there, actually everybody knew me. That's where I'd received my waitress experience. I had also waited tables at a ritzy restaurant but nothing compares to being a bar wench.

I actually liked the job when I was twenty-one to twenty-three. It was great money for just working weekends, but it was the same thing every weekend. About the only time something different happened was when *I* started a fight.

Fighting isn't my nature, but being fondled by drunken men is not appealing to me either. The guys would get plenty of warnings before I decked them. That caused me a bit of trouble with some of the women too. It seems some of them didn't like their boyfriends being taken down by a girl. I would have to

Color Me Grey

4

explain to them they should be mad at the man for not keeping his hands to himself. The first time I tried to explain the situation to a girlfriend she would hear none of it. I felt bad for her, but I had to defend myself. That kind of thing hardly ever happens now though. I decided to keep looking for another job. Going back to the Skylight was not an option.

The next few ads below the 'Bartender at the Skylight' were restaurant and bar related so I skipped them and the next ad was listed in bold ink:

Person wanted with specialized training.
Exciting and highly paid position.
Inquire at 1324 Plaza Dr. Suite 73
Monday through Saturday

What was this? It sounded interesting. Now, I'm pretty cocky and arrogant, in case you haven't figured that out by now, so I thought I would try it out. Just to see what the heck it was all about. It was probably a listing for a cruise ship attendant. That could be a fun job.

I sat skimming the paper and sipping my espresso for another twenty minutes. I watched people come in, order their coffee and either leave or sit to enjoy the few minutes of leisure time they afforded themselves.

I would usually walk away with some great gossip, but then I would feel so guilty about eavesdropping that I couldn't bring myself to tell anyone. I usually knew a lot about the people in the neighborhood just because I went to the coffee shop and sat for a while each weekend and sometimes in the evening during the week.

The gossip was different depending on the time of day. In the morning you would hear about what the wives had been doing in the area. Noontime was a combination of housewife banter and working stiffs talking about the job, bosses and co-workers. The evening was a lot of teenage type of gossip, which was by far the juiciest and not always about teenagers. That's where I got most of my information about the people in my neighborhood.

I always knew quite a few people when I walked in but, because I rarely went in without a book or something else to read, I was usually left to my own devices. Every once in a while someone would invade my space. If I'm truly reading, prepare to feel my wrath but, if I'm just eavesdropping, I don't usually get that upset with the distraction. I've never really been that much of a talker, so people rarely tried to chat with me anyway. About the only time someone tried to converse with me was when they had an argument about which planet was closest to the sun or who was the sixteenth president. I could always give them the answer.

Today most everybody was involved in home-related talk and not involved in any deep discussions about the surface of Mars or the existence of black

J.C. Phelps

holes. Nobody bothered me the entire time I was there. They must have been able to tell I was seriously contemplating something. This job offer in the paper had me intrigued. I got up, dropped my Styrofoam cup into the garbage can and out the door I went. I jogged home so I could get downtown before lunch time and check out this job.

Chapter Two

I pulled into the parking garage of 1324 Plaza Dr., paid my fee and found a spot right away. I had changed clothes before I left my house and was wearing something appropriate for a job interview. Nice skirt, nice shirt and heels. I had pulled my hair back away from my face with a large barrette. I wanted the out-of-the-way look, but still wanted to leave the length.

I had never been in this building before and had been missing out! The floor in the lobby was black and so shiny I was afraid people might see up my skirt. I went to the main desk and asked for Suite 73. I was pointed to the elevator and told to get off at the seventh floor and take a left.

"There are only three suites on that floor so you shouldn't have much trouble finding the right one," Mr. Rent-a-Cop told me.

I did as I was told and sure enough, there was Suite 73 right in front of me. I stood outside the door for a second. There were no windows or even a sign to state what kind of office this was so I wasn't sure if I should just walk in or knock. I opted for the just-walk-in approach. This had to be a business, they were asking for applicants.

I swung the door open slowly and walked in to see a woman with blonde hair about twice my age sitting at a desk. On the name tag sitting in front of her it read Gabriella. She was on the phone and nodded in my direction to let me know she had seen me. I looked around and saw the front office was quite small. There were some filing cabinets in the corner, the main desk with Gabriella sitting at it and no windows. There was nothing to tell me what kind of business this was. There were chairs to sit in and I was on my way to one of them when I saw *him*.

I stopped breathing. Now that's a man I thought! He was about 6' 3" and just perfect. A body that wouldn't quit, short dark hair, but I couldn't see his face. His office door was open and he was standing at the window looking down at the world and talking quietly on the phone. He was wearing a tight army green t-shirt, slightly faded jeans and motorcycle boots. Strange, this building and this office just screamed suit and tie. I stared at him for a full thirty seconds before I caught myself. That wasn't like me. I'm good at being sneaky, but something about this man made me lose it.

"Can I help you?" the woman at the desk asked with a smile in her voice. She had obviously seen my mouth open. I quickly composed myself and answered her.

"Yes. I'm here to apply for the job listed in the paper."

She looked taken aback by what I said and made me wonder even more at what kind of job I was going to apply for.

"All right, please take a seat and I'll get the paperwork together for you." She stood and started toward the filing cabinets.

I headed toward a seat that had a view. I couldn't help myself; it was like looking at a train wreck but in a good way. I had never in my life seen a man that affected me the way he did just by his appearance and the way he held himself. He was away from the windows now and looking into the front office at me. He looked to be a few years older than myself putting him still under thirty but over twenty-five. His complexion was darker than the average white guy, but his features were hard to place. He most definitely wasn't Oriental or black. He didn't look to be Hispanic and he was definitely not the type you would easily forget. Dark eyes from where I was sitting, but he wasn't close enough for me to get all the little details. He had a trendy design of facial hair. His sideburns were long and angling over his jaw, but not the fluffy, thick kind of sideburns. His were nicely and neatly trimmed into a thin line just along the jawbone. How interesting.

While I was ogling what I assumed to be her boss, Gabriella came to me with the paperwork and asked, "Do you know what kind of job we are offering?"

I looked her straight in the eye and said, "No. I just saw it in the paper and thought it sounded interesting. I don't know if I have the qualifications but I thought I might check it out. I'm recently unemployed."

She smiled softly and gave me the eyes that said she was sorry but was sure I wouldn't be able to do the job they were offering.

"We don't usually hire women for a job of this type. I couldn't begin to explain everything that would be required of you, so if you wouldn't mind filling out the paperwork I can see if I can get you in with Mr. White. He will be able to explain better." She passed the application form, and about thirty other sheets of paper that were filled front and back with questions, over to me.

As she walked back to her desk, she said over her shoulder, "If at any time while filling out the paperwork you feel you won't be qualified for the position don't feel obligated to stay." She sat down at her desk and said, "Mr. White is quite busy and the only position he's hiring for at the moment is the one you are applying for; we'll keep your application on file for six months in case there are any future jobs that you may qualify for."

"Sure, thank you," I said and began to fill out the application. It was a normal application asking for past work history, education and such. I had it filled out in less than two minutes and Mr. White was still on the phone but had

Color Me Grey

looked in my direction more than once. I hadn't looked up from the application but I have quite good peripheral vision and saw him turn toward the door a couple times.

I got to the rest of the paper work and was a bit shocked at the questions. They were questions like, "Do you think it's what you know or who you know?" The type of questions that are meant to figure out your personality. I didn't know what they were looking for so I wasn't sure as how to fill out the questionnaire, so I just told the truth. I answered that I thought it was both, so on and so forth.

The next batch of questions was all of a military nature. "How long would it take you to field strip an M-16?" "How would you take control of a small country?" That kind of thing. What kind of job was this? I answered all those questions too. This was becoming more and more interesting. I might like this job, if I got it. It seemed to me that they were a little against the woman being in this work environment though.

I will admit, not too many women had the military training that I had without actually going into a branch of the military. They definitely wouldn't be out yet at my age and have the training completed. Well heck, I'll admit it; probably *no* other woman had the training that I did. This job might be just what I was searching for.

I was beginning to wonder what kind of company this was. I had been curious before I reached the office building, but everything from the marble floors to the man in the other room had piqued my interest immensely.

Within fifteen minutes I had filled out the entire batch of paper work and walked up to Gabriella to give it to her.

She stopped typing on her computer, reached for my application, then said, "Thank you, we will let you know if something comes up." And then went back to typing whatever it was that she was working on before I walked up to her desk.

I said, "I thought you would see if Mr. White would be available to talk to me if I filled everything out."

This got her attention and she looked through the papers to make sure I had filled out everything and left nothing blank. After about a minute she looked up at me and said, "Please take a seat. I can't believe you got it done that quickly. I'll take this in and he'll let you know if he would like to speak to you."

I felt a surge of excitement. Soon I could be sailing away on a beautiful cruise ship and getting paid for it. This could be ship security or something. I should have done something like this a long time ago. This was fun.

I went back to my seat with a view and watched Gabriella hand Mr. White the stack of papers. He was still on the phone and had put his hand over the receiver. He looked from Gabriella directly at me. I could see that he had a questioning look on his face. He told her thank you and she headed back toward her desk. I saw the mysteriously handsome man hang up the phone and look in my direction one more time as Gabriella shut the door to his office.

"He should be with you in less than half an hour. He always likes to look over the entire application before he speaks with someone," she said through a smile as she was sliding back into her chair. She had gotten over her surprise and was genuinely enjoying this. "Do you really have that kind of experience?"

"I've had training on everything listed, yes. But I've never put it to use other than playing war games with my instructor", I admitted.

"Well, I think you shocked him and I don't think I've ever seen him shocked at anything. If you get the job this is going to be great. I'd love to have another woman around. I get tired of seeing nothing but customers and men who take too many steroids."

I kind of liked Gabriella and didn't mind looking a little stupid in front of her so I came right out and asked, "What kind of business is this?"

This brought another shocked look and then a smile. "You really are something. First, you come here without even knowing what kind of a job you are applying for, then you are more than qualified and then you tell me you don't even know who it is that you'll be working for," she said as she shook her head. "We are a bit like a private investigation outfit, but we do other things as well. Recovery of people and property, surveillance, and sometimes we even break into banks, sometimes. The company name is White and Associates."

Wow! I didn't even know this place existed. I have tons of book knowledge and physical training, but when it came to the real world I was a bit sheltered. I had been kept at home most of my childhood and only had the past five years or so of being in the *real* world. College doesn't count, it's not even close to the real world unless you work your way through and I had had my way paid in full before I even stepped foot on campus. I worked at a computer all day and didn't have much of a social life so I still wasn't really in the world of the living. Not to mention I still lived at Mom and Dad's. I got some stuff off TV but other than news, how much of it are you supposed to believe? Then it sank in…

"Break into banks?" My voice was an octave higher than normal.

"Oh, sorry," she giggled. "Not to steal things, but to test the security system for the bank," she said with a large grin on her face now.

"Oh," I said regaining my normal voice. I worked my way back to my seat no longer with a view and sat down. Gabriella went back to typing with a grin and I waited.

I didn't have to wait long. Mr. White buzzed Gabriella on the intercom within five minutes and in this absolutely wonderful voice said "Gabriella, send in Ms. Stanton please." Very businesslike, but deep and smooth like butter. His voice was as good as the rest of his body. I now knew who I would fantasize about, at least until I got to know him better. Once you know a person well enough it seems like they aren't usually worth fantasizing about. I was going to

Color Me Grey

take advantage of this one before I found out he was a putz. Bosses usually turn out to be putzes.

Gabriella gave me a funny look that I couldn't decipher, almost scared but yet sympathetic and still hopeful. "Good luck." She said this with some emphasis that made me think she really wanted me to get the job.

I walked into Mr. White's office. He was in his chair facing the windows away from me, but the shades were drawn. I had all the confidence in the world. Then he turned around and I lost it. My confidence went south, right out of my toes and onto the floor in a little bubbly puddle. My brain quit working, all I could think of was how sexy he was. Get a hold of yourself I told myself. He's just a man, good looking, but just a man.

I stood there looking at him in his chair and he waited for me to sit. Finally he said, "You can take a seat."

Quit being such a dork I thought as I sat in the straight-backed chair directly in front of his desk. It seemed to me the office had changed in the short time since I had looked in on it from the front office. I didn't remember seeing any other chairs in the room and now this one was right here. The chair was ugly wood and uncomfortable without upholstery and placed just out of reach of the desk. It stood out from the rest of the décor of the office. Very unlike the rest of the room. There was a heavily cushioned black couch not far from Mr. White's desk and four other chairs in the room that matched the couch and looked very comfortable.

This reminded me of the times Chief Slade had screamed at me in a mock interrogation. Was that what this was, an interrogation, not an interview? Weird. I set my mind to be interrogated just for fun and practice. I put my small knowledge of yoga to use. I tried to slow my heartbeat and listened to myself breathe. He was just sitting there with an inquisitive look on his face directed toward me, like he expected me to say something.

Chief Slade had yelled and screamed at me that you DO NOT speak until you are spoken to. I didn't dare speak even if this wasn't an interrogation. I felt the fear that Chief Slade had told me about, but I had never felt it with him across the table. My dad was paying him so he wasn't all that scary. He might smack me a good one in the back of the head, but he would have never drawn blood or broken bones. This guy was different, he had that look. I hadn't noticed it before because I was so infatuated with his rear end and mysterious looks. But I noticed that wild look now. I could tell he wasn't just mysterious, he was dangerous. If this really was an interrogation, I was lucky that I hadn't sat before I was told to do so.

As the minutes ticked by my fear grew but my gaze didn't falter. Mr. White didn't even blink. It seemed like hours had passed. 'This is pretty strange,' I was thinking when he said, "Good. Now, Ms. Stanton, what branch of the military were you in? I didn't see it listed on your application." The dangerous look was still there but pushed a little deeper than it had been just a moment before. His eyes were still dark and boring a hole into my soul.

I was still afraid to talk but I managed to tell him, "I've never served in the military, sir."

"Where did you train at?" he asked with raised eyebrows. The dangerous look wanted to return but he kept it subdued.

"I was lucky enough to come from a family with means and I received my training at home from Chief Slade, sir," I replied.

This brought a look of surprise that was quickly suppressed. "Is that so? I served under Chief Slade myself. I didn't know he'd gone into the practice of servicing the civilian sector."

The last sentence was spoken with a hint of sarcasm and disbelief. This wasn't going too well. I got the distinct feeling he was looking at me as an enemy and not a potential employee.

"I'm sorry, sir," I said. "My father is affiliated with the Navy. That's how and why I was lucky enough to be a student of Chief Slade."

"Your father would be...?" Again with the eyebrows.

"Admiral Robert S. Stanton... sir," I replied. I hadn't been involved with my military training for some time and was a bit rusty and actually had never been perfect. Maybe this wasn't such a good idea after all.

"Admiral Robert S. Stanton? Now that's very interesting. Didn't he leave the service before he reached Admiral?"

"Yes and no, sir. I'm not sure as to his exact title, but I do know that he is and has been for some time now a commissioned Admiral, sir." What an idiot I was. I was twenty-four years old and I didn't know what my dad did. Why didn't I know? I had never really questioned it before because I had never had to explain it, I guess. As soon as I got home I was marching straight over to his house to ask him what the heck he did for the government!

"I see." He started to look through the mountain of paperwork like he understood and the fact that I didn't have a clue was explanation enough. "Have you ever been employed to work a job like this one?"

"No, sir. I don't believe so. I'm still a bit unsure as to what this job is though, sir," I repeated trying not to sound insolent.

"You will know what it is when and IF you are hired to do the job," he said in a matter of fact tone.

I nodded my head once to show that I understood. The fear was beginning to subside a bit. The dangerous look had wanted to show itself again with the mention of Chief Slade, but the mention of my father sent it deeper and that put me at ease, somewhat. Good ole' Daddy, watching out for me from everywhere.

"Thank you, Ms. Stanton," Mr. White said by way of dismissal. "I will be in touch within the week one way or the other." He gave me a small smile and my fear of him disappeared. How did he do that? He was GOOD. Definitely fantasy material.

Color Me Grey

I stood up from the chair, said thank you and walked out of his office, shutting the door behind me.

Gabriella jumped at the sound of the door shutting. The worried look still on her face.

"Wow! I thought you would have been out of there long before now."

"Why, how long was I in there?" I asked.

"An hour and a half," she said with disbelief. Then she got a sly look on her face and said, "What did you *talk* about?"

I was still in a daze with the news that it had been an hour and a half and didn't catch her implication. I said, "He just asked me about my training and my father."

"Oh, honey," she said. "I think you've been traumatized."

I took a deep breath and let it out slowly. "I'm fine. Just surprised," I said. "This is not what I expected. He said he'd be in touch within the week to let me know one way or the other." I shrugged.

"What? He will let you know one way or the other? Sweetie, you have the job. I'm almost sure of it. He never contacts people that don't already work for him. He has me do it. Either that or you made one hell of an impression."

"Yeah," I said. I was still in lah-lah land as I walked out the door and got onto the elevator. I got across the shiny marble without a thought of my panties being seen by anyone and got in my car. I was home before I knew what had happened.

What a rush. I can't remember the last time I had so much fun. Yeah, I was scared out of my mind, but it sure beat data processing! I didn't care whether or not I had a job working for scary, sexy Mr. White or not. I would find something to do. I just couldn't go back to sitting in front of the computer all day.

This called for a celebration so I took a nap with a plan of going to the coffee shop later this evening to catch up on gossip and then maybe onto the Skylight later.

Chapter Three

I woke up around 6:30 PM, a little later than I had planned. I could get something to eat at Sal's Sandwiches, next to the coffee shop when I got there. I changed my clothes into celebrating clothes. I poured myself into a pair of jeans and put on a shirt that showed cleavage. I decided I wanted to go all out so I let my hair down and curled the ends of my hair in to give it a little more volume.

7:00 PM. I could get to the club and get a good seat to watch people if I just got a sandwich and went straight to the club.

I got into my car and thought about it before I pulled out of the driveway. I might want a drink. I could call a cab while I was eating my sandwich then I could have a drink if I wanted to. Any excuse not to drive. I got out, relocked the doors and started to walk to the sandwich shop. I looked down and considered changing out of my high-heeled boots, but what was the point. You had to sacrifice to look good and I was going to sacrifice my feet tonight.

I was walking the length of the driveway and noticed a dark car parked not far from the entrance. As I got closer I could tell what kind it was. It was a black Crown Victoria with generic rims and tinted windows. I couldn't see inside but had a feeling there was someone sitting behind the wheel. Most days I might not have even noticed the car but today was strange and my senses were heightened after my interview with the peculiar Mr. White.

I decided that I was being paranoid but still picked up my pace to the sandwich shop about a mile away. Just as I thought, the car stayed put as I rounded the corner of the estate. I began to think of the day's events and my decision to quit my job. Maybe I shouldn't have quit. That wasn't a very responsible thing to do. Mom and Dad had been harping on me to be more responsible before I got the data processing job, now they were going to start up again. Oh well, maybe I would get this new job and surprise them.

The inquisition at White and Associates had worn me out and I had forgotten to walk over and ask Dad what exactly it was that he did. I had asked him before but he had never given details and I wanted details. No more, "A little of this and a little of that," and answering my questions with questions of his own.

I had walked a couple of blocks toward my destination when I spotted a black Crown Victoria parked a block away in front of me. It had tinted windows

14

and generic rims and the same license plate. The license plate was nothing special, I just notice these things from time to time without knowing that I did it.

I promptly turned around and hiked back to the guesthouse to change my shoes. I was pretty sure I was being followed but by who and why was a mystery. I had my thoughts, but they seemed unfounded. No matter how strange the interview was I didn't think they would waste time following me around. Who did that kind of thing anyway? White and Associates, that's who. That's what Gabriella said, surveillance, recovery of people and property and breaking into banks.

What had I gotten myself into? I should have just walked out. Granted, I was thoroughly enjoying myself wondering what was going on and trying to figure it out, but I still wasn't sure that constantly watching over my shoulder was the kind of life I wanted to lead.

As I was marching home I toyed with the idea of staying home for the night, but by the time I got to my door I was determined to see this through. It wasn't in my nature to back down, even if it was in my favor to do so. You know the saying, "Curiosity killed the cat." I thought of that often but I was still alive. My curiosity always prevailed over my good sense. This time was no exception. I felt I could take care of myself as long as I knew what I was dealing with.

No matter how curious I was, I was always careful. I chose to call the cab from the safety of my place instead of the open payphone at the sandwich shop or my personal cell phone.

The wait for the cab would be about fifteen minutes so I figured I'd call Sal's Sandwiches and place an order so it would be ready when I got there. I could eat it in the cab on the way to the club.

With any luck, the person in the car would follow me in there. He or she would be easy to pick out in there because I should know everyone else. New comers to the Skylight, that weren't with a regular, stuck out like a sore thumb.

I heard a honk out front so I quickly put on my running shoes and stepped out into the night. I couldn't see the end of the driveway from my front door so I didn't know if the black car was waiting for me again or not. I kept my eyes open for the few minutes it took to get to Sal's but no sign of the car. I was a bit disappointed but relieved at the same time.

There was nothing unusual at Sal's either. I paid for my turkey club and headed back for the cab waiting outside. Out of the corner of my eye I saw the black car parked in the lot up a bit from where I was standing. I got in the cab and asked the driver to take me for a ride before he dropped me off at the Skylight.

"No problem, Ms. Stanton," he said. I had obviously used this taxi service before. I suppose that's why my Mustang was still in pretty good shape. Other than back and forth to work I didn't drive often. I preferred to walk if the weather was good and my destination wasn't too far or I would call the cab company so I could pay more attention to the scenery.

I wanted to make sure the Crown Victoria was really following me and not just cruising around in the neighborhood. That happens from time to time. I live in a very nice side of town and people sometimes came just to see how the other half lived.

The Crown Victoria pulled out of the lot just as we rounded the corner of the block and headed our direction. I kept my eyes open and saw it several times, sometimes in front of us, sometimes parked in a lot that we were passing. It was almost as if there were black Crown Victoria's with the same plate all over the place.

When we finally came to rest in front of the Skylight I looked around and saw my admirer pull into a spot down the street. I paid my driver and crept out of the cab. I walked inside a little faster than I normally would have and then caught myself just inside the door. I stopped and took a deep breath, smoothed the front of my shirt and walked down the dimly lit hallway to the main area.

The Skylight had been a warehouse before it was changed to a club. The owners had added a gigantic skylight directly above the dance floor, hence the name. The building was set up almost like it was two different businesses. When you first came in the door you were confronted with the bathrooms on the opposite wall and a mediocre hallway extending about fifty feet to the main bar area. The two extremely large bathrooms took up a quarter of the building's length and most of the width. As soon as you emerged from behind the old time swinging doors at the end of the hall, you found yourself in a mix of loud people, loud music and strong drinks. They had quite a large round bar situated toward the middle of the building. The bar was surrounded by tables and then at the end of the building was the dance floor and stage that always had a live band. Along one side of the building were high-backed booths that afforded couples more privacy than they should have in a bar. Give people enough to drink and they will do a lot of things they really shouldn't do. I usually steered clear of the booths but thought tonight might be the night for me to sit there.

I quickly scanned the room. Most everyone was out tonight. There were a few new faces so I made a mental note to remember they were here before I was. I hadn't told anyone where I was going so the people already here shouldn't be looking for me.

I found myself shaking as I walked to the booths to find a suitable hiding place. This wasn't a game, this was real. If it weren't White and Associates it could be a kidnapper. My parents did have money after all and were well-known for spending tons of it on me, their one and only child.

I was grateful for my training; otherwise I may never have noticed what was happening. At the same time, my training had never really prepared me for the possibility that I might truly need it someday. Of course I fantasized about saving the world James-Bond style but then I was never placed in any real

Color Me Grey

16

danger. The closest I had ever come to real danger was when I was involved with the drug crowd in college. Some of those people are really rough, but they aren't professionals either.

I was scanning the booths and found my old tutor and best friend, Colin DeLange. His mother is deaf and I had asked if he would tutor me in sign language when we were younger. At first I just wanted to be around Colin. He was a few years older than me and not at all hard to look at. By the time I got the basics down for signing we had grown to be very good friends.

Over the years we had remained best friends. We might not have seen each other for months but we could always fall right back into the friendship. I walked toward him and he smiled. Colin had joined the Navy a few years ago and was considering making it a career like his dad. He had already been in for eight years and had just re-upped for another four. Sometimes when Chief Slade was drilling me, Colin would come over to benefit from his services. I think our Dad's had worked out a system that Colin would tutor me for lessons from Chief Slade. Colin's tutoring would have gone on without the extras that my dad paid for but my dad really liked Colin. I think our parents had conspired together hoping something other than friendship would blossom between us. I guess Colin could be considered my first boyfriend, but there had never been anything sexual between us. We both thought of the possibility, I'm sure. It was just an unwritten rule that we were to remain friends and in no way did either of us want to jeopardize that friendship.

Colin had one of those personalities that you just couldn't dislike. He smiled easily and was very charismatic. When he was around I was drawn to him like a bee to honey. He was always happy and hardly ever had anything bad to say about anyone or anything. I reached the booth and he stood to give me a welcoming hug.

He immediately sat to where he could see the door. Chief Slade may have gone a bit overboard with the training for watching your back. I knew I had to sit there too. I was sure the person following me would be in soon, if not already here. I skootched in next to him. He looked at me a bit funny so I mouthed at him, "I want to see the door."

Colin was an expert at reading lips, not only did he have the benefit of growing up in a deaf house hold, he had been given specialized training in the Navy for just such things. I think my father played a roll in Colin's good luck in the service, but if anyone deserved to be treated well it was Colin.

"What's going on?" he mouthed back at me with his hands up already signing what he had just said. Having a friend that signs and reads lips to sit with at the Skylight was nice. I didn't have to leave my voice behind in the bar when I left. The music was permanently loud and a person had to yell to be heard.

"I think I was followed," I said in my normal voice.

J.C. Phelps

This brought an incredulous look from Colin. "Are you getting paranoid in your old age? Or did Master Chief Slade visit you lately?" He smiled. "MASTER Chief?" I said. This was a new development. "How long has he been a Master Chief?" I asked.

"A few months." Colin had stopped signing everything he was saying making me work to read his lips. Once a tutor, always a tutor I guess.

I wasn't so good at reading lips, but I could usually catch enough words to make out the main topic of conversation.

"Is that the guy?" he said nodding his head in the direction of the door.

I looked away from Colin toward the door and he most definitely wasn't a familiar face. He was scanning the room. I don't know if he was looking for me or if he was just checking out the scene. I involuntarily slouched in my seat.

"I don't know," I said to Colin.

Colin sensed my nervousness and both of us were quiet as we watched the man pick a seat at the bar. He could see us and we could see him. He was quite a large man with a rough face and a sandy blonde military-style haircut. He reminded me a little of the actor Dolph Lundgren, except he wasn't as refined looking. We watched him order. "Bud please," Colin repeated.

Colin and I had spied on people like this before; this was nothing new to me. I think it was Colin's way of trying to teach me to read lips better, but it was my way of eavesdropping on conversations across the room.

The bartender, who happened to be my one and only ex, Anthony, was working. I didn't harbor any hard feelings for him anymore, but he steered clear of me all the same. I had caught him with one of the other waitresses in the women's bathroom one night. I had been infatuated with Anthony and very naïve. I had been taken by total surprise. When I saw them together, her on the sink with him in front of her admiring himself in the mirror, I pulled him off of her and then literally picked her up over my head and threw her out of the bathroom. Anthony had grabbed me to stop me from going out to finish the job but I just flicked him away like a fly. By the time I had gotten away from Anthony and out the bathroom door, the little floozy still hadn't gotten her panties up from around her ankles and there was a crowd building. I squared off with her but she was horrified so it took some of my anger away.

About that time Anthony came out of the bathroom. He was furious and grabbed me by the hair and whipped me around. He backhanded me and I was slammed to the floor. Some of the men in the club were on their way to take care of the woman beater, but I beat them too it. I stood up, bawling like an idiot, and grabbed his arm. I had it pinned behind his back before he knew what hit him. Then I forced him to his knees. "Apologize to me," I had regained my composure and said this in a quiet voice.

"What? Let go of me you bitch!" he yelled back at me.

I wrenched his arm harder and heard it snap. Oh shit! had been my thought at the time, but only for a millisecond. I leaned down toward his ear and spoke

Color Me Grey

18

into it so he would hear me over his screaming. "I said apologize to me, you prick. I can make it worse or you can make it better by just apologizing to me like a gentleman."

Anthony couldn't say, "I'm sorry," enough. He was still apologizing while they put him in the ambulance. For some reason breaking his arm made me feel better. He probably could have pressed charges against me but decided against it because the witnesses there would have told the cops that I had broken his arm after he hit me. I walked around with a black eye for about a month after that. Then I became a bitter single girl working in a bar and came unglued any time someone touched my butt. I eventually gave up the job for the greater good of the public. Anthony finished college and continued to work part time at the Skylight. As far as I knew, his sex life has never been the same.

Women talk and they all knew about how he hit me that night. Some women gravitate to that kind of thing, but the ones who do are already attached to the man who is beating them. My sex life was non-existent after that because I imagine men talk too. Nobody wanted a girlfriend that might break your arm.

Colin nudged me to get my attention, "I said, they're talking about you."

"What are they saying?" I asked him. Before Colin nudged me I had been intent on the two of them at the bar, but now my eyes were locked on Colin's lips.

"Army Boy wanted to know if Anthony knew you. I can't tell what Anthony's saying though. Do you suppose he's telling him about how you kicked his ass?"

"Probably more like how he's had me. That's more Anthony's style," I said.

Colin and I both went back to watching them talk with Colin translating Army Boy's words.

"Really?" "Is she here?" This turned Anthony around to point in our direction. "Thanks." Then Anthony saw to his other customers.

We could clearly see Army Boy and he could see us. He was a bit stunned to see the two of us staring right at him. He was made and he knew it.

Colin yelled in my ear, "Go to the other side of the booth, I'll keep an eye out and tell you anything else he says. He doesn't need to be staring at you." I could tell he was a little upset at the situation. Sometimes I thought Colin was in love with me but other times he was just my big brother watching out for me.

I got out of the booth and moved to the other side. This bothered me because I couldn't see Army Boy anymore. I turned in the seat and got up on my knees to look over the back like little kids did when you were in a Perkins or Denny's booth trying to eat your breakfast. Colin grabbed me by my pants pocket and pulled me back down before I could get my head up over the back of the seat.

"What is going on?" he asked.

J.C. Phelps

" I don't know." I told him about the Crown Victoria and how it had followed me around and how I was pretty sure Army Boy was the person operating the vehicle. Then I told him about the job interview with White and Associates. I told him about Mr. White and the interrogation. I yelled all of this to him over the band because he wouldn't take his eyes off the bar and Army Boy.

Colin finally looked at me when I finished my story and said, "Are you kidding me? What the hell have you gotten yourself into?"

"I don't know. I'm just glad that you were here so I could tell you about it. I'm actually having some fun with this, but it would be more fun if I knew exactly what was going on."

"Well, I guess you could go up to the guy and ask him what he's doing here asking about you. You're in a public place and I think he probably wouldn't try anything here," Colin said.

"Yeah, I suppose I could."

I started to get out of my seat and Colin put his hand up and said, "Wait, he's making a call."

I sat back down hard. Great, now I was going to have a chance to think about the confrontation with Army Boy. It was always harder to build my courage up than to just jump in with both feet without thinking. If I had just gone right then and there I wouldn't have even thought about it until it was over. Telling Colin about my day had put it in a new light. All of the excitement was starting to fade and be overshadowed by the fear and worry that I felt.

"Yeah, boss." Colin was giving me the one-sided conversation being held at the bar. "I have a problem." A small pause, "The Skylight on 1st and Main." "Alright."

"I wonder what that was all about." Colin said.

"He called his boss and told him he had a problem," I said a bit peevishly.

"I know that, I meant what does that mean for you. Man, you need a nap or something," Colin yelled over the music.

A waitress had strutted to our booth now that we weren't on the same side anymore. You learn quickly at the Skylight to leave the couples in the booths alone until they are on opposite sides of the table. It was Sara McNenny. She had started working here shortly before I quit. I liked her well enough, but we weren't close.

"Hey guys," she said. "Can I get you anything to drink?"

Colin ordered his regular, a tap beer, and I butted in and ordered a shot of whiskey and a Coke back. This brought surprised looks from both Colin and Sara. I rarely drank anymore and it usually spelled trouble.

"Be right back." And then Sara started her bar wench walk up to Anthony to fill our order.

Colin was giving me a look so I said, "What, I've had a rough day. I'm over twenty-one, I can legally drink." He was still looking at me. "Alright," I

Color Me Grey

20

said. "I'll be good." I gave him the most sincere smile I could muster. "Hey, I could have ordered a bourbon," I added.

"This is true," he said. "I'll make sure you get home safe." Then he grinned because he knew I would probably be just fine once I had some liquor in my belly.

I began to watch the band. The big white sign with changeable letters next to the stage read, "Incompetence." What a name for a band. I hadn't heard of them but they were doing a pretty good job. Not too incompetent.

Colin had kept his eyes on the big guy at the bar. Then Sara returned with our drinks. I took my shot straight from her tray and threw it back and said, "Will you bring me two more?" I handed her a fifty for the lot and sat back to await the arrival of my other invincibility potions.

"You're going to be sorry," Colin said.

"I know it, but I have to gather up enough courage to go face off with the guy. Besides, I get a little flirty when I drink so I think I might be able to flirt the guy to death." I smiled. I hadn't drunk alcohol in several months and I was already feeling the effects of the first shot.

"Here you go," Sara said with a concerned look on her face. "There's a guy at the bar asking about you. Is everything alright?" she asked.

I didn't pick up either of the two shots sitting in front of me yet. I just sat there looking at them. Sara laid my change on the table and turned to leave.

I yelled over the noise, "Sara!" She turned back to our table. "Everything's fine. Maybe you could try finding out who he is 'cause I don't know. Oh, and keep the change," I said laying it back on her tray with a genuine smile.

"Thanks. I will," she said and went about her business of selling booze.

"Colin, just ignore him. I'll take care of it later. I'm sure you didn't come here tonight to baby-sit me," I said.

"Not a bad band," he replied. "If you drink those other two shots, I'll dance with you," he said with a big grin.

I was a pretty good dancer. Mom had made me take dancing lessons along with the etiquette classes. I hated it then but was grateful now. Colin wanted me to be drunk on the dance floor because I was more fun that way. I was pretty reserved until you chipped away at the inhibitions with whiskey.

I slammed down the second whiskey and caught a gag in my throat. I sipped my Coke for a few minutes watching the band, letting my stomach settle.

"Hurry up with that last shot," Colin hollered at me. "I'm in the mood to dance."

Peer pressure. I grabbed the whiskey and brought it to my mouth then quickly moved it away. I could smell it and that made my stomach turn. Just slam it and you'll be over it. You're the stupid one who ordered it in the first place. I thought to myself. I lifted it back to my mouth being careful to take a deep breath before it got too close and then swallowed it down. I was feeling the effects of the first drink but not the other two yet.

J.C. Phelps

Colin stood up and led me to the dance floor. By the time we had waded through the tables and people I was feeling the second shot and had forgotten all about Army Boy at the bar.

After the first song I was feeling really good and cockier than ever. I told Colin I was going to use the restroom so he mouthed, "Be good," at me then began to dance with another girl that we knew from the club.

I walked a straight line to the bathrooms not even glancing in the direction of Army Boy because I had totally forgotten about him. I really had to pee. I made my way down the hall to the women's restroom. They were large enough that there was rarely a line and I found no line as I got there this time either. I washed my hands and entered the hallway to go back to the fun.

There was a man in the hall just this side of the swinging doors but the lighting was low and I'd had enough to drink that I didn't recognize the form. It looked familiar, muscles on a sleek frame but it just didn't register. He was facing me; casually leaning on the wall with his arms folded in front of him and had one leg crossing the other. I kept walking toward him. I was on top of him before I recognized him.

"Mr. White," I said coolly by way of greeting as I passed him going through the doors. My voice was even and short, but my heart was racing. Mr. White! He gave me a small nod with a small grin attached to it. Then he followed me through the doors. I put a little more swing in my walk and calmly and coolly nodded to Army Boy at the bar. He didn't seem to like my acknowledgement and pinched his lips together. The word *oops* and the *F word* both came to mind. I kept walking like I knew where I was going. You wouldn't have known it by watching me slowly scan the room, but I was frantic, trying to locate Colin. I didn't see him anywhere so I made my way back to our booth.

I slid in the side facing the bar to keep an eye on my pursuers. I should have been scared sober, but that didn't work with me very often. You really had to scare me. This came close but not quite there. I saw Mr. White sitting next to Army Boy at the bar and they were speaking. At least now I knew who the hell had been following me. I still didn't understand why though.

I was concentrating on Mr. White's lips. He said something like, "Happen. I you her you." Hell. I needed to find Colin! I scanned the dance floor. He was there. I got up and started for him. He saw me and came my direction, clearly able to see that something had come up. We met on the edge of the dance floor.

"What's up?" he asked with concern on his face and in his voice.

"Ok," I said as way of calming myself down. "Let's go out on the dance floor, I'm wired and need to get rid of this energy. I'll tell you out there."

The band was playing a fairly slow set so we were able to blend in and still talk. I made sure Colin was facing the bar. "Is Army Boy still sitting at the bar?" I asked.

"Yeah, but there's another guy sitting and talking to him."

Color Me Grey

22

"That's Mr. White," I said.

"No, I know him. I can't remember his name but it's not White," Colin said. "I recognize him from the service. He was of a pretty high rank, Petty Officer 1st class, I think."

"You know how bad I am at the ranks. I can never remember what's what," I told him.

"Well, Master Chief Slade is one rank under being a commissioned officer."

Commissioned officers took tests to become commissioned, if I remembered right. What I did remember was commissioned officers were on the top third of the rank ladder.

Colin went on, "Petty Officer 1st class is only a few steps below Master Chief." I was still a bit confused, but I understood that Mr. White wasn't Mr. White and had some extensive military rank.

"So what does that mean?" I asked Colin. "Well, the guy you call Mr. White started the service about the same time I did and has since gotten out. I think he did two tours which is eight years and then he got out a higher rank than I am right now," Colin said.

"Are they talking," I asked.

"Not since you told me they were there."

"Would you please translate if they start?" I asked.

"Wouldn't miss the chance." A big grin plastered to his face. I think Colin had a shot of whiskey or two while I was in the restroom.

We danced a couple more songs and then the band picked up the pace again. The effects of the alcohol were getting to me. I began to forget about the two men at the bar again and was really getting into the music. Of course I knew they were there, how could I totally forget after seeing Mr. White waiting for me in the hall? Music just had a strange effect on me and I started to relax again and enjoy myself.

That's not the whole truth either. I knew Mr. White was watching and I was putting on the best show possible without being obvious. I envisioned him coming up to me on the dance floor and one thing leading to another and then it cut to me waking up in his bed.

Colin and I were working up a sweat and I asked him, "Have you been watching?"

"Non-stop and neither one of them have taken their eyes off you."

"I'm getting tired. Let's go back to the table," I suggested.

"Whatever my lady wants," he said as he bowed to me.

I bowed back and then he followed me off the dance floor. We wormed our way back to the booth and sat watching Army Boy and Mr. White at the bar.

Army Boy had a disgusted look on his face but Mr. White was just sitting there with hardly any expression at all. A hint of a question loomed in his eyes, but that was it. Neither one of them took their eyes from our table.

J.C. Phelps

Colin told me to move to my side of the booth so we could get another drink. Might as well, I thought. I wasn't going anywhere until they did or I had enough courage to confront them.

We sat for a while before Sara noticed we were again on separate sides of the table. She sauntered over and asked if we needed something.

Colin ordered a shot of tequila and a tap beer. I knew he'd had a shot of something while I was gone. Tequila was his choice of invincibility potions. I ordered another whiskey with a Coke back and asked Sara, "Did you find anything out?"

"Not really. I went over to him and tried flirting, but he must have it bad for you because he didn't even notice I was there."

"Thanks," I said and off she went to fetch our drinks.

We sat there quietly, me staring at Colin and him at the bar.

"This is like a stare down," he said as Sara reappeared to drop the drinks off. Colin paid this time. It was his turn. Sara was disappointed because I was a much better tipper. I pulled another dollar out of my pocket and put it on her tray at the same time Colin put his empty shot glass up there and she walked away a bit happier.

"Here we go," Colin said starting to sign and simultaneously repeating what they were saying. "How many has she had?" "Four, including this one."

"Wow. They are really paying attention," I said. Colin didn't hear me over the music.

"What have you found out?"

"Not much, I think she's who she says she is. She lives at the Stanton estate. She eats at Sal's Sandwiches. She IS a woman."

"No shit, I noticed that at the office." This brought a smile to Colin's face and redness to mine. "How and when did she find out your were tailing her?"

"I don't know. Her and her friend over there were looking straight at me when I sat down at the bar."

"Shit"

"What?"

"Can you see what he's doing over there?" Colin's smiled broadened. He knew we were busted but hey, we busted them first. "Sign language. She didn't list that on her app. Let's go. Please tell Ms. Stanton thank you for her time and that I will be in touch with her tomorrow."

Colin motioned Sara over and bought us each another shot. My last shot was still sitting in front of me and I wasn't sure I could handle that one not to mention the one on the way. I was about to put my head down when Sara showed up with our drinks. Great.

Colin chugged his down and I did the same with one of them. I asked Sara to wait and drank the other one. For a few seconds I was afraid that I might have to make a run for the bathroom but my stomach settled down again. I was thoroughly drunk.

Color Me Grey

24

Colin asked me if I would like to dance and I told him to find someone else, I was going home.

"That's too bad. You were starting to turn me on out there before." he said with an impish grin. "Are you going to be alright?" he asked.

"Yeah," I said. "I'll call a cab and be home in bed in no time."

"I'll go call the cab, you stay here. Then I'll come get you when they get here." He could tell I had drank several too many. "By the way, I'm proud of you. No fights tonight." Then he smiled and walked away to make that call.

I sat there watching the band and dancers swim around the room for what seemed a long time. I seemed to have trouble gauging the time today. It seemed like it had been at least an hour before Colin came back and said, "I'll walk you out."

I had a reputation to uphold, so I said no thanks to the offer of him pretty much carrying me out of the bar. I thought I did fairly well walking through the crowd, down the hall and out the door. I was aware of Colin right behind me to the swinging doors and I suppose because I didn't run into anyone or the walls he allowed me to walk the hall alone. I stepped outside into the fresh air and took a deep breath. I was beginning to feel a bit better. The cab wasn't at the front door like I had expected though. I walked back inside and called the cab company and arranged for another car.

Back outside I sat on the brick planter that surrounded the building, trying to concentrate on what had happened that day. A black Crown Victoria pulled into the parking lot directly across from me. Army Boy stepped out with a nasty look on his face.

"Hey!" he said to get my attention.

"Leave me alone," I said. "I'm pretty drunk and not in the mood right now."

He walked up to me and hovered above me. "You made me look like a fool today. I want to know who told you that I was following you."

I sighed, "Man. Nobody told me! You and that car were right outside my driveway when I was walking to Sal's," I said. "I didn't think anything of it until I saw you parked up the street a couple blocks away after I had left you behind."

"Is it true that you were never in the military?" he asked.

"Yep," I said trying to sound tired. It was all in the attitude most of the time.

"What the hell makes you think you could become an associate in White and Associates?" he asked rudely. "I'm in the running and you made me look stupid."

"I don't think I made you look stupid. You did that all by yourself," I said standing up. This guy was beginning to annoy me. I stood up a little too fast and got a bit woozy. I did a step forward and caught myself on his chest.

J.C. Phelps

"Excuse me? Did you just put your hands on me?" he said bobbing his head back and forth. All he needed to do now was put his hands on his hips to complete the look.

"Look, Army Boy," I said. "I told you I'm drunk and I just stood up too quick."

"How did you know I was in the Army? Who the hell are you?" He reached for me and I ducked out of the way. While I'm down here, I thought, I'll just knock him off his feet. I struck out with a sweep of my leg and brought him down hard. I was back on my feet and almost sober. I was quite a lot slower than I normally would be and that pissed me off. I should give up drinking all together.

I wonder if Colin knew this guy too. How else would he know that he was from the Army in a town full of Navy men? What a creep, he could have told me.

Army Boy was back on his feet and he was acting like a boxer, jumping around with his fists covering his face.

Boxing was never one of my interests. He jabbed at me and I sidestepped. He almost missed me. I wasn't fast enough and he caught me in the shoulder. I went down to the pavement, but hey, here I was again. I struck out again and again he went down hard. Some people never learn.

I got back up and so did he. Now he was really pissed. I think I could see steam coming from his ears and nose. I laughed in spite of what I was facing. I put him at about 230 pounds. That meant he outweighed me close to 125 pounds. This guy could NOT hit me anywhere substantial.

I gave my head a shake while he danced around. I bet we looked like a pair of idiots. I was trying to clear my head of the whiskey but it wasn't working. How the hell was I going to take this guy down? If I hit him square in the jaw I think I might break my hand and he would squash me.

"What's wrong with you man?" I asked, trying to buy myself some time to think. He had another coming at me before I could think of anything so I dropped and he missed me again. Guess what, I'm back. Down he went again. Didn't his mother teach him to think ahead?

I was up and on top of him before he could get back up. I had both of his arms behind him and pulling for all I was worth. He was a brute and I couldn't get him exactly where I wanted him. He stood up and I was getting a piggyback ride. Being the cocky person I am and drunker than a skunk, I hollered, "Giddy up, bitch!"

Army Boy was turning around in circles so I checked out the scenery. No crowd yet, thank goodness, but standing against a black 1969 Mustang, with his arms folded and a disapproving look on his face, was Mr. White. All right, now I'd had enough. I released my captive and jumped down.

"Time to get down to business," I said quietly.

Color Me Grey

Army Boy had resumed his fight position as well as I. He was jumping around, doing some elaborate dance and I stood there completely relaxed on the outside and a ball of energy inside, waiting for his next move.

"Are you serious about hurting me?" I asked him while he skipped around like a fool.

"You're damn right." Then he took a wide swing at my head. I ducked and thought, 'this is too easy'. I didn't take the opportunity to knock his feet out from under him this time but instead I ended up behind him.

He twirled around. I could see Mr. White behind him still with his arms folded in front of him but with a slight smile on his face.

"You're dead!" Army boy screamed and ran for me. I took a small step to the side and he ran straight into the side of the Crown Victoria. I couldn't help it, I giggled.

I hadn't been in a fight for close to a year now and it had been several years since I had sparred with someone with a little more experience than a street fighter or a drunk. Army Boy spun himself around again.

"Are you getting dizzy?" I asked. I had my hands in my back pockets to show that I wouldn't hurt him if he quit. "If you want to persist in this you're going to end up getting hurt. You know that don't you?"

He yelled something that I couldn't understand and I don't think he did either. Then he started bouncing around again.

"You know, if you keep jumping around like that you're going to make yourself tired. And it bugs me," I added.

He took another swing but this time aimed for my middle. Getting smarter. Only I caught his fist in mid swing and pushed back hard on his hand. His wrist cracked and I winced. I never liked breaking bones.

Army Boy screamed and clutched at his arm. At least he had quit jumping all over the place like a hyper poodle. "You bitch!" he yelled. "You broke my wrist."

"Are you done then?" I asked.

"Fuck you!"

Mr. White walked over toward us and Army Boy got a surprised look on his face. He hadn't even known that Mr. White had been in the lot watching us, but I was sure he had started Army Boy on his way to beat on me.

"Nice job, Ms. Stanton," he said. He nodded somewhere off behind me.

"Please call me Alex. And what the hell was that?" I yelled. Then two men, one with a similar build to Mr. White and the other with more muscles walked, up beside me.

"Let me introduce you to Leonard." Mr. White indicated Army Boy.

"Nice to meet you." Then I looked to Mr. White and said with my hands on my hips, "I don't appreciate being set up."

"Set up?" He raised his eyebrows at me.

J.C. Phelps

"Yeah, set up. There was no reason to sick your dog on me." I was getting frustrated.

"I didn't sick anything on you," He replied calmly. "I was waiting to make sure you made it home safely."

"So you think I can't take care of myself?" I asked incredulously.

Mr. White's hands came at me quickly trying to grab for my arms. I deftly maneuvered away. We made a half circle within his circle of goons then he reached up and grabbed my shoulder that Army Boy had tenderized. I saw spots and the next thing I knew I was laying back on the hood of his car with him leaning over the top of me. I wondered if he carried his gun in the front of his pants. I hoped so, kind of. We lay there for some time, with me breathing hard and him hardly breathing at all. We were looking into each other's eyes and I felt an energy there. The question was, did he feel it?

"You cheated," I said finally.

"No, I took advantage of a situation," he explained.

"Yeah," I said by way of dismissal and he let me up.

"This is Mr. Black and Mr. Blue," Mr. White said with a grin.

I gave him a sidelong glance. Then he said, "I think it's fun to put them together on jobs, what with their names."

He got a smile out of me.

"I'm quite impressed," he said. "I didn't expect you to be too proficient in fighting, considering your size."

I stood there in a daze from the way he smelled and didn't catch much of what he was saying.

"I'm sorry, Mr. White," I said. "I'm really drunk and I think I'm going to be sick, please excuse me."

I went back inside just as the cab was pulling into the lot. I didn't have time to tell the driver that I would be right back so I ran in to use the restroom. After a few minutes I came out of the stall and washed my face. I felt better except for my shoulder.

I walked back outside to find the cab was no longer there. Black and Blue were gone and so was Leonard. The Crown Victoria remained and so did Mr. White.

I was too exhausted to go back in and call a cab so I did my sexy walk over to Mr. White. Maybe my premonition on the dance floor could come true yet. I couldn't help it. I had been celibate for almost a year and everyone knows, once you've had it, you want it again. I had had some chances but I was chicken and they weren't pushy enough. I would have given in eventually.

"Would you mind giving me a ride?" I asked. "I don't know what's up with the cabs tonight. They won't wait for two minutes."

"Leonard sent the first one away and I sent the second one away," he replied. "Get in." And with that, he was behind the wheel of his beauty.

Color Me Grey

I poured myself into the bucket seat and buckled myself up. "You know where I live?" I asked.

"Yep."

Chapter Four

I woke up in my bed still in my clothes from the night before. I don't know how Mr. White got me in here, but he did. I sat up and then fell right back down onto the bed from the pain. I had a monster headache and I didn't think I could move my arm. I looked at the time on my alarm clock. It was 7:00 AM on a Sunday and I was awake. What the heck was wrong with me? I must have gotten home fairly early.

I made myself get out of bed to take some ibuprofen. Then I managed to get my clothes off. I put on a t-shirt and went back to bed.

The phone woke me up at 11:00 AM. I got out of bed and the hangover was gone, but my whole left side hurt, not just my shoulder or arm, I hurt to my toes.

I picked up the phone. "Hello?"

"Good morning." It was Mr. White.

My heart skipped a beat and I got that giddy feeling again. "Good morning." Chief Slade had taught me to keep an even voice through most anything. Never let your voice give you away.

"How are you feeling?" he asked. It seems Chief Slade had taught White the same tactics.

"Better," I said. "How did you get me into the house?" I asked.

"I found the keys in your pants. It was a challenge to get them out though." I blushed. "I'm sorry about falling asleep in your car," I said.

"Not a big deal. Do you drink often?" He asked.

"No. It gets me into trouble. If I had been sober I could have avoided that fight all together."

"I see. Put some ice on that shoulder and be at the office by 6:00 tomorrow morning." And he hung up. Great. I was too tired to even think about getting up at 6:00 in the morning.

I grabbed an ice pack out of my freezer and pushed it to my shoulder. I winced and hoped he hadn't broken anything. Other than the time Anthony hit me I had never been hit before in a fight and I hoped I was never hit again. I was only a little stronger than the average woman of my size but I was quick. That was my greatest asset, my quickness. It gave me an advantage because I could get out of the way before I got hit.

Color Me Grey

Well, at least I didn't have a black eye. When I came home with the black eye that Anthony so graciously bestowed upon me, my mother flipped. She was furious. When I walked in the door she drew in a deep breath and in that Motherly concerned voice said, "What happened? Are you okay? Did you get into an accident? Where's your car?"

"Anthony hit me." That was all I was able to get out before she was out the door. I guess she drove to his dorm and when he opened the door she clocked him in the nose. Then she told him, "There, now that aught to teach you to hit a girl." And with that she turned and walked away. I heard all of this whispered behind my back everywhere I went. Mom never told me about it and neither did Anthony.

By the time she got home I had explained it to my dad. I wouldn't have told him but he caught me leaving and asked what happened to my face. After I explained what happened he said, "Well, I'm glad you broke his arm. A man that would hit a woman unprovoked should be put down." And by put down he didn't mean down to the ground he meant put down like when you have to shoot your horse because it broke it's leg.

I sat on my couch flipping through pages of the latest book that I had been reading but I just couldn't concentrate on it. I was dying to get over to the main house to talk to Dad. If Colin knew Mr. White maybe my dad did too. Also, I wanted to grill my Dad about his "job."

I got to thinking about that, I didn't even know where it was my dad went to when he went to work. He didn't hold a regular job with nine to five hours, Monday through Friday either. He came and went on whatever day of the week it happened to be. He spent most of his time in his office at home though. There were times he was gone for a few weeks, but that happened less frequently now.

I collected myself up off the couch and walked to the main house. I walked through the back yard to the back door. The main house was a good distance from the guesthouse. I could be having a rave at my place and the main house would be oblivious to any goings on.

I went in through the back door into the kitchen/dining room. The house was mostly open and I could see through the kitchen and the living room to the front door. There were rooms to my right. The laundry room connected to the kitchen, then under the staircase, leading to the second floor, was the main bathroom. The second floor was nothing but bedrooms and bathrooms. There was a hallway between the laundry room and main bathroom, which lead to the other half of the house where I would find the library and my dad's office.

My parents were nowhere to be seen. Mom was probably working in her shop outside. She had recently gotten herself some power tools and was currently into woodworking. Dad was more than likely in his office.

J.C. Phelps

I walked through the hall toward the second half of the house. The library was as large as the living room and about a third of the kitchen. My dad's office was nestled into the remaining part of the house.

I knocked on the door and Dad said, "Yes?"

I walked into his office. He was sitting at his computer in his overstuffed chair. I sat down on the couch at one end of the room and took it all in. It was a dark room but not uncomfortable. The floor was a dark wood that matched the walls. The two large windows that looked out onto the back yard had heavy, maroon curtains that were drawn shut. The walls were lined with bookshelves that were full with books of all shapes and sizes.

"What's on your mind?" my dad asked looking up from his screen. He looked at me through his glasses, but over his reading glasses. Instead of going in to get a new pair of glasses that he could read with and see day-to-day with, he wore reading glasses over his regular glasses. It made him look comical.

My dad had been slowly adding to his middle area for the past few years. His hair was becoming salt and peppered and he had begun to get that papery old-people skin. But to me, my dad would never be old. He was the smartest person I knew and I had a lot of respect for the man.

"I want to know exactly what you do," I said nodding toward the computer on his desk.

"You know what I do," he said and looked back to his work.

"Dad," I said in that singsong little-kid way.

"Well, honey, I do so many different things I couldn't begin to explain. Is this really important? I have things to do."

"I know you are an Admiral, but are you still in the service?" I asked.

"Yes and no. I work for the government, but I'm not quite in the military," he said. I could tell he was trying to find the right words to satiate my curiosity, but not really tell me the full truth. "Let me put it this way, if there were a war tomorrow, I would be working for the military and the government, but I wouldn't go to fight. At my age I couldn't anyway, but even if I were a young man they wouldn't send me. I'm too important." This last sentence was said with a hint of humor and an eye roll. I was sure it was true, but he found it funny somehow.

"When you leave, where do you go?" I asked.

"Why all these questions?" he asked back.

"I want to know. I was asked yesterday what it was you did and I couldn't explain it and it bothers me," I replied.

"Who was asking?"

I told him about the newspaper ad and how I had gone downtown to be interviewed. I didn't go into complete detail about Mr. White and the interview itself.

"What's the name of the company?" he asked.

"White and Associates."

Color Me Grey

32

"Do you know what they do?"

"I'm not exactly sure. I was told they're kind of like a private investigation outfit," I explained.

"Well, kind of," my father replied.

This made me sit up straighter. "You know who they are?" I asked.

"Yes, I hire them from time to time. I'm not so sure I want you working for them," he said.

"Why, what do they do?"

"A little of this and a little of that." Back to the same old explanations but not for himself this time. "It's a dangerous job, honey. I like you doing data processing."

"Well, I quit," I said with a bit of defiance in my voice. "I'm tired of sitting in front of the computer all day and not having any excitement." My dad brought out the child in me.

"Alright. If that's the way you want it," he said turning his head to the side and lifting his hands in an "I give up" type of gesture. "Just make sure you are prepared to do the job."

"I'm trying to. Mr. White had me followed yesterday," I said, thinking I would get a rise out of him.

"I suppose he did. I imagine you are under surveillance right now." He sat back in his chair and put his hands behind his head so it looked as if his ears had somehow sprouted elbows. "Don't get undressed anywhere but the bathroom. I imagine they have installed video and audio into the guesthouse. I know Mr. White, as you call him, and I'm sure he'd be a gentleman and leave the bathroom private. Probably the bedroom too, but you never can tell." He said all this like it was normal conversation.

"What!!!" I was on my feet and my face was hot.

"Honey, sit down. If you want this kind of job you've got to live with some sacrifices at first," Daddy said.

"It doesn't upset you that someone came onto your property and messed around with your stuff?" I said, still standing.

"It's not the first time. You said you wanted to know what I do for a living and you are about to find out." I sat down to listen to the rest of my father's words of wisdom. "When you were younger I had hopes for you to follow in my footsteps, but as I get older I find that all I really want is grandchildren. I had hoped you had gotten over wanting adventure and were ready to settle down. Now I can see you were trying to become domesticated but are unhappy with it. I had always hoped you would be more like me but you are just like your mother. She was impossible until I got her pregnant."

This was all news to me but it still didn't give me a full picture of anything.

"Who is Mr. White? Colin told me he knew his name isn't White."

"Mr. White. He is a Navy man. Right now he's out on his own, but he still has ties. His real name is classified."

J.C. Phelps

I gave him my exasperated look and said, "How can you joke around right now? I'm involved in something and I don't have a clue and I'm asking for your help."

"You take things too seriously. If they know you are my daughter you'll be safe," he said.

"Fine, so what's his real name?" I asked.

"Rick Malone. He's from this area; in fact I think you two have probably met before. I had him and his father over when you were about twelve. That would have made him... let me see..." He typed for a second on his computer. "He's twenty-nine right now so he would have been seventeen then."

I remembered that day! I had a few guys that I fantasized about late at night when I was all alone. Mel Gibson, Harrison Ford, Sean Connery, the guy from "A Knights Tale" and the guy who was in my backyard for one afternoon. I remembered him. I couldn't believe this. I KNEW him. Well, not really, but in my dreams. Now the feelings made more sense. He had affected me in a similar way back then. I spent the whole day sitting in the garden watching him. His father, my dad, Colin's father and the two boys were all there talking shop. That was just a year or two before Colin joined up and I think that's what they were talking about that day. Until that very day I had always thought I would marry Colin, but after seeing this guy, Colin was no longer in the running for forever.

In my fantasies I had run into him on the street and he immediately fell in love with me. Now I had run into him and didn't even know who he had been. I wondered if *he* remembered that day? I hoped not. I had changed considerably since then. I didn't get boobies and a figure until I was sixteen. I'm sure he had seen me as nothing but a little girl back then and I hoped he didn't see me that way now.

"So what exactly do you hire him to do?" I asked.

"Lots of things. Sometimes I need someone to be relocated and I enlist White and Associates to get the job done. I am not going to get into the details with you. That would be a breach of ethics."

"Fine. If you were Malone would you hire me?" I asked.

"That's not fair. I know you better and differently than he does. I can't answer that question." Sometimes talking to my dad irritated me. He was so technical with his answers; you had better word it just right to get a decent answer out of him. He was the master of avoiding questions.

"Dad, try to put yourself in his shoes and if you can't, would YOU hire me to do the jobs that Malone hires out for?" I asked.

He thought for a second. "I can't imagine you not being my daughter, but as my daughter I would hire you. But I would have to make sure you got proper training. Does that satisfy your question?"

"I guess so. I'll let you get back to your work. Thanks, Dad," I said and turned to walk out of the room.

Color Me Grey

34

"Don't forget about the surveillance devices I told you about. If you find them, don't take them down either. They will just come back and re-install and you won't know where they are."

I walked out of the room to go back to the guesthouse. These past two days had been more hectic than I had ever experienced before. I thought I was pretty cool and knew a lot before yesterday. Now I was beginning to question everything.

One thing that bothered me was the way my dad took this in stride. He had always been my protector and now he didn't even care that I was being spied on. He seemed to think it was funny. Maybe he was getting senile. I didn't really think that. My dad could lose the use of every part of his body but his brain would still continue to work, and work well.

I got to my place and hesitated before I went in. I knew quite a lot about computer technology and had done some research into spy technology so I figured, if they had money the devices were probably pretty small, otherwise they would be easy to find. The things would have to have some way to get power and the easiest way was to use battery-operated devices. The only problem is the batteries die and you have to replace them. It's not a big deal if you plan to do surveillance for a short period, but I didn't have any idea how long they planned to spy on me.

I walked around the outside of the building searching for unexplained wires. I found some wires coming out of the house and went in to find they were kosher. I looked around and found a little black device attached to the lamp on the end table in the living room. I put it back where I found it and continued my search. I spent the rest of the day ferreting out six audio bugs and five cameras strewn throughout the kitchen and living room.

The guesthouse was not tiny, but it was only big enough for one person or maybe a couple. There weren't that many places to hide things. The floor plan was open like the main house except for the one bedroom and bathroom.

Dad had been right about not finding any in the bathroom or the bedroom. For that, I was thankful. I would have had to move out. There are certain things I don't want people to know about me unless I choose to share them. What my body looks like under my clothes is one of those things.

Most of the devices I found were wired into the main electrical lines in the house, so that was not at all reassuring. A person could do surveillance indefinitely that way. From what I could tell by the angles of the cameras there wasn't a spot in the whole house they couldn't see, including the bedroom and bathroom if I happened to leave the doors open.

I cleaned up the mess I had made while conducting my search and flopped down on the couch. I sat there for a while pretending to read, but I couldn't shake the feeling of being watched. I got up off the couch with my book, put some shoes on and left for Sal's to get supper.

J.C. Phelps

After I had eaten my sandwich I went to the coffee shop to have some privacy. I stayed there long after I finished my book. I finally made myself head for home. I immediately scanned the area for vehicles that seemed out of place. I saw several that I wasn't sure about, but nothing popped out at me. I was continuously looking over my shoulder all the way home. When I got there I couldn't bring myself to go inside. I sat outside in my car for a long time. I woke up with a terrible pain in my shoulder and neck and decided to go inside.

I went straight to my room and shut the door and set the alarm clock for 5:00 AM. I slept in my clothes for the second night in a row.

36

Chapter Five

The alarm was going off but I couldn't seem to pull myself out of bed. I laid there for a long time listening to the constant beeping. Finally I got mad enough at the sound to roll over and turn it off. I looked at the time. It was 5:09 AM.

I suppose I should get up, I thought. I went to the bedroom door to make sure it was shut tight. I took off my clothes and inspected my shoulder. I had put off looking at it because I was afraid of what I might see. The bone could be showing and then I'd have to go get it taken care of. It was swollen and the bruise looked like the fist that hit me. I was satisfied I wasn't going to die so I started to get dressed.

My shoulder ached. My neck ached. My mind ached. Getting dressed was a chore but I managed to get on jeans and a t-shirt. Putting on my socks and shoes was a bit harder.

I had lain in bed awake for a long time last night thinking. I couldn't seem to get things straightened out.

I wanted to be excited for today. I wanted my normal cockiness to return. I just wanted to be able to walk around holding the world in my fist again. Invading the privacy of my home really put a crimp in my style. The events of the past couple days had me whirling. The world was not at all what it had been. I had been queen of the roost before, but now I was just a person being spied on, followed and left in the dark about everything.

I had thought I was so smart. Granted, I still knew more than the normal person walking the street about computers, dancing and military maneuvers but I wasn't sure how much good it was doing me. Sure I was bored with being a data processor but I wasn't sure I wanted to live a life where people could be watching me at any time. I was pretty good at acting cool when other people were around, but I was human after all. Once in a while I might feel the need to pick my nose or pass gas. I could no longer do these things without the whole world knowing that I did it.

All right, get yourself out of this funk, I told myself. I opened the bedroom door and went straight to the bathroom and shut the door. I brushed my teeth, washed my face and pulled my hair back into a braid. I didn't know what was on the agenda for the day, so better to be safe than sorry with the hair. Braids were always good. They looked nice but kept my hair out of the way. I thought my braid helped me look a little like Lara Croft from the "Tomb Raider" video games.

J.C. Phelps

I was an avid video game player and wasted many hours in front of the computer or TV killing things and finding treasures. Lara Croft was one of my favorites. She had that accent. I had tried but I just couldn't do it. I didn't care for Angelina Jolie as Lara Croft, her lips were too big, but considering what Hollywood had to offer, she had been the best choice by far. She could play the tough part and still be sexy. The only person who could have played Lara better would have been Lara herself. I longed to be just like Lara, accent and all.

I stood in the bathroom and debated on whether or not to call a cab to take me downtown. I finally opted in favor of the cab. I walked out to the living room, picked up the phone and called. I went back into the bathroom and shut the door. I put the lid down on the toilet and sat there waiting for the cab service to show.

Within ten minutes I heard a honk. I stepped quickly from the bathroom to the front door. I looked out and saw a primered black 1970 Plymouth Barracuda in my driveway. I looked closer and saw that it was Mr. Blue in the driver's seat. Imagine that. I suppose someone overheard me call the cab company and sent Mr. Blue instead.

I stepped outside and walked to the car. I let myself in the passenger's door and said, "Good morning, Mr. Blue."

"Good morning, Ms. Stanton. How's the shoulder today?" he replied.

"It's been better, but I'll live," I said.

Mr. Blue had light brown hair that was cut short in the back but his bangs fell into his eyes. His eyes were ice blue and had a hard quality, as did his face. He was clean-shaven but his facial hair must have been coarse because you could see the hairs wanting to poke out through their pores. He looked to be in his mid-thirties. I would have guessed him right at 6' tall and about 180 pounds. He was wearing a black suede jacket over a tight t-shirt and I could clearly see that he worked out. I hadn't seen so many buff men in my life as I had seen in the past couple days. Still, Mr. Blue didn't get under my skin like Rick Malone did.

He popped a rap CD into the stereo and jacked the volume. This ended all chance of conversation but that was fine by me. I was busy worrying about who it was on the other side of the camera lens watching my every move. I hope it wasn't Mr. Blue. I hoped it was Malone.

I didn't know if I should let Mr. White know that I knew his real name yet because I didn't know why they used aliases in the first place. My training had taught me not to divulge information unless it was necessary. I decided to be polite and wait it out.

We pulled up to the attendant at the parking garage and he just waved us through. Mr. Blue parked in an open spot with the letters BLUE spray-painted with blue spray paint on the cement in front of the spot. I looked down the row and saw WHITE, BLACK, GREEN, BROWN and RED all spray-painted in their corresponding colors. The spots were filled with all types of vehicles. The

Color Me Grey

black Mustang was in front of WHITE. In BLACK was a large black SUV. GREEN drove a little yellow Miata. BROWN had a dark gray pickup in his spot. RED drove a red Camero.

I followed Mr. Blue through the lobby with the shiny black marble and happened to notice he was carrying a gun in a shoulder holster by way of the marble. He nodded to Mr. Rent-a-Cop at the front desk.

"Mr. Blue, Ms. Stanton," desk security said by way of greeting. This shocked me a bit. I had been here once and the guy already knew my name and I hadn't given it out. I smiled a greeting back.

I got on the elevator with Mr. Blue and I was glad he didn't seem to be the talkative type. He stood in the elevator in an "at ease/parade rest" position. His arms were clasped behind him, his feet were perfectly in line with his shoulders and he was looking straight ahead. He had no expression on his face whatsoever. He would have made a great poker player. I had always wanted to play poker professionally but I usually had a cocky half grin on my face or I just looked mad. I could never get my face to go void of all expression.

I felt butterflies flitting around in my stomach now. I really want this job, I think. Actually, I'm not sure if I want this job as much as I want to know what the job is.

The elevator came to a stop and we walked down the hall to Suite 73. I expected to see Gabriella sitting at her desk, but it was empty.

"She doesn't come in until 8:00," Mr. Blue said. He walked straight for Mr. White's door, opened it and went in. My feet wanted to falter, but I made myself stay right on his heels.

The office was dark and empty of people. I had expected to see Mr. White and the rest of the colors when I walked in.

Mr. Blue gestured to the desk, where Mr. White had been sitting during my interview. "Sit here. You will find everything you need on the desk. Someone will be back for you later." And he left.

The first thing I noticed on the desk was a computer. I better leave that alone for now, I thought. There was a stack of papers on the corner of the desk with a pencil on top.

I flipped through them and they were more questionnaires like the ones I had already taken. I got to work on them. There were a few questions that had me stumped. One that I didn't answer fully had to do with military ranking, of course. All in all I think I did a good job. Filling it all out took me about and hour and a half and still no activity other than me.

I sat for about five minutes thinking about turning on the computer. I imagine Mr. White had cameras in his office. What the hell, I thought.

I reached around back and switched it on and prepared to snoop. No luck, it was password protected. Time to put to use my computer knowledge. I had spent more time in front of the computer in my life than I think I had slept. I hacked the password in less than thirty seconds.

J.C. Phelps

Pretty normal files for a business, I guessed. Accounting programs, that type of thing. I wasn't finding anything useful though. I decided to check the e-mail. No new messages. Damn. Did he even use this computer?

I got online and hacked into the database for the closest Naval base. You'd think government computers would be hard to hack but they aren't, if you know your way around. I know this is illegal, but I know how NOT to get caught. I typed in my dad's password and voila… ACCESS GRANTED.

When hacking a government computer it's handy to have the highest security pass available and the rightful owner of my pass was probably still in bed at home. If dad was out of bed before 8:00 he rarely got onto his computer before 10:00 AM. I was counting on that right now. If he logged on while I was still connected there would be a conflict and I would be busted. Then I would have to sneak around some more to find out his new password. Not to mention I could go to jail. I didn't know if my dad could get me out of that kind of trouble. I might even get him into some trouble of his own and I really didn't want to do that. I typed Rick Malone in the search box and waited for the computer to search its files.

It seemed to be taking longer than it should. I was still waiting when it dawned on me the military would know him better by Petty Officer 1st Class Rick Malone. I punched in PO1 Rick Malone. It took a matter of seconds for me to get a nice picture of PO1 Rick Malone aka Mr. Richard White, aka Whip. Navy Seals, Covert Ops. Discharged with honors, blah, blah, blah. Get to the good stuff. I skimmed down the page to where his current address was listed: 1324 Plaza Dr., Suite 73. Shit.

The door to the front office opened. I immediately logged out and started to play solitaire on the computer. I had done this before and the solitaire bit worked like a charm. The trick is to have the game open on the computers desktop before you really get down to business. That way when you close whatever you are messing with, the solitaire game is right there for you to start playing. Not a bad idea to play for a second before you begin too, that way there are moves made on the game and it looks like you have been playing a while and not doing anything else.

It was Gabriella. She walked into Mr. White's office and said, "Oh. It's you. Ms. Stanton right?"

"Yeah, hi," I said while I quit the game and turned off the computer like it was mine. Don't act guilty and people won't think you are guilty. I hope.

"I figured someone would be here because I was called to work and don't normally come in on Mondays. I'm glad it's you," she said with a happy smile.

"Mr. Blue brought me in this morning and told me to fill out these forms." I pointed at the papers on the desk.

"You have them done?" she asked.

"Yeah. I've been waiting for someone to come back and get me," I said.

Color Me Grey

40

"You're quick with the paperwork, that's for sure," She said as she walked toward the desk to pick it all up.

"Come on out here and I'll call someone to come get you." She was walking back to her desk and I was right behind her.

"They normally wouldn't be back until around 9:00, but then again, it normally takes a candidate until 10:00 to complete this stuff." Gabriella set everything on her desk, motioned me to the chair on the other side and picked up the phone.

"I'm going to call Mr. Black," she said holding the receiver up. She got a sly look on her face and said, "I LOVE his voice, so I call him whenever I get the chance. I'll put him on speakerphone so you can hear, but you have to be quiet. Okay?" Her voice got quiet with the last two sentences, like Mr. Black might hear her.

I smiled and nodded that I would be quiet.

She dialed a number and a very deep voice said, "Hello?" I remembered Mr. Black from the parking lot at the Skylight and his voice fit. Mr. Black had nice muscles. I remembered he'd had a shaved head and a serious look. He was nice looking and his voice added to his charm.

"Hello, Mr. Black," Gabriella said.

"Do you have me on speakerphone again Gabriella?" he asked.

"Well, yeah, but I have my hands full right now," Gabriella said walking to the filing cabinet and putting my paperwork inside.

"I'll wait," he said.

"Alright." She shut the drawer and walked back to the phone and picked it up.

"I know," she said. I imagined him reminding her how much he hated to be put on speakerphone. I had had that same conversation before. I didn't like the speakerphone either unless I was on the receiving end.

"Ms. Stanton is finished with her paperwork and is waiting for a ride. Okay, see you then." And she put the receiver down.

She stifled a giggle with her hand and said, "He's my favorite. Just wait till you see."

"We've met," I told her. "He didn't say anything though. You were right, he does have a great voice." I smiled.

"He said it shouldn't be much more than half an hour. I am so excited!" Gabriella said.

"I can't believe I'll get to work with a woman again. I'd hoped you'd come through and here you are." She put her arms out like she was demonstrating a product for a commercial.

"I don't know if I have the job yet. I haven't even had my second interview," I told her with doubt in my voice.

"Honey, they NEVER let anyone into the office alone that doesn't have the job. I'm just glad it wasn't that creep Leonard," she said.

J.C. Phelps

"Don't say anything, but what you are going through now is like a type of initiation. Mr. White likes to know what you can and can't do and how well or how badly you do it. He'll have you trained to his liking in no time."

"So what job am I being hired for?" I asked.

"Mr. White will put you on the jobs that you are best suited for. Sometimes they hire for single jobs, but I think you are to become a permanent fixture around here." She looked around suspiciously and added with a smile, "You really made an impression on him Saturday. As soon as you left he called in all the guys for a meeting. I don't think everyone has been here at the same time EVER. At least not when I've been here or when the sun was shining." She had been leaning over her desk at me while she had said this and now she sat back.

"I think they were just looking for someone to take on a couple of jobs they've got coming up, but I think you made Mr. White want to take in another partner. That's the only reason I can think of him calling in everyone."

"He's quite the hunk though, don't you think?" she threw at me.

"I guess so," I said trying hard not to blush but failing.

"He's a lady's man though, so don't get attached. I've heard the guys talk. Mr. White never says anything but the rest of them do. He's a heartbreaker, that one," she said with a disapproving look.

We sat and chatted. I decided I really liked her. She was full of juicy tidbits and wasn't afraid to share them. After about forty-five minutes Mr. Black came in the front door.

Chapter Six

Mr. Black was about 6' 3" tall and had the look of a gangster. He had shaved his head and it looked good on him. His eyes were almost black and unforgiving. In the parking lot of the Skylight he had been sporting a look that said he was cooler than cool and he wore the same face today. He pointed down at me and in his rough, deep voice and said, "Up. Let's go." He hiked his thumb toward the door.

I got myself right up out of the chair with no hesitation. His demeanor demanded it. He was already out the door, but I made sure to be right behind him.

The elevator ride was uneventful and we went directly to Mr. Black's SUV in the garage. He unlocked the passenger's door and opened it for me. I stepped up into the vehicle and he shut the door for me.

We ended up in front of my place and Mr. Black got out and met me as I came out of the vehicle. He opened the back passengers door and pulled out what I thought had been his dry cleaning and a manila envelope. He handed me the bag-wrapped clothes hanger and said, "That's a business suit for you. I think we got your size right." He still held the envelope as he walked me to my door.

"You need to wear that suit for this job. You have forty-eight hours to complete your assignment." He handed me the envelope and said, "Everything you need to know is in here. Good luck." With that he was gone.

I got into my house and went directly to my room. I hung the outfit on the door and sat on the bed and opened the envelope. Inside I found a piece of folded paper and a floppy disk.

The paper read:

Subject:
First Federal Bank
17721 1ˢᵗ Ave.

Objective:
Find and retrieve file name FALSEPRETENSE

Notes:
You must find a way to get this file from the bank's computer database from inside the bank.
It must be brought to the office by 0930 hours, Wednesday.

J.C. Phelps

Use of excessive force is not an option.
This is a covert act and is to go undetected.
Use of excessive force is not an option.
This is a covert act and is to go undetected.

Okay. I had to break into the bank's computer and steal a file. I could do this from home! I suppose the bank was testing its people for security reasons. Now all I had to do was figure out how to get on one of their computers. Getting the file would be easy. Think.

I started to get undressed to put on the suit. I had my shirt off and my pants undone when I remembered the cameras staring down at me. I quickly slammed the bedroom door and finished putting on the suit. It was a perfect fit and quite flattering.

I had formulated a plan within half an hour of sitting on my bed. I made a quick phone call to my dad to get the ball rolling and stepped out the door.

I had decided I didn't want to take a cab. I might have to sit in the car for a few minutes before I went in to get up the nerve and the driver might get suspicious of me.

Within the hour I was at my destination. I found a parking spot on the street not far from the main door and went directly into the building. I went straight to the island loaded with forms so I could check things out. I grabbed a deposit slip and began to fill it out so I would be doing something else other than looking around. The security guards were posted on either side of the main door. Both of them had their thumbs in their front pockets making their elbows stick out and they were casually scanning the room.

When I finished filling out the form I went to the appointment desk and asked to speak with an officer because I wanted to make a substantial deposit. I was directed to the waiting area and did just that, waited. It only took a couple minutes for an officer of the bank to come and get me. I followed him back to his office and sat down.

He said, "How can I help you today?"

"I would like to make a transfer from another bank and start a new account here," I said and handed him the deposit slip.

His eyes widened at the sight of the sum and said, "This should be no problem, Ms. ...?"

"Miss Stanton," I said. "This is my dad's account, I hope that won't be a problem."

"If he has authorized the transaction it should be no problem," he replied, pushing buttons on his keyboard.

I waited while he put the information in. He had a baffled look on his face. "Is there a problem?" I asked.

"This doesn't seem to want to work Miss Stanton," he said. "I better go get my supervisor. Please stay here, I'll be right back." He left the room.

Color Me Grey

44

I got up and quietly shut the door and ran around to the other side of the desk. I had the file right in front of me but there was no floppy disk drive on this computer. Shit, shit, shit. I didn't have much time so I quickly set up a Hotmail account. I labeled it stealingfromu@hotmail.com and used the password "firstfederal." I was going to e-mail it to myself. I hoped it wasn't a huge file. It must not have been because it didn't take long to get it to go through. I barely got sat back down before the officer and his supervisor came back to the room.

"Ms. Stanton, there seems to be a problem. The account number you gave us does not exist. We have called the other bank and they do have an account for a Mr. Stanton but there is not an authorization to transfer funds," the supervisor explained.

"I see," I said, putting a mad look on my face. "May I use your phone?"

"Of course," the supervisor said and handed me the phone. He punched the nine and said, "There, now you can make an outside call."

I dialed my house and said to the answering machine, "Daddy, they say you didn't authorize the transaction." I waited for a second trying to look more and more frustrated. Then I said, "Well, you could have told me that before I came down here and made a fool of myself. I'll talk to you later. Bye." And I hung up the phone.

"I'm sorry," I said. "My dad already transferred me money into a different account at his bank. I'm really sorry that I wasted your time."

"No problem. But Miss, if this wasn't a misunderstanding you could be in some trouble. You should make sure your father knows his bank will be calling him to let him know of the attempted activity," the supervisor said.

"I'd hope so," I said and walked out the door.

I had a hard time not running from inside the bank. I walked a little faster than normal. I wanted to get into my car and speed away. I did pretty well until I got a couple blocks away in my car. Somehow, my foot wanted to plant itself to the floorboard with the accelerator underneath it.

When I reached my house my nerves had settled a bit. I went in the bedroom, made sure the door was shut tight and changed out of the suit and back into a t-shirt and jeans. I hung the suit back on the clothes hanger and neatly spread the black plastic bag over the outfit, just as I had received it. I made sure I had the floppy disk and drove back to the office.

Gabriella wasn't at her desk and Mr. White's door was closed. I went to it and knocked lightly.

"Come in," Mr. White replied.

I opened the door and stepped in. I began to walk to the couch to set the outfit down.

"Close the door behind you please," he said. I saw a playful look cross his face.

J.C. Phelps

While I was doing that he asked, "Do you have some questions on your instructions?"

"No. I think I have the file," I said.

If I hadn't been watching for the surprised look I wouldn't have seen it. It was apparent on his face for less than a second.

"Bring it here please," he said putting out his hand.

"It's not here but you should be able to access it from your computer." I walked to the couch and laid the outfit down.

"Those were not your instructions," he said.

"I understand, but the computer at the bank didn't have a floppy drive." I handed him the empty disk. Our hands touched and we both hesitated for a moment.

He reached over and put the disk in his computer's floppy drive and motioned me over.

"Get me the file please."

I leaned in slightly to turn on his computer and the heat of his body made me a little shaky.

I looked toward him when the computer asked for the password and he just looked back at me. 'Fine,' I thought and typed in his password. I logged onto the Internet and looked up the Hotmail address I had created at the bank. As I was doing this all I could think was, please be there, please be there. I got logged on, typed in the password and started to download the file onto the floppy disk.

"Fairly impressive, Ms. Stanton," he said making me jump.

I looked to him and he had a smile on his face. It was a complete smile, not a sly grin that I had seen before. It was a wonderful smile and made me melt.

The phone rang and he picked it up. "Yes?" he said. "Yes, she's here. Really? Yes I have it in my possession." Then he hung up.

"That was Mr. Black. He lost you coming back from the bank. Seems you have a lead foot." His smile was still there.

"Thank you for a job well done. Welcome aboard, Ms. Grey. Please have a seat while I finish this up," he said, still smiling. He picked up the phone and dialed.

I chose to sit on the couch. His call was to the bank manger reporting our success and finishing up all the little details. I didn't pay all that much attention to his conversation because I was trying to get used to my new name.

Mr. Black walked into the office just as Mr. White ended his conversation with the bank. He hovered in the door while Mr. White told me what lay ahead of me.

"From now on you will be at my beckon call. Do you understand that?" he said, all trace of the smile gone from his face.

I automatically picked up on the change and answered appropriately, "Yes, sir."

Color Me Grey

"I will give you jobs as I feel you become suited for them. You have the benefit of some good training, but it's not thorough enough." he added.

"Mr. Black will get you started."

Chapter Seven

Mr. Black ushered me out of the office building to his waiting SUV. Again he opened the door for me. I climbed in and waited for him. As soon as he got behind the wheel he handed me a cell phone.

"Call your Dad. Tell him you will be gone on company business. No loose ends," he said.

I did as I was told and we left the garage for parts unknown. We stopped for gas just as we were leaving town and he filled both tanks. He returned with a plastic grocery bag and set it in the back seat.

"There's water in the bag, but pace yourself, it's a long trip," he explained.

I assumed that meant we weren't going to be stopping for a potty break any time soon. I didn't have any idea where we were going or why. Talk about being on a "need to know basis." If I were driving I'd need to know.

"Do you want me to drive the first shift?" I asked.

"Nope," he said.

I thought I would have gotten a little more info than that. He could have said, "No, no need for shifts." I guess that would have been too much information for my brain to handle. Oh shut up and quit whining I told myself. No need to pick on the Neanderthal man.

I actually didn't mind Mr. Black. He was a man of few words but he seemed very polite, a little intimidating, but polite. He had opened the car door to let me in and shut it behind me both times I had ridden with him. I think if I waited to get out of the vehicle when we stopped he would come open my door without a second thought. I know some women find that offensive nowadays, but I found it charming and endearing. It demonstrated respect.

We had been driving for a few hours and not a word had been said. Mr. Black apparently didn't want to listen to the radio either. I had tried to turn it on and he had smacked my hand away. I was getting bored. It was getting dark and I had a tough time seeing any scenery.

"Get some shut-eye. It'll be a while before you get another chance."

The sound of his voice in the quiet vehicle made me jump a bit. I lowered the seat back and closed my eyes. I lay there and listened to the song of the tires on the road for a long time. I couldn't fall asleep. The seat wasn't really too uncomfortable, it was my mind doing aerobics.

I must have dozed off because the next thing I remembered was the door to the SUV swinging open and Mr. Black ordered, "Up. Out."

I immediately and instinctively followed orders. Mr. Black pointed at the ground in front of me. "Put it on."

There lying at my feet was a green canvas backpack and a pair of hiking boots. I also found a green army-type jacket to wear. I put the boots on and felt the tenderness in my shoulder. I pulled the jacket on and snatched up the backpack and immediately regretted it. That thing was HEAVY and didn't help my shoulder any. I guessed it weighed at least fifty pounds.

I shrugged it on and noticed the sun hadn't been up for too long. There was a mist hanging close to the ground and the sky had a pinkish hue. We weren't even on a road. No road to be seen. Somehow Mr. Black had gotten this big SUV through the close trees.

"Keep up," he said and marched off into the woods.

I was in decent shape and didn't have much trouble keeping up for the first few hours. I was enjoying the scenery and occasional wildlife sighting. Then slowly my shoulder started aching, my feet hurt and my back was killing me. I slowed a bit and was falling behind when Mr. Black yelled, "I won't wait. Keep up or fail." I seriously considered stopping a few hours later. I was silently crying as I plodded on behind Mr. Black. Tears were rolling down my face but I didn't dare make a sound. I was exhausted and almost passed out more than once. We must have traveled at least ten miles when we came upon a stream.

Mr. Black stopped and said, "We'll take a brief, rest here." He reached for his canteen in the side pocket of his backpack and said, "You better drink some water, but not too much, you'll get sick."

I reached around to take my pack off and he said, "Leave it on, you won't be able to pick it back up." He came over and took my canteen out of my pack and handed it to me.

"Remember, not too much," he repeated and then began to dig in the pack again. He handed me Vaseline, foot powder and a pair of socks.

"Change your socks, Vaseline between your toes and foot powder in your socks and shoes," he said.

I sat down and went to work changing my socks and following the rest of his directions.

"I'll be back with lunch," he said and disappeared into the woods. I hoped he'd be gone for a couple of hours. Maybe he would run back to Sal's and bring me a club sandwich. Hey, if you're going to dream, dream big. Maybe he was running to a payphone to order in pizza. Pizza sounded good. I had my shoes back on and Mr. Black wasn't back yet. Thank goodness for small favors.

"Lunch." I woke up to Mr. Black's voice. I had been using my pack to lean on and had my legs stretched straight out in front of me. My mouth had been wide open and was dried out.

J.C. Phelps

Mr. Black had built a fire and had something on a stick, holding it over the flame. It looked to be a mammal or reptile of some sort. It had no head or tail, but it had four juicy looking legs.

I thought I had been in pain from Leonard's punch the other night, but I literally fell to my knees while trying to stand up. I was on my second attempt when Mr. Black appeared at my side. He extended his hand and helped me up. He had been harsh all day so this change in attitude was a bit surprising.

"You've done good today. I've not met many men that can do what you just did and not complain," he said by way of explanation.

He went back to the fire and pulled some meat off the creature and handed it to me. I did my best to wipe the ashes and burned pieces off but ended up just shoving it all in my mouth.

"Pace yourself," he said. It was hot, so I spit it back into my hand and started to eat more like a lady. There was a bit of a wild taste to the meat but it was pretty good. I wondered what it was but thought better of asking. After I was full I would ask what I had just ate. I wasn't a picky eater, but I had found the *idea* of some foods made me gag. I would rather not eat a reptile, but if this was a lizard of some kind I may have to change my mind.

Between us we picked the bones clean in about five minutes. Mr. Black put out the fire and said, "Let's get a move on, we have a long way to go."

"What did we eat?" I asked while I stood.

"Squirrel," he replied.

Poor thing, I thought. Squirrels were cute little things. I pictured one sitting on a log, his tail twitching like they constantly do. Didn't taste all that bad though.

Once we started moving again it was a new kind of pain. I ached everywhere, but it was a dull ache. I no longer checked out the scenery or occasional wildlife sighting. I watched the back of Mr. Blacks hiking boots go up and down. I concentrated on his footfalls and matched them step for step. I counted them, lost my place and started over again.

Mr. Black stopped and I stopped. I noticed that it was almost dark. Maybe we were going to stop for the night. Don't get your hopes up, it's probably just dinner break I told myself.

He took his backpack off and started to remove the bedroll that was fastened to the bottom. I stood there and watched him, not fully comprehending what was going on. He rolled it out on the ground and then came up to me and took the pack off my back and did the same with my bedroll.

"Help me find some firewood," he said when he was done.

He got up and went one direction and I went the other. I came back with an armload of dead twigs and he had already gotten the fire started.

"Is this enough?" I asked, my voice hoarse.

"Yeah. Get some rest. We'll eat in the morning." With that I laid down and promptly fell asleep.

Color Me Grey

"Breakfast." Mr. Black nudged me with his boot.

I sat straight up and looked around. Where was I? Shit, now I remember. Damn, I thought maybe I was in hell. No such luck.

"What time is it?" I asked him.

"Time for breakfast," he said. Smartass, I thought. I wasn't in the best of moods this morning or evening or whenever it was. It was as dark as it could get. The only light available came from the fire and the eerie eyes in the distance.

"What's out there?" I asked.

"Don't know for sure. Maybe wolves. Most likely deer," he said.

Great, wolves. I ate the jerky he handed to me and sipped on my water. All the while I kept my attention on the eyes around us.

We sat in silence and waited for the sun to come around to our side of the world again. Slowly the mist formed on the ground and the brightest stars started to fade. Eventually the sky turned from a black to a bluish gray. Then the first hints of pink and orange began to show on the clouds. Mr. Black had put the fire out sometime between black and gray so we could fully appreciate the sunrise.

"On your feet," he said before the sun was visible. I felt cheated. I stood and all the aches of the previous day came back. I had a little trouble lifting the pack but managed to get it up alone. I had to use one arm because the bruised shoulder hurt too much. I couldn't make that arm move without breaking into a sweat. I had to do some special maneuvering. I leaned down and put my injured arm under the strap and then turned around and hiked the whole thing up on my other arm. Then I adjusted the strap for the bad arm.

Mr. Black was already marching away through a particularly thick stand of trees. Once inside the stand I couldn't see more than a few feet in front or to either side of me. I managed to catch up to Mr. Black with no problem. His pace was a lot less brisk this morning, more of a casual stroll.

I strolled along behind him and before long we came to the edge of the thickly placed trees. Not more than one hundred feet away stood a small cabin. Was this our destination? I hoped so. I loved the outdoors, but I was too tired to enjoy it. A nice bed, or lumpy bed for that matter, would be wonderful.

We strolled up to the door and Mr. Black went in. I stood on the porch and thought about it. We had been hiking less than fifteen minutes. We could have been here last night. I wouldn't have had to sleep on the ground. I could have gotten an extra fifteen minutes of sleep. My anger was building as I thought about how close we had been to the cabin all along.

"Why didn't we just hike to the cabin last night?" I asked with a hint of frustration in my voice.

"I like to camp," he said.

"You like to camp?" I replied with my eyebrows raised.

J.C. Phelps

"We made good time yesterday but the program calls for a night in the woods," he said.

I decided it would be best not to pursue this line of questioning much longer. Mr. Black was, after all, at least three times my size. I didn't want to provoke him because I didn't know exactly what he might do. He had me guessing. One minute he could be a major hard ass, the next he was helping me out.

I walked into the cabin and looked around. It was about the size of my place, maybe a bit bigger. It looked as if it had been used recently. The outside of the cabin led me to believe the place hadn't seen people in years. The inside was different. It was by no means elaborate, just the basics. A refrigerator and stove in the kitchen. A wooden table that was big enough to seat six comfortably. Two recliners, a couch and books in a bookshelf along one wall but no TV. There were five bedrooms, each with a single bed and not much else. And one bathroom with a toilet, sink and shower.

Mr. Black had taken off his pack and set it on the floor next to the table. I did the same and asked him, "What now?" I was eyeing the bathroom. I'd love to have a shower and then maybe a nap.

"Get cleaned up," he tipped his head in the direction of the bathroom. "When you come out I want to take a look at that shoulder," he added.

"I'm fine," I said walking toward the bathroom. I didn't like to admit to any kind of fault or liability I might have. As far as I was concerned I was darn close to perfect. Besides, the only way he could inspect the area was if I had no shirt on and being without my shirt in front of Mr. Black made me nervous.

"All the same, I *will* take a look," he replied in a voice that made me believe he would see my shoulder if he had to hold me down to do it.

"You've got fifteen minutes," he added as I shut the door behind me.

Fifteen minutes, I thought with disdain. I locked the door. I thought about taking my time then thought better of it. He would probably just break down the door.

I hurried out of my clothes and started the shower. I half expected to have nothing but cold water, but it warmed up quickly. I found soap, shampoo and conditioner and used a bit of each. After I finished washing up I got directly out of the shower and found clothes on the toilet lid. They were nicely folded and had a toothbrush sitting neatly on top. I dried off and wrapped my hair up in the towel. The pants were loose fitting, tons of pockets, comfortable and black. The shirt was a black tank top and my shoulder was nicely displayed. That ended the worry of showing private parts to Mr. Black. My hiking boots were set on the floor next to the toilet with fresh socks rolled up inside. The boots completed the outfit. I looked like a bad ass with a towel on her head. I found toothpaste on the back of the pedestal sink and brushed my teeth. I didn't have a hairbrush. Shit. I imagine Mr. No-hair didn't think to bring a brush. Oh well, I used my fingers to get at the tangles and pulled it into the all-purpose braid.

Color Mc Grey

I stepped out of the bathroom and Mr. Black was in one of the bedrooms rummaging around. I walked to the door of the room and watched.

"This is your room," he said. My pack was lying on the bed. It was open but it didn't look like it had been unpacked.

"Take this outside and empty it," he said motioning to the backpack on the bed. I went and picked up the pack and glanced inside. It was filled with ROCKS. ROCKS!

"Rocks!?" I repeated out loud. Then I looked at Mr. Black.

"Did I carry these rocks all the way up here?" I asked in disbelief. Rocks, I thought again.

"Yep." That's all he had to say was, yep. Fine, I thought and I stomped out of the room to dump my rocks outside.

I stepped outside and it was still early morning. I hefted the pack out a ways from the cabin in hopes that Mr. Black wouldn't find the rocks to put them back in my pack later. I wonder what *he* carried up here, probably just the necessities. He wasn't undergoing training.

I went back into the cabin and Mr. Black was walking out of a different bedroom toward the bathroom. He turned and said, "Now, empty mine." He pointed to his pack still on the floor by the table. It looked like the side pockets had been gone through but the main body of the pack looked undisturbed.

I walked over to it while he shut the bathroom door. I reached down to pick it up and it didn't budge. I ended up having to drag it to the door. The damn thing was filled to almost overflowing with rocks. Who was this guy? I got it to the deck but didn't want to drag it down the stairs. It would make too much noise and Mr. Black would know that I had to drag the thing. I started pulling out rocks and pitching them out away from the cabin. At least the guy was working hard, the same as me, I thought. I found a new respect for him as I emptied the pack. Some of the rocks were large enough that I had to pick them up with both hands and carry them away from the building monkey style. I had my arms stretched almost to the ground in front of me and my back hunched over. I finally got the last of the stones out of his pack and went back inside.

Mr. Black was sitting at the table when I walked in.

"Come here," He had placed a chair in front of himself and was pointing to it.

I went over and sat in front of him. He reached over and moved the strap of my tank top to the side.

"Nasty," he said. "But you'll live." I looked down at my shoulder and it actually looked better than it had before. Not more attractive, but better. It had started to get a greenish hue to it and I thought that meant it was healing. He put the shirt back into place and stood. "Let's go."

We went out the door and started another march out into the woods. We followed some sort of trail. I figured animals must have made it because there didn't seem to be people anywhere close. Before too long we came to a large

J.C. Phelps

clearing that held a beautiful lake. The water was clear and the bottom was made up of pebbles. I was enjoying the fresh air and the beauty of it when Mr. Black pointed to a buoy out in the water.

"Get out there."

I sat down to take off my boots and he said, "Nope, just go."

I started for the lake and looked back at him over my shoulder. Mr. Black just stood there waiting. I put my boots in the water and my feet didn't get wet. They must be waterproof boots I thought to myself. The water got deep quick and within two or three steps it was up to my knees and cold. I could feel my body tensing up and the goose bumps all over. I kept walking toward the buoy and when the water reached hip height I dove in and took off for the middle of the pond. I was an all right swimmer. I had taken swimming lessons as a kid and Mom and Dad had a pool that I loved to lounge at. Swimming fully dressed with heavy hiking boots was quite different than a swimsuit though. The boots wanted to go to the bottom of the lake and walk me to the buoy. I finally reached it and I looked back to shore to see Mr. Black wave me in. I swam back to shore and plodded out of the water looking like a drowned rat.

"Again," he said and sat down on the small beach. If I had known that I was to be tortured I wouldn't have taken the job. Funny, I thought, I didn't actually take the job, it took me. I hadn't had any control of my life the second I had stepped foot into the office of White and Associates.

I slogged back into the lake and headed back for the buoy. I knew what was coming when I headed back to shore so when I reached the shallows where I could stand again I just turned around and started another lap and began counting. I wonder how many he's going to make me do?

I was exhausted and afraid I was going to drown. I was holding onto the buoy and trying to catch my breath. The wind had picked up and the water had some waves hitting me in the face making it hard to not swallow water with each breath. I was at lap fifty and didn't know if I could make it back to shore. My legs were burning and didn't want to move with the lead boots hanging onto my feet. The sky was beginning to darken and that gave me hope. I had made good time on the first few laps but had slowed a little with each lap and now I was holding on for dear life at the buoy. I was afraid if I went back to shore Mr. Black would send me right back out.

I'm NOT going to drown myself for this I told myself and swam back to shore with renewed energy. I walked up out of the water thoroughly soaked and freezing. Mr. Black was still sitting on the beach and I stomped past him toward the cabin. I didn't care. He could say whatever he wanted. I was going back to take a shower and go to bed.

Mr. Black got up and followed me back to the cabin. I was leading the parade now. He was right on my heels. I could hear him behind me, but I didn't dare turn to see his look. He didn't say a word though.

54

I walked into the cabin and went straight to the bathroom and shut the door. I took a long hot shower and when I came out I found clean sweat pants and a t-shirt on the toilet waiting for me. I dressed and walked out into the kitchen and on the table was a steaming bowl of stew in front of Mr. Black and one across the table for me. He was sitting with a book in his hands and when he saw me he put it down and said, "Let's eat."

I sat down and ate the wonderful stew. I had never had better tasting food in my life. I hadn't eaten since the jerky this morning. I sat and chewed the pieces of potato and carrot that I had just put in my mouth and waited for Mr. Black to say something about me being a *quitter*.

"Well?" I challenged him after a few more bites of my stew.

"Well what?" he asked back.

"Aren't you going to say something about me quitting today?" I threw it right out there.

"Do I need to?" he asked as he put his head down and took another bite of his stew.

"If I had stayed out there another minute I would have drowned," I said defensively.

"You know your limits. Just remember, the outcome is only as good as the input," he replied and the conversation ended there.

I was worried. He didn't say much about anything, but I wanted to know if he was upset that I had just quit out there. I mulled it over while I finished my stew. I got up to wash my bowl. Mr. Black had since cleaned his bowl and the rest of the kitchen and had gone to bed. I walked to my room and flopped down on the bed. I really think I would have drowned, I thought to myself. I truly believed it too. I wasn't exaggerating in the least. I fell asleep content that I had done the right thing but was more determined to do better.

The next couple of weeks went by pretty much the same way. Every morning I got up and did laps in the lake, fully clothed until I could probably have swam back and forth to that buoy indefinitely. Mr. Black seemed to give suggestions instead of orders. I guess it was up to me on what kind of shape I wanted to be in. Running was added to my daily exercise and other things like sit-ups and push-ups. I did my fair share of chopping wood too. At first I was a bit afraid I was going to miss the log and drive the axe into my leg but I got the movements down.

One morning when I reached the lake Mr. Black was already there waiting for me in a black, tight fitting scuba outfit. There were two air tanks sitting beside each other on the beach. He handed me an outfit of my own and said, "Change over there," and pointed toward the trees.

After I got the outfit on I went back to the beach and Mr. Black explained to me how much the air tanks held and how long it would last. He gave me all the little details about the art of scuba diving. It was the most I had heard him talk. After about an hour listening to him we got into the water and I got my first

J.C. Phelps

scuba lesson. After that my days were filled with the same exercises, except a scuba lesson was added every afternoon. In the evenings I was given books on scuba diving and told to study them. I had never scuba dived before this and found it was completely wonderful. Eventually we started diving after dark until I was proficient at all aspects.

I had become accustomed to waking before daybreak, so when I opened my eyes it was still dark. I went to the kitchen and started coffee. I always slept with my bedroom door open but Mr. Black kept his shut. I didn't know if he was in there or not.

I was sitting at the table thinking about how strange it was that I had only been there a month and it had seemed like a lifetime. I was sipping my second cup of coffee getting motivated to start my day. The sun had just started to peak over the jagged horizon. Then I heard a helicopter in the distance. It took me a second to realize it was getting closer. I stepped outside and saw Mr. Black standing in front of the cabin looking to the sky. The helicopter reached us and hovered above for a few seconds and then headed toward the lake.

Mr. Black walked past me into the cabin and I followed. He went straight to his room and began to pack. He told me, "Get packed. It's time to go."

I did as I was told and packed everything I had been using into the backpack that had been sitting in the corner of my room unused. Mr. Black and I were finishing up when a man entered the cabin.

Mr. Black met him half way across the cabin and they grabbed each other's wrists in a sign of gruff affection.

The man had a boyish quality and seemed to smile easily. He said, "Great to see you man." Then he sent a glance my direction.

"So this is Ms. Grey," he said to Mr. Black.

"Yep." Mr. Black now looked to me and said, "This is Mr. Brown."

Mr. Brown had already let go of Mr. Black's wrist and walked my direction. He had brown hair and eyes. His eyes were friendly and happy. He was dressed in the same type of attire that Mr. Black and I had supported for the past month. He had deep dimples on either side of his smiling mouth. He reached for my arm and gave it the same shake he had given Mr. Black. He didn't carry the bulk that Mr. Black did, but again, he was in good physical condition.

"I think Mr. White misses you guys," he said with a grin. "Actually, we have a job to do so I was sent to pick you up. You all set?" He looked to Mr. Black.

"Good to go," he said and started for the door.

I went back to my room to grab my pack and followed Mr. Brown out the door. We walked the distance to the lake. The three of us got into the helicopter and Mr. Brown flew us off the mountain.

Color Me Grey

Chapter Eight

I had thought we were at the end of the Earth, but as it turned out we hadn't been all that far away. Mr. Brown flew us back to the office building in less than an hour and a half. He landed the helicopter on the helipad at the top of the building and we all got out and trooped into the building to the elevator.

Once in the elevator Mr. Brown asked Mr. Black, "So, how'd it go out there?"

Mr. Black looked at him but didn't say anything. The question was asked with a level voice but I got the impression Mr. Brown was hassling Mr. Black about me.

"Mr. White was getting antsy. I think he was wondering what you and Ms. Grey were doing out in the woods." This was a definite rub.

Mr. Black's jaw started to twitch. I had never seen it do that. I must not have ever made him mad. Mr. Brown was getting under his skin though. I wasn't appreciating the implication either. I decided it was time for me to speak up. I didn't need to be compliant anymore. I was in my element once again.

"Excuse me, Mr. Brown," I said and he turned to face me. The grin fell from his face when he saw the expression that I was wearing. "I don't appreciate the implications you are making. Mr. Black is a perfect gentleman and I am *not* easy." He just stared at me with a dumbfounded look until the elevator doors opened. My gaze didn't falter until he turned and left the elevator.

I turned to look at Mr. Black. He was *smiling*. Not a cocky grin that I had become used to seeing around these men, but a genuine smile. It was a great smile. I wondered why he didn't do it more often.

Mr. Black followed me out of the elevator and reached the door to the office in time to open it for me. I stepped in and there was Gabriella. I could see her eyes brighten when she saw Mr. Black. I could understand her appreciation for him better, now that I had spent some time with him. I still didn't know him well, but I knew him well enough to think he genuinely was a good guy.

"...to speak her mind," I heard Mr. Brown say from inside Mr. White's office. I looked inside and saw that half grin on Mr. White's face.

"Please take a seat Ms. Grey. Mr. Black would you please come in and brief me on your progress?" Mr. White said raising his voice enough so we would be sure to hear him.

J.C. Phelps

Mr. Black stepped into the office and shut the door behind him. I had seen the questioning look in Gabriella's eyes so I had taken the seat directly in front of her desk.

I could tell she didn't know what to think of me anymore since I had spent an entire month with the man of her dreams.

"So what was it like, spending an entire month with him?" she asked.

"Okay, I guess."

"You look different. You look…tougher," she added.

"I'd hope so," I said. "Mr. Black had me up at the crack of dawn *every* morning." I stuck my tongue out and she giggled.

"You are *so* lucky," she said. "I wish it could have been me."

"No you don't," I said. "You want romance not ass chewings." Mr. Black had *never* chewed my ass, but I thought it sounded good.

"I didn't realize how much I had missed him until I saw the two of you walk through the door," she said. "Isn't that silly? He wouldn't even give me the time of day and I'm infatuated with him."

"I don't think that's silly. I feel the same way about another man," I said back.

"Who?" she said and got a sparkle in her eye.

Shit, now what do I tell her? *I've got it bad for Mr. White.*

"When I was twelve, this guy came over to my place and I haven't been able to forget him since," I said. It *was* true.

"Do you know where he's at?" she asked. Then the door to Mr. White's office opened up and Mr. Black came out. He turned back to Mr. White and said, "No. My way or I don't go." He pointed at me and said, "Up, let's go."

I obeyed. You couldn't say no to that finger pointing at you.

We got to the car garage and Mr. Black's SUV was in it's rightful spot. He opened my door and then stepped up behind the wheel.

"How'd this get here?" I asked.

"Mr. Brown and Mr. White brought it down off the mountain the morning we started our hike," he said.

"What's going on?" I asked.

Mr. Black didn't say anything. His jaw was twitching again. I looked forward and waited to see if he would want to tell me about it before we got back up on the mountain. I know I hadn't been gone but a few hours but I was already beginning to miss the fresh air, the exercise and the solitude.

"Are we going back up to the cabin?" I couldn't stand it; I wanted to know.

"Nope. We're on our way to do a job," he replied. "Mr. White wanted to leave you behind on this one, but I told him no. On-the-job training is the best kind there is." Mr. Black had started to talk in longer sentences since I had started my scuba training.

Uh-oh. I wasn't sure I wanted to cross Mr. White, even if I was with Mr. Black.

58

"What's the job?" I asked.

"We need to pick someone up," Mr. Black said. I let a silence fall upon us and the next thing I knew, we were in my driveway.

"What are we doing here?" I asked.

"We need some info and you'll be able to get it from here," he said.

We got into my place and it was just as I had left it a month ago. Mr. Black walked directly to my computer and turned it on.

"I need you to hack into the office's computer and pick out a file for me," he said.

"I don't know," I said as I walked to the computer. I sat down and began to *hack*. I just couldn't resist a challenge. In a matter of seconds I had the office system open on my computer. Mr. Black told me the file name he was looking for and I found it right away. I downloaded it onto my computer and my phone rang. I jumped and logged out.

I answered it on the third ring. "Hello?"

"Ms. Grey," It was Mr. White. There was a heavy silence. I waited, then said, "Yes?"

"I'm sorry. I'm about to make a decision that could affect the company. The job that Mr. Black wants to take you on is for a client that specifically asked that you not be involved," he explained. What kind of client would even know about me? My mind reeled. DAD! He had said that he hired White and Associates from time to time.

"I don't want to do anything to jeopardize our standing with this client, but I also don't want my clients telling me how to run the company," Mr. White said and I could tell he was frustrated.

"I'm going with Mr. Black on this because I will *not* be pushed around or bullied," he said. Then after a short pause he added, "I hear you did great at the cabin." Mr. White continued, "It's hard to impress Mr. Black and you certainly did. He told me that you made it to the cabin in just one day. No one else has done that on their first hike. Pretty impressive, Ms. Grey."

"Thank you," I replied.

"Mr. Black also says you're the best scuba diving student he's ever had. Good thing, because this job requires it. You have exactly one week to prepare. Make use of it." And he hung up.

Mr. Black had been standing and watching me. His cooler-than-cool look back on his face. When I hung up the phone he raised his eyebrows at me.

"That was Mr. White," I said.

"And?" Mr. Black asked me.

"He said he wasn't going to let a client tell him what to do," I repeated. "Oh, and we have a week to prepare."

"Right," he said. "We better start then." He sat in the chair at the computer desk and started to read the file. "Do you have anything to eat in here?" he

J.C. Phelps

asked. I scrounged around and found some canned tuna in the cupboard and some bread in the freezer. I made us tuna sandwiches on toasted bread.

By the time I had lunch fixed Mr. Black had printed out the file and was sitting on the couch. I brought him two sandwiches and sat down next to him and ate mine. He finished his food and looked at me.

"I want you to know you did a good job out there."

I had felt uncomfortable when Mr. White told me this on the phone, but coming from Mr. Black, it was pure torture. I wanted to impress Mr. Black and do a good job, but this kind of thing was hard for Mr. Black and it made me uncomfortable to be putting him in this kind of position.

"I'm glad Mr. White suggested giving you a color. As far as I'm concerned, it's one of the best decisions he's ever made. But I need to know a few things about you. I need to know how you handle yourself in a fight and would you be able to kill if you needed to?"

This caught me entirely off guard. Could I kill someone? I really didn't think so.

"I don't know, probably not. It depends, I guess," I said fearing I would ruin his opinion of me but knowing how I felt when I ended a fight by breaking somebody's bones.

"We'll have to work on that," he said. "Let's go."

He took me to a gym. It was full of big men and women. Both sexes had muscles larger than they should be. Mr. Black fit right in, but I stuck out like a sore thumb. Before he took me to the cabin I had been in good shape and now I was in even better shape, probably the best shape I could be in. I just didn't have the muscle mass that these people had.

There were boxing rings and mats spread all around the building. All of them were being used by sparring partners.

"Hey, Black!" A monstrous black man came up to us.

Mr. Black nodded his hello back to the huge man. They grasped each other's hands each with a grip that would have crushed heads.

"Ms. Grey, meet Helix," Mr. Black told me. I smiled at him and he eyed me up and down.

"Damn! You are one *fine* lady," Helix said and then looked back at Mr. Black. "What'cha needin', man?"

"We'd like to use one of your mats," Mr. Black said.

This brought a large laugh from Helix. He threw his head back and a great big "HA!" came from deep inside.

"Man, you know I don't run that kinda place," he said grinning from ear to ear. He looked at me from head to toe again. "She sure is fine, don't you think she deserves someplace private?" He looked from me back to Mr. Black.

Mr. Black had a look that would have made me turn and run if it had been directed at me.

60

"Hey, man." Helix backed down. "I didn't think you was serious, man. Sure, just let me get one cleared off for ya." He walked to the nearest mat and hollered for it to be cleared.

Mr. Black and I put on sparring paraphernalia then squared off on the mat and he said, "Let's go."

I said, "I never throw the first punch."

He lunged at me. Shit, he was quick. I managed to step out of the way, just in time.

"Good, but you're going to have to start it this time," he said. Helix was standing at the side of the mat enjoying the show.

He yelled, "Get 'em, girl!"

I dropped and tried the leg sweep, but Mr. Black jumped over my leg and had me down on the mat before I could stand up to my full height again. I heard Helix laugh off to the side.

Mr. Black got off me and helped me up and said, "Did you see how I did that?"

I nodded yes and he said: "Now you try."

I stood waiting for the leg sweep. I jumped at just the right moment and was on top of Mr. Black in an instant. He just stood there though with me hanging off of him. Helix was laughing so hard he started to cough.

"I had this same problem with Army Boy," I said as I jumped off Mr. Black.

"There are tricks to it. You have to put pressure here, and here." He touched me in a couple of places that I remembered Chief Slade had shown me years ago.

"Pressure points," I said.

"Exactly," Mr. Black said. "Get ready."

"Same thing?" I asked.

"Nope," he said as he came at me. He was throwing punches and kicks and I managed to block them all. I had achieved a black belt in karate and had done just as well in kickboxing. I managed to grab his foot with one of his kicks and flipped him over. He went to the mat on his stomach. He jumped up and I saw that smile for a second time.

"Now we're talking," he said and came after me again. He had me face down on the mat. "Mix your styles and you'll throw off your opponent," he said.

This went on for about thirty minutes and we both had worked up a good sweat when I noticed the gym had become quiet except for Mr. Black's voice. I looked around, all activity had ceased and all eyes were on us. Mr. Black motioned over a woman that must have been from South America, from somewhere around the Amazon.

Amazon Woman came forward and stepped onto the mat. She came toward me slowly then lunged for me. I sidestepped and she hit the mat. I jumped on

J.C. Phelps

top of her and applied pressure to one of the recently remembered pressure points. She pounded the mat until I let her up. She stood back up and started throwing punches. Not one of them hit their mark. She did connect with my body, but never where she had been aiming. I went after her with punches and kicks and backed her off the mat. We both knew the etiquette of fighting so as soon as she stepped off the mat I backed away. She got back onto the mat and tried the same thing as I had just done. I found her hand with one of her punches and had her down on her knees in a matter of seconds, being careful not to break her wrist.

Mr. Black came up to us and told her, "Thanks." Then he waved over a guy that looked like he lived in the gym. I had noticed him in one of the boxing rings when we first came in.

He started the boxing dance. I didn't understand that. To me it was a waste of energy. I stood and waited for him to make a move. He danced around and waited for me to make a move. I finally gave in and went after him with punches. He counteracted with a kickboxing style that I had never come across before. He was so fast that I got confused as to where he might strike next. He dropped to the floor and used my move. He swept my legs out from underneath me but I jumped right back up and made my move. As I came up off the floor I jumped into the air and did a round house kick at his head. I knocked him cold. He fell to the floor and a couple of other guys came to his aid. They shook him awake within seconds, but he bowed to me and left the mat.

Mr. Black came up to me and said, "Not bad, but you should NEVER be hit. Let's go." He nodded his thanks to Helix whose bottom jaw was practically touching the floor.

When we got back into Mr. Black's SUV I said, "What exactly is this job?"

"Mr. White has been contacted by a client that we have done business with before. We've been asked to collect a certain someone. The man we will be picking up will *not* want to come with us. This client is a part of a public entity that cannot be involved with this kind of action. We have to sneak in and do this without anyone being the wiser, including the crew."

"The crew?" I asked.

"Yes, Mr. Brown will drop us about a mile from a boat that will be transporting our target. We will have to swim to that boat, board it without being seen and get the target off without alerting anyone to our presence," he explained. "All you need to do is follow my lead." We pulled into my driveway again.

"Take the rest of the day for yourself," Mr. Black said. "I'll be here first thing in the morning."

I jumped out of the black SUV and walked into my place as he drove away. I made some show of going inside but as soon as he was out of sight I took off for the main house. What the hell was my dad's problem? I was going to find out.

Color Me Grey

Dad was in his office, as usual. I put my knuckles to the door and knocked, then went straight in. I didn't even wait for the "Yes?" to come through the door after I knocked.

"How long have you been back?" he asked with enthusiasm.

"I just got back not too long ago," I said.

"So, how's the new job? What have they got you doing?" he asked.

"Not bad. I'm in training right now. Chief Slade was tough, but not this tough," I replied. If he was going to be sneaky, so was I. Dad knew I wasn't stupid, but sometimes he didn't think I would figure things out. I actually wasn't sure beyond any doubt that Dad was the "client."

"You were gone a month and all you did was train?" he asked raising his eyebrows.

"Yep," I said.

"Mr. White throw anything your way since you've been back?" he asked.

Okay Dad, I thought. Now I *know*.

"Nope. He recalled Mr. Black though," I said.

"Hmmm," my Dad said. "Do you think he'll be putting you on any kind of job any time soon?"

"Maybe, but I'm not sure. Who knows, I could be shipped off any day for any thing," I said. "Mr. Black leaves in a week and he'll be picking me up to train until then. Then I think I'm to go somewhere else and complete training," I lied. "I think I was supposed to go out on this job with Mr. Black, but something must have happened," I added and the implication was thick.

"What do you think happened?" he asked.

"I think someone stuck their nose somewhere it didn't belong," I said.

"Hmmm," he said again.

"Where's Mom?" I asked. I knew he wasn't going to come right out and say anything and I didn't want to either. He always had a way of getting me to tell the truth, eventually.

"She's taking classes for something or other," he said. "She's been busy while you were gone. I think she's going into business for herself. Trying to sell her woodworking. I was skeptical of her creations at first, but it turns out she's quite artistic," he said with a smile.

"Well, that's good," I said. "I suppose I better let you get back to work. I just wanted to let you know I was home. Love you," I said as I walked out the door.

"Yep, me too." The word *love* rarely passed his lips.

I walked back to my place and went inside. I decided I'd kill some aliens on my computer for a while, then I played some cards. I had missed technology while I had been away. Soon it was getting late so I went to my room, glad to be able to sleep in my own bed again.

Morning came and I was showered and ready to go when Mr. Black pulled up the driveway. I met him outside and got directly into the SUV. We drove back to the gym where we had been the day before. I felt the eyes on us as we walked up to Helix.

Mr. Black said to him, "Same as yesterday."

Mr. Black taught me several new moves. We battled each other for most of the morning without a break.

Then Mr. Black said, "I'm going for lunch, you keep practicing." With that he was gone. I was left standing alone in the middle of the mat. Helix came over to me and said,

"Ole' Mr. Black don't bring women in here. What are ya, his new girlfriend?"

"No. I work with him," I said.

"So you single?" he asked.

"No," I lied.

"Too bad, you're damn nice to look at. Let me round ya up some sparring partners. There's lot's that want to try their luck with you," he said waving over a couple of people.

Soon the mat was surrounded by the entire gym. They weren't just watching, they were standing in line. I guess they didn't appreciate a new comer, especially my size, coming in and showing them up. I took them down one at a time. Some got in a few good shots and by the time I noticed Mr. Black standing and watching with his smile on, I was sore. I still had a few butts to kick but he walked onto the mat and escorted me to the waiting bags of fast food.

"You're getting better," he said as he handed me a burger. "Just remember, don't get hit. You're not big enough to take the force some of these people put out." With that, he started eating.

In between bites he said, "We'll go running and you can come back and finish up the rest of these guys tomorrow." We finished our lunch and took off to go for a run. We ran until late afternoon and then he took me home.

When I got home I found some books lying on my couch that hadn't been there before. I picked them up and a piece of paper fluttered to the floor.

I retrieved the paper and read it:

Ms. Grey,
I thought these books might be of assistance to you. Enjoy.

The books spanned several topics including one on the art of stealth and one on yoga. I sat down and began to read.

I woke up on the couch the next morning and readied myself for another day at the gym. Once there, I finished off the rest of the crew waiting to get in their shots and then Mr. Black and I worked out together for the rest of the day.

When Mr. Black dropped me off at my place he said, "Take tomorrow off to let your muscles relax a bit. We're going to have a big swim and I don't want

Color Me Grey

you tired before we start. I'll be here Friday morning to pick you up. Be ready."

Chapter Nine

I woke at the break of dawn Friday morning. I checked outside for Mr. Black but he wasn't here yet. I took a shower and dressed. Still no Mr. Black in the driveway.

I paced around the house for a while. Finally I decided to fix myself something to eat. I still didn't have much in the house for food and I didn't dare walk to Sal's and miss Mr. Black, so I put peanut butter on some saltines and drank a glass of milk for breakfast. I got up to look for signs of life in the driveway. None yet and the sun had been up for at least an hour.

Okay, calm down, I told myself. I took a few deep breaths, closed my eyes and sat on the floor. I put myself in the lotus position, you know the one…where you sit with your legs bent at the knees and put your feet on top of your legs. I kept my eyes closed, but my ears were tuned for sounds on the driveway. All quiet on the front and I was beginning to relax when the phone rang.

I got up and answered it. "Hello?"

"Good morning." Mr. White's voice came across the line. It was quiet and sexy.

"Good morning," I returned. "Where's Mr. Black?" I asked.

"He's to have you here around nine so I would imagine you have some more time to relax. " He said. I heard a hint of amusement in his voice. "I see the books are being used, especially the one on yoga."

The cameras! I had forgotten about them. How could I have been so stupid!

"When are you going to take the cameras out of my place?" I asked. I tried not to be too abrupt, but failed.

"So you found them?" he replied, more like a statement than a question.

"Yeah." Like duh! "I found them the day after Army Boy and you attacked me." Again, a little too abrupt. I took some deep breaths. "So when?" I asked with more control of my voice.

"When I get around to it," he replied.

"Thank you for telling me when to expect Mr. Black," I said and hung up. Then I promptly turned around and gave one of the cameras the bird. I had an urge to go straight to my room and slam the door but I resisted and sat back down and resumed trying to relax. While I sat there all I could think of was how stupid that had been. How immature. The last thing I wanted to do was lose my cool in front of Mr. White. Well, I had stopped myself from flipping off all of the cameras one at a time. That was the only good thing I could think of about what I had just done. I sat for quite a while with my thoughts, but eventually I got off the floor and went to the couch and started to read. Not any of the books that had been left on my couch though, I was protesting.

Mr. Black finally showed up and we headed to the office. We went straight to Suite 73. I felt silly for what I had done earlier this morning. I also was pretty sure it wasn't always a good thing to hang up on your boss. I had been nervous about the job before, but now I was nervous about seeing Mr. White and what he might say. I hadn't told Mr. Black about the early morning conversation because I had felt like an idiot.

We walked into the office and Gabriella was not there. I figured her work schedule must be flexible. Mr. White's door was open so we went straight in. Mr. White was at his desk and on the couch was Mr. Brown. Mr. Black and I each took a seat in one of the chairs closer to the desk.

Mr. White looked at me with a glint of childishness in his eye and that cocky half grin on his face. I looked back to him with a semi-pissed off look. I was mad at him, but had in reality been glad it had been him who was doing the surveillance.

"Ms. Grey, Mr. Black," he greeted us.

Both Mr. Black and myself gave him a small nod. Mr. Black was starting to rub off on me.

Mr. Brown sat leisurely on the couch, with his arms spread over the back. He was kind of cute, but I still hadn't gotten over the remarks he had made before. I looked to him and he smiled at me. It was an infectious type of smile, impish.

"Alright everybody, let's get down to business." Mr. White said. "Mr. Brown will fly you two to Florida where you will get a hotel room and wait. We've been told the target has been planning a cruise on his yacht. He won't be leaving international waters and that's where we come in." He looked to Mr. Brown. "When I receive confirmation that his yacht is underway, I will contact you with the exact coordinates of the drop." Mr. White turned to Mr. Black and myself. "You two are to board the yacht and seize the target." He handed a manila envelope and a small silver case to Mr. Black. "When you acquire the target you are to get him overboard and wait to be picked up by Mr. Brown." He looked at us all one at a time, "Is this clear?" he asked.

We all nodded and stood to leave. I waited until Mr. Brown and Mr. Black had started for the door. I somehow felt I needed to follow them out and not lead them out. I was making my way to the door when Mr. White said, "Ms. Grey will catch up. Ms. Grey please take a seat." Shit, I thought.

I sat and Mr. Black shut the door behind him as he left. I hadn't been alone with Mr. White since the day of the *interview.*

J.C. Phelps

"I just wanted to wish you luck," he said. I was flabbergasted. I thought I was in for it. He continued, "If you follow Mr. Black's lead and you really are as quick a learner as he says you are, you'll be fine." He had a soft smile on his face and a look that I thought might be concern. Nah. I got up to leave and he added, "By the way, that kind of sign language is frowned upon." He had exchanged the soft smile for a devious grin, just when I was beginning to like more than just his looks.

I left the office and both Mr. Black and Mr. Brown were waiting at the elevator for me. Mr. Black wore a questioning look but Mr. Brown was grinning again like that day in the elevator.

"He wished me luck," I said. Oooh, sometimes I made myself so mad. Why did I say anything? It wasn't any of their business. I had been so much more composed before I met this gang of men. What had my life become?

I thought about that during the entire flight to Florida. I had been pretty well off before I decided to spice up my life a little over a month ago. I thought about what I would be doing right at that moment if I hadn't quit my job as a data processor and was glad that I had fallen into this.

Things had always come easily to me my whole life, but this was a challenge. Chief Slade had worked me hard, or so I thought. Mr. Black had worked me until I had wanted to die, but I had enjoyed it.

We got checked into an obscure motel several hours later, all three of us in the same room. I thought I had heard Mr. White wrong or it was a slip-up when he said *a hotel room* but I guess not. The room was definitely nothing special. It had an unpleasant odor of many different bodies. There were two double beds with orange bedspreads shining up at us. I immediately went to the bed closest to the bathroom and claimed it. The two men were going to have to sleep together.

We had left our equipment in the chopper and it was just the three of us in the room with one bathroom, two beds and one TV. I had never been very good at waiting. I got bored and usually ended up pacing, and a few hours later I found myself getting an annoyed look from Mr. Black because I was doing just that, pacing. He had been reading what was in the manila envelope.

I sat on my bed and said, "Sorry. I can't help it."

"Yes you can," he said, emphasizing each word and went back to reading. I looked at Mr. Brown and of course he was wearing that perpetual smile of his. I bet he slept with a smile on his face.

"Someone at least find the remote," I said getting up to search for it myself. Mr. Brown stood up and handed me the remote saying, "Here ya go."

I snatched it and said, "Thanks." I turned on the TV and sat watching for almost half an hour before Mr. Black handed me the manila envelope and said, "Memorize these, then we'll go over the plan."

I opened the envelope and took out the paperwork. Inside I found several pictures, each with descriptions underneath, but no names. Above one of the

Color Me Grey

68

pictures was the word *TARGET*. He had a dark complexion and looked to be either Hispanic or Indian. I memorized all the faces and descriptions then I came to the floor plans of the yacht. Mr. Black began to explain exactly how he wanted this done by pointing to places on the floor plans.

When Mr. Black had finished with the details he asked, "Any questions?"

"Who is this guy and why are we picking him up?" I asked.

"Terrorist." He answered both of my questions with one word.

The rest of the evening was nerve racking for me, and the two men were not enjoying my company at all. Finally Mr. Black said, "Calm down, Ms. Grey." I decided now would be a good time for me to get ready for bed. I went into the bathroom and shut the door.

I started the shower and heard voices in the main part of the room. Neither one of the men had spoken other than to tell me to quit being annoying since we had arrived. I quickly undressed and stepped into the shower and listened at the wall. I could hear pretty well. One of them said, "Now tell me why we have to all be in the same room." Mr. Black, I think.

Then Mr. Brown said, "Malone wanted it that way." Malone meaning Mr. White.

"I don't get him lately," Mr. Black replied.

"It's her. You know how he is with women,"

"Not like this,"

"I guess, but he's been acting weird since the day she showed up in the office. That's why I think it's her. I think he's dying to get in her pants but doesn't dare because she's not just another woman," Mr. Brown said.

"He better not even think about it," Mr. Black said.

"Oh, someone is testy about the Ms. Grey subject," Mr. Brown said.

"We *need* a woman on the squad and I don't think we could have found a better one," Mr. Black explained.

"Is that why you're so protective of her?" Mr. Brown asked with sarcasm in his voice.

"Yes. Believe what you want, but I think she has the potential to be better at this job than even Malone," Mr. Black said.

There was silence after that, so I showered for real and thought about what was said. So Mr. White might be attracted to me. That was good, at least for my fantasy life. I had never thought of him in terms of real life. It would be complicated. Oh well, I just won't think about real life with Mr. White. As for Mr. Black, I knew what he said were his intentions *were* his intentions. We had a big brother-little sister thing going, kind of. I just couldn't imagine myself with as much potential that he thought I had. I always thought I could do anything, but I'd never been confronted with these kinds of challenges. Lately though, my biggest fear had been disappointing Mr. Black. That was something I didn't want to do.

J.C. Phelps

I stepped out of the shower, dried off and put my clothes back on. Then I went back into the room with the beds and men. Mr. Brown said, "About time."

I got under the blankets and threw the bright orange bedspread to the foot of the bed and watched TV for a while before I drifted off to sleep.

When I woke the next morning Mr. Black was sitting on his and Mr. Brown's bed watching a show on fishing. I got myself out of the bed and pulled up the blankets and outdated bedspread and went straight to the bathroom to do my morning brushing of the hair and teeth.

When I came out of the bathroom the television was off and Mr. Black was sitting on my bed along with the little silver box that Mr. White had handed to him the day before. He said, "Mr. White called last night and we are to head out around 10:00 tonight. When we get on the chopper we will change into our gear. We are not using tanks, but snorkels. Do not put your fins or face mask on until we're in the water. First of all, you need to know how to get into the water safely from the helicopter. We'll be dropping from the air and it's very important you cross your arms in front of yourself." He demonstrated by putting each of his hands on the opposite shoulder.

My eyes cut to the box and he said, "I'll get to that in a minute. Don't forget the arm placement and point your toes down or you'll break your feet, ankles and possibly legs. After we hit the water we'll put on the rest of our gear. We may encounter some large swells. If this happens, ride them up and swim down them otherwise you'll tire yourself out. Okay, the box. It contains Phenobarbital, which is a sedative. We'll use it to put the target to sleep so he'll be easier to handle. Any questions?"

"Not right now," I replied.

Mr. Brown showed up with breakfast and a deck of cards not long after I had received my instructions. We ate and played poker. I was the only one without a dime, so they each fronted me a few dollars. We played poker until around 6:00 PM and then the pizza we had ordered showed up. I bought because I had won the most money. I even paid back what had been fronted to me. After we ate we lounged around and waited for the right time to leave for the helicopter.

"It's time," Mr. Black's voice woke me. I had fallen asleep while waiting. Mr. Brown was gone again. Mr. Black explained he had gone to check us out of the room and he'd be back soon. We sat in the rented car and waited and I began to get nervous again. This was something I had pictured myself doing, but only in the fantasy aspect of my world.

We had been in the air for about fifteen minutes when Mr. Black handed me my equipment and suit. Along with the normal attire he handed me a wristband that looked a bit like a large watch. He explained that it was a GPS tracking device that also included a homing beacon. He showed me how to use it and which buttons were for what. Mr. Black secured it to my wrist and then put his own on. I waited for him to turn his head before I started to get the suit on. It

70

didn't take me long because I was afraid he might turn his head back or worse yet, Mr. Brown might sneak a peak. Only Anthony had seen me without clothes since I had become a woman and I wished he hadn't. I wasn't ashamed of my body. I thought it was actually rather nice, but there was always the chance that someone would find some flaw and broadcast it.

We flew low over the water. Sometimes close enough that I was afraid that we might hit it. It took less than two hours for us to reach a spot where Mr. Brown began to hover.

"This is it!" he yelled over the noise.

"Remember what I told you!" Mr. Black yelled and jumped from the helicopter.

I followed right after him, no reason to stand and think about it. I crossed my arms and pointed my toes and still hit the water hard. It was cold and black. When I surfaced I was disoriented and confused. Mr. Brown had already piloted the helicopter away and I didn't see Mr. Black in the darkness. I pulled on my mask and began to pull on my fins when I saw a faint green light a little ways off. I swam toward it and before long I saw Mr. Black bobbing in the water. When I reached him he said, "I'm going to drop this light now." And he let go of what looked like one of the glow sticks kids carried on Halloween.

"From now on we'll use red chem. lights instead of green. It's harder to see red light at night unless you're looking for it," he explained. He reached over and attached a line to my waist securing us together. He started to swim away and I matched him stroke for stroke. We swam for about an hour without a break, and then Mr. Black stopped and checked his wristband. I saw a small green light shining from his arm even though he was trying to shield it.

"Start watching for the boat's running lights. We should be there anytime now." With that he resumed his repetitive strokes.

I had been keeping my head down and not paying much attention, but now I swam with my head above the water, watching for any light. There were thick, rolling clouds in the sky, but the moon peeked out once in a while. About another half an hour of swimming and I spotted lights on the horizon to my right. I tugged on the line that was attached to my waist and Mr. Black stopped his advancement. He turned and looked at me and I pointed to the distant lights. He nodded once and adjusted his direction. I fell into the rhythm of his strokes once again.

When the lights were considerably closer he stopped and said, "No talking. We don't want to alert anyone to our presence. Grab and go and stick close."

"What happens if we get caught?" I asked.

"We'll have to take care of it, so don't get caught," he replied.

We'd have to 'take care of it'? I figured that meant we would have to kill someone. I most definitely didn't want to have to do that. Don't get caught, I told myself.

J.C. Phelps

They say crime doesn't pay, but this criminal owned an eighty-four foot yacht. We boarded the ship at the rear as planned and found the small motorboat in its place at the back of the boat. Mr. Black motioned me to one side of the boat and we lifted it to the edge of the yacht and were beginning to set it gently into the water when I dropped my end making a rather large *splash*. Mr. Black ushered me around the side of the yacht and we stood in the darkness for a moment straining our ears to hear if anyone would come to investigate. No one did, thank goodness.

We continued on with the rest of the plan by quietly walking through the empty rooms making our way to the stateroom where the target should be sleeping. Our plot hinged on the hopes that everyone would be sleeping or at the helm at this time of the morning. Our luck held as we crept through the first deck, which held the living quarters such as the dining room. We got to the stairs leading to the birthing floor and heard a bathroom being used. We stood at the top of the stairs and waited until we heard some doors open and shut. Slowly Mr. Black started down the stairs with me right behind him. At the bottom of the stairs it was quiet, but light filtered out from a nightlight in the bathroom.

Mr. Black reached to his utility belt and pulled out the little silver box. He opened it up and inside was a syringe and a small vile of a clear liquid. Using the little light filtering out from the nightlight he filled the syringe. He replaced the vile back to the box but not the needle. We resumed our slow pace to the stateroom at the back of the ship.

Mr. Black stood at the door for a moment listening and then quietly opened the door. There, lying in the bed was the target. This is too easy, I thought with glee.

Mr. Black and I went to the side of the bed and he motioned for me to get ready to cover the target's mouth so he couldn't scream out when he felt the needle stick him. I motioned I was ready.

He grabbed the target's wrist just as I leaped onto the bed. I put my knees onto the man's arms and shoulders and my hands over his mouth and held on tight. He put up a bit of a fight but was soon quiet again, breathing evenly.

I looked to Mr. Black and he was replacing the syringe back into the silver case. I crawled off the man in the bed and went to the door. Looking out carefully, I noticed everything seemed right. I turned and nodded to Mr. Black, who now had the man on his shoulder.

Slowly I opened the door and made my way back to the stairs, making sure Mr. Black was still right behind me. My heart was bursting from fear and excitement and it was all I could do to control my breathing. We slipped up the stairs and back out on the deck. Cautiously we started to make our way back to the awaiting motorboat when we heard noises coming from our destination. Mr. Black set the target down and motioned me to stay put. My eyes had become

Color Me Grey

readjusted to the outside light and I saw a man trying to pull the small motorboat back onto the stern of the boat.

Mr. Black was on top of him before the guy knew it, but somehow he managed to slip from the grasp of death and knocked the silver box out of Mr. Black's belt at the same time. I saw the box fall and open on impact and the syringe rolled across the deck. The man had it in his hands before Mr. Black knew it was gone. The man came at Mr. Black with the syringe. He stuck the needle into Mr. Black's leg and scurried away from him. Mr. Black was on his way to finish the job when he faltered and went down on one knee. The next thing I knew he was lying motionless on the deck.

What the hell was I supposed to do now? I thought. The man was inspecting Mr. Black by the time I got up behind him. I had been quiet and he didn't know I was there. I reached out and grabbed him around the neck, cradling it in the crook of my arm. I grabbed onto my forearm with my free hand to secure my grip. Mr. Black had just recently taught me this maneuver and it had the choice of several outcomes. The man could either be choked into unconsciousness or death or I could move my arms just a bit and I would break his neck.

The man wriggled under my grasp and clawed at my arms. His feet were kicking wildly and I knew choking was not an option. He was making too much noise. I squeezed just a little tighter and not only heard the crunch and crack of breaking bones but felt it in my arms and chest.

I was immediately nauseous but repressed the urge to run to the back of the boat and empty my stomach. Instead, I set the limp body down on the deck and went to look at Mr. Black. I was worried when I reached his side that he may no longer be alive because he had told me the syringe held at least three doses and too much would be lethal. But was relieved to hear a smooth stream of air going in and out of his lungs. The syringe was still in his leg and there was a little of the clear liquid left in it. I pulled it out of his leg and retrieved the silver box and its spilled contents and replaced them all into Mr. Black's utility belt.

This took me a little while and I became aware of the time I was wasting so I hurried and dragged Mr. Black to the waiting motorboat. Somehow I managed to get him inside. Then I returned to where I had left our target and dragged him to the motorboat. I had to fight with his and Mr. Black's limp bodies to get them both in the boat and not spill either one of them out but I handled it.

Next I had to get rid of the body, but I was afraid it would float and the rest of the inhabitants of the yacht might find it. I decided to bring it with us. I slid into the water. Grabbing the dead man by the shirt I pulled him off the deck as quietly as I could. I kept a hold of the man's shirt as he floated next to me, and then untied the motorboat. Then I began to push the boat forward and pull the man behind me. I did this for what seemed like a very long time until I felt I was far enough away from the yacht to stop for a rest. I could still see the running lights in the distance but I figured it was a good sign that no new lights had appeared in the darkness.

I crawled up into the motorboat next to the sleeping men. Still holding onto the casualty, I tried to rearrange arms and legs so I could eventually get to the motor. I didn't dare start it up until I could no longer see lights in the distance. With one hand I repositioned the target and Mr. Black so I had full access to the motor and then I sat watching the lights grow smaller. I don't know how long it had been or exactly when I couldn't see the lights anymore. I had been sitting in the boat rolling with the waves and just realized they were gone. I pried my fingers from the dead man's shirt and left him floating at the side of the boat.

The sky had begun to lighten and I wondered how long I had sat oblivious to the world around me. I was worried about Mr. Black. He had said that too much of the sedative could be fatal and from what I could tell he had gotten more than one dose. I started to move toward him to check his breathing when the target grabbed for me. Instinctively I struck out and managed to hit him in the nose. His head went back sharply but he brought it forward again and lunged for me. Fighting in that small boat was awkward. We grabbed at each other and punches landed randomly and rocked the boat. He had me down on the floor of the boat and was choking me. I had somehow slipped under Mr. Black's legs and about all the target could see of me was my face. My arms seemed pinned underneath the hulking Mr. Black but I was able to get at the silver box on his belt. I worked the syringe out of the box while I fought unconsciousness from the strangle hold the target had on my neck. I was frantically trying to get my arm up high enough to deliver the remaining sedative to the target. Everything was going dark and I saw little white lights dancing in and out of my vision. My eyes started to roll into the back of my head involuntarily and I knew that I had to get this over with or I was dead. With a burst of adrenaline I pulled my arm free and stuck the needle in the target's back. He immediately let go of my neck and tried to reach for the needle. I got myself free from Mr. Black's limp body and sat coughing. The target was still wrestling with himself trying to get the needle out when he slowed and then slumped over Mr. Black's legs face down.

I reached for the syringe and noticed that there was still some liquid left in it, so I pushed the plunger to empty the remaining amount into the target. I didn't want him waking up again until the chopper arrived. After I was sure the needle held no more, I pulled it from his back and replaced it in the silver box that was still half attached to the utility belt.

I sat back in the boat and wondered where the chopper was and wanted to kick myself because I had forgotten the homing device. I switched it on and waited. The dead man still bobbed near the boat, but I didn't notice much of anything until I heard the sound of a helicopter. I scanned the horizon and saw a small black dot. I turned the engine over and it caught on the first try so I headed for the chopper.

Color Me Grey

A rope with a harness attached landed in the water not far from the boat, almost hitting the dead man's body who, for some reason was still hanging around. I got myself back into the water and pulled the boat in the direction of the waiting rope. When I reached it I brought it back on board the motorboat with me. First I hooked up the unconscious target and he was hauled up. Then I hooked up Mr. Black. Finally I attached the rope to myself and let myself be hauled to the chopper.

Mr. Brown was in the pilot's seat once again, but Mr. White had joined him. He had been the one hauling up all the bodies, including mine.

He looked at me and said, "Good job. Who's that?" He gestured to the dead body floating near the boat.

"He must have gotten tangled in the rope." I had forgotten to bring in the rope that had held the motorboat to the back of the yacht.

The chopper had already headed back to land and I sat watching for Mr. Black to make a move.

Chapter Ten

The target regained consciousness just a couple hours into the flight, but Mr. Black remained unresponsive. My main attention was on Mr. Black, but it seemed odd the target was submissive. When he awoke he just looked around and said nothing. If I had found myself in a similar predicament I think I would have been yelling and screaming for answers. He had wriggled in his bonds for a few seconds but then his eyes met Mr. White's. The target didn't move much after that. It had seemed as if something passed between them. Maybe it was the stern look Mr. White gave him.

Mr. Black was still under the influence of the sedative when we landed at an obscure helipad somewhere in the desert. I didn't know where we were but it looked like a small military base. A high chain link fence was topped with rolled barbed wire, surrounded the installation. There were a few large buildings that looked like hangers for aircraft, but no runways visible.

As soon as the helicopter touched down, Mr. Brown cut the engine and three men in black fatigues ran up to us. Mr. White escorted the target out the door of the helicopter and the three men saluted him. He just nodded at each of them and marched the target toward a building not too far from us with the three men in tow.

The building was built from brick and unmarked. It looked somewhat like a convenience store without the large glass windows and doors in front. Instead of the glass it had a heavy metal gray door.

Mr. White disappeared into the building with the target and one of his escorts. The other two men in black fatigues planted themselves on either side of the heavy door.

I looked down at Mr. Black and his eyes were open and he was studying my expression.

"Did you get the target?" he asked in his normal voice.

I just nodded.

"Good," he said and sat up. I could tell he was somewhat light-headed by the way he swayed while sitting there. He looked to Mr. Brown who had moved to the back of the chopper next to me.

"What happened to the guy?" Mr. Black asked me, meaning the man who had stuck him with the needle. I didn't say anything and Mr. Brown picked up the question for me.

"I don't know what happened, but when we got the signal from Ms. Grey's homing beacon and not yours too, Mr. White thought he'd better ride shotgun," Mr. Brown explained. "Mr. White is usually close by when we do a job like this one," he directed at me. Then he looked to Mr. Black again and said, "When we got to the little boat there you were snoring and drooling and so was the target and there was a man floating around the boat face down in the water." They both looked at me.

"The guy somehow got a hold of the syringe and got you in the leg," I told Mr. Black.

"Well, what then?" Mr. Brown said wanting to hear all the details.

"So I broke his neck," I said with a sick sound in my voice. All conversation stopped there until Mr. White returned to the chopper.

"I see you're awake," he said to Mr. Black. "You can tell me about it when we get back." He looked at me to let me know I would have to explain too. Seconds later we lifted off the ground and headed for home.

The flight home took the rest of the day and most of the evening. I wasn't paying attention to the time. I was worried about how to explain what had happened. I didn't want to make Mr. Black sound incompetent because it was a fluke It was pure luck that the guy got to the syringe. I know if he hadn't, everything would have been ok and I wouldn't have been the one who killed someone.

We finally reached the office and Mr. White told Mr. Brown that he'd be in touch. Mr. Black and I followed him down to the office and each took a seat while he eased himself behind his desk. There was silence for some time and I became even more uncomfortable. I didn't let it show though. I knew I had to keep a tight control on my emotions right now because if I didn't I would just fall to the floor and cry.

"So, what happened?" he asked Mr. Black.

"I dropped the syringe on the deck while trying to subdue a threat. The threat retrieved the syringe and stuck me with it," he said and then stopped.

Mr. White looked to me and said, "You're going to have to fill in the blanks for me. I want it from the beginning. From when you hit the water," he added.

I started with the story being sure not to miss a single detail. I told him how we saw the boat and swam to it and how the plan went perfectly until the man was pulling the motorboat back onto the deck of the yacht. How Mr. Black went after him and wasn't seen. How the guy had knocked the box to the deck and retrieved the syringe. How Mr. Black continued to fight until the sedative took hold. Then I paused. I was having a hard time with this. Mr. White came around the desk and sat on it right in front of me. He said in an uncharacteristically gentle voice. "Then what? I need to know."

I looked to Mr. Black and he had a sympathetic look on his face too. I should have been grateful but it pissed me off What was I, a sissy girl? The looks and the tone in Mr. White's voice snapped me right out of the funk I was

J.C. Phelps

in. I straightened my spine and said with no feeling at all, "So I got up behind him and broke his neck. Then I loaded Mr. Black and the target into the motorboat." I continued with my story all the way up to the chopper retrieval. I even left in the part about the dead guy getting caught up in the rope I had left hanging off the boat. It was the truth and they wanted *all* the little details.

When I had finished Mr. White stood up and returned to his seat at the desk. He said, "I am not happy with the way this turned out you two. However, Ms. Grey you did the right thing by toting that body away from the yacht. Mr. Black…" Mr. White looked at him and continued. "I am aware some things can't be controlled and this seems to have been one of those situations. I'm glad you held out to have Ms. Grey be your backup. I don't think you could have chosen a better partner. All this said, I am putting you two on the back burner for now." He folded his hands in front of himself and said, "Mr. Black, you are to return to your training of Ms. Grey. She still has things to learn before I can trust the two of you on another mission."

Mr. Black looked perturbed at being *put on the back burner.* But I was relieved. I needed a break from the real world for a while. I seemed to do better in fantasy anyway.

Mr. White added as we got up to leave, "Mr. Black, I will give Ms. Grey a ride home tonight."

Mr. Black looked a bit shocked at this but just left me there without another word. I was horrified. Why would Mr. White want to take me home? Many thoughts entered my brain, the first of which was sexual, but that was shot down immediately when I remembered how we had botched the mission. The next thought was the one that seemed more reasonable. I was going to get into more trouble. If it had been anyone else besides Mr. White or Mr. Black that I was going to get into *trouble* from I would have just blown it off, but I didn't want to come off as inept to these men. I wanted to fit in. I had never wanted to fit in more in my life! I had tried everything to become a part of this and it seemed to be the most suitable to my true self.

"Ready?" Mr. White asked.

"Sure," I said, unable to hide my nervousness.

He led me out of the building and actually opened the door on his Mustang to let me in. He climbed in behind the wheel and the sound of the engine was reassuring. It reminded me of my car and I realized I actually missed it.

We left the lot but he didn't take me home. He drove to a spot known to teenagers for necking. It had a beautiful view of the city below and a steep drop at the edge of the parking lot. He got out of the car and came around to my door. I was distressed and hadn't even gotten out of the car yet.

He opened the door and said, "Come on out."

I stepped out with caution and he laughed. It was a sound that I had never heard before. It was quite pleasant and reassuring. He said, "Don't worry. My intentions are honorable." He flashed his rare smile at me. After he shut the

Color Me Grey

78

door to the car he went to the hood and laid back on it. I followed suit and lay back next to him. We sat for a long time gazing at the stars not saying anything. Finally he spoke up. "Ms. Grey, the reason I brought you out here was so we could talk like people and not like boss to employee. The men and I are very good friends and this wouldn't work if we weren't. I would like to set up a similar relationship with you." I had no reply; I was caught entirely off guard.

"Do I make you nervous?" he asked through his smile.

Rarely could I pull off a lie so I said, "Kind of."

"Well, that's good."

Where was he going with this? It gave the impression of flirting but I had a hard time believing it. Maybe Mr. Brown was right and Mr. White was about to try his luck. Well his luck with women was about to turn. I was certain if this evolved into a sexual relationship I would be out of a job very quickly and also without a boyfriend. Speaking of jobs, I had NEVER been paid for anything. Money wasn't that big of a deal for me because everything I needed was paid for by Mommy and Daddy, but I didn't relish the idea of working for free.

With a bit of an attitude I said, "Am I ever going to get paid? Or do you not pay for training?"

"Yes, Ms. Grey. You should have already received your first check. I know you weren't home long before we sent you on this job so you probably didn't get a chance to check your mail. I will be cutting checks for this job in the next day or two. The company posts a fee for each job and keeps a small percentage plus expenses. Which leaves the larger percentage of the fee to be split among the players."

"Players?" I asked.

"Yeah. You and Mr. Black were the players for this job."

"What about Mr. Brown and you?" I asked.

"We were expenses this time. The players who do most of the work get most of the money," he explained.

"Oh, I see." That sounded fair to me. We sat for a while longer and watched the sky.

"So, what's everybody's real name?" I felt him jump slightly at my voice.

"Well, you already know my real name. To find out who the others are you're going to have to ask them or do some more snooping around," he said.

"Is there a time when you guys call each other by your real names?" I asked.

"Not on a job. When we get together for other reasons we may or may not. It just depends on the mood at the time," he explained. "I suppose I better get you home, the sun is going to be up soon." He started to sit up.

"Can we stay to watch the sunrise?" I asked. I had gotten used to watching the sun lift it's head over the world around me while I was out at the cabin and was missing it right about then.

"Sure," he said and relaxed back down onto the hood of his car.

J.C. Phelps

"How many people have you killed?" I asked out of the blue. I could pretend that it didn't bother me for only so long and I was beginning to feel more comfortable around him. The scent of him still made me a nervous wreck, but I trusted him.

"I don't know," he said quietly. "More than my fair share. It gets easier, but what really helps is knowing why you're doing it. In this line of work you kill or be killed. There is no better reason to kill than to stay alive."

For some reason I trusted his motivations for taking the jobs he did, but I asked anyway, "Do you take every job that comes your way?"

"No. I have to believe in the cause. I don't mind bending the law from time to time, but I won't take a job to do a hit on someone's husband or wife. Is that what you meant?" he asked.

"Pretty much," I said and we fell silent to watch the sunrise.

When it was fully light we got back into his car and he drove me home. I stepped out of the car and felt better about the whole situation. I said thank you and was about to shut the door when he said Mr. Black would be picking me up in a couple of days and then reminded me to check my mail.

He drove away and I went directly to Mom and Dad's to collect my mail.

Mom was in the kitchen at the table painting her latest creation. It was a small shelf she had already stained but was now adding some finishing touches.

"Hi!" she said happily. "I haven't seen you for a long time."

"I know," I replied just as happily. "I like your shelf, you did a great job."

"You know what it is? Your dad can be such a pain. He pretends to not know what my stuff is. I knew he had to be pretending. How could you not know this is a shelf?" she said.

I smiled. My dad and mom were the perfect couple. I had only seen them argue once and it was over me. As I got older my mother had voiced her opinion to me about my dad's shortcomings, but then she would end it with some thing like, 'I suppose I should be used to it by now,' or 'I still love him though.'

"Do you have my mail?" I asked Mom.

"Yes. It's over there on top of the microwave." She pointed with her paintbrush.

I walked over to the small pile of letters and flipped through them. Credit card application, then another, and another, bank statement and then I saw it. The return address was stamped:

1324 Plaza Dr.
Suite 73

I tore it open and looked at the check. Wow, I had no idea! Wow! If I kept working for these guys I would soon be independently wealthy and I wouldn't *need* Mom and Dad's money.

Color Me Grey

"What's that?" Mom asked motioning toward my check.

"It's my paycheck," I said with pride as I handed it to her.

"Oh, my. Your dad told me you were working for these people," she said.

Great, here it comes. She's going to tell me that it's too dangerous and girls shouldn't be doing that kind of work and when was I going to find a good man to marry.

"I'm glad that you found something that you can like," she said, handing the check back to me. "You're doing something that I would have loved to do."

What!!! My mom, go kill people! I don't think so.

"It's okay, I guess," I said.

She smiled and went back to her painting. I hugged her and said thank you for keeping my mail. Then I went straight to my car to set up a new bank account. I wanted to keep track of the money I made separately from my allowance afforded me by my parents. My plan was to mooch off them for as long as I could. Mom and Dad had given me lessons with money as I grew up, you know... 'Here's your allowance, put half in the bank and do what you want with the other half. Just remember once it's gone it's gone.' I actually could have been a shop-aholic but I was careful with what I spent my money on. Usually I found myself wanting the high-priced items like a car and a good stereo and a great computer so I saved more than I spent. It had become a habit to hoard rather than to spend. I'm not saying I didn't splurge on stupid things, like going to the bar. Fancy underwear that I would never share with anyone was a downfall of mine. I just didn't do it as much as I used to.

I got everything settled downtown and headed for home. The excitement of receiving my first paycheck and the shock of seeing the balance of that check had begun to wear off. I thought about the dead guy and quickly pushed him out of my brain and decided to fantasize about Mr. White. I got to a part in the fantasy where I said 'Oh, Mr. White' and it killed it for me. From now on I was going to have to use his real name, Malone, in my fantasies. Not that it was all that much better either.

Upon reaching my driveway I noticed I was exhausted. I wondered why. It wasn't even noon yet. Then I remembered I had been up for a day and a half. I decided I'd go in and go to bed.

When I got to my bedroom, I made sure the door was shut tight before I changed out of my clothes into some sexy pajamas. I had an urge to walk around in front of the cameras, like I forgot they were there, but I hadn't forgotten they were there. Out of all the experiences I'd had since joining the company, the cameras affected me the most. Well, other than having to kill a man.

That brought back the vision of the guy floating face down in the water. I tried to push it out of my head but it wouldn't go. I suppose I'm going to have to face it eventually, I thought. I retraced every part of the mission trying to find a way to not kill the guy What if I hadn't dropped the end of the motorboat, if

J.C. Phelps

Mr. Black had waited to see if he'd leave. All those and other thoughts came to mind but my reasonable side shot them all down. The guy must not have heard the splash or he would have been there sooner. Mr. Black knew what he was doing and the guy probably would have conducted a search of the deck after finding the motorboat the way it had been. Every way I found to change the outcome, I found to be flawed. I guess it had been unavoidable. That helped me a little. I finally fell asleep with the image of the dead man floating around in my skull.

I woke up early that evening and decided to go to Mom and Dad's. I hadn't been around them much lately and I really missed them. Independence had always been my middle name, but I still liked to be around my parents. They were good people. Mom should have dinner ready soon anyway.

When I reached the back door of the main house I could smell spaghetti. I hadn't had spaghetti for a while. I walked in and there was Mom, sitting at the table, painting. Dad was at the stove stirring the noodles.

"Is Dad cooking?" I asked incredulously.

"No, he's just checking the noodles for me," Mom said. My parents were a bit old fashioned. My dad would probably starve if he had to cook and my mom didn't trust him to cook either.

"Here, Dad," I said taking away the spoon he was using. He looked relieved and went to sit at the table.

"Are you going to clean off the table before we eat?" he asked Mom.

"Yes, honey. I just want to get this little part... done... right... here," my mom replied and then stood and began to clean off the table. I drained the noodles and started to dish them up on plates for us. I got Dad's plate put together and then Mom's.

"Did you make garlic bread?" I asked.

"I knew I forgot something," Mom said.

"Oh well, no big deal," I said and dished up my own plate.

We sat at the table like a normal family and Mom talked about the projects she was working on. She had a sign to make for the nice couple down the street. She was thinking about going to a craft fair, she just didn't know if she would like to sit there all day. Then she began to tell my Dad about my paycheck. How excited I was when I opened it, how much it was. All the details about how I practically ran out to go get it cashed.

"I hope you didn't spend it on something stupid. That's a lot of money to be carrying around if you didn't spend it." Dad said to me.

"I didn't spend any of it. I put it in the bank." I said like a little kid who had just gotten in trouble for something she hadn't done.

"Oh, well good. Does this mean I can cut your allowance off?" My Dad said.

"No!" I yelled. I hadn't caught the sly look on my Dad's face until after I shouted.

Color Me Grey

82

Him and Mom both found it funny. The rest of the dinner was nice and we talked about other unimportant things. I helped put the dishes in the dishwasher and headed home.

It wasn't time for bed yet, so I decided to play on the computer for a while. As I was killing aliens I toyed with the idea of checking out the rest of the guys real names. I was mostly interested in Mr. Black, but I thought the best way to find his out would be to ask him. I felt guilty just thinking about spying on him. Respect was a big part of our relationship. He gave me my fair share and I had tons of respect for him.

I pushed myself away from the computer before I found myself doing something that I would feel bad about later. I decided I'd call Colin and catchup. We talked about my new job. I gave him all the details about the training and the bank job I had done. I left out the recovery mission where I had killed a man though. I didn't feel like talking about that anymore.

The next couple of days were pretty much the same. I spent quite a lot of time with Mom and Dad. I even started making a sign of my own to hang on my wall. I had borrowed some paint and brushes from Mom and brought them home so I could work on my sign in the evenings.

It was late evening and I was painting on my sign to keep myself off the computer. Every time I sat at the thing I wanted to go snooping for names. The phone rang so I set my brush down on a paper towel I had at the table and got up to answer it.

"Hello?" I said into the receiver.

"I'll be there to pick you up late tomorrow morning." It was Mr. Black.

"Okay," I said. "What are we doing?" I asked.

"Going back to the cabin," he responded.

"For how long?"

"Don't know. Until you learn what I have to teach," he said.

"See you then," I said and he hung up. He seemed a little short with me and I hoped he wasn't mad at me for screwing up the mission. You know what, I told myself, I *didn't* screw up the mission. I *finished* the mission. It didn't help, I still felt bad about how the mission had turned out. I thought on that while I went back to painting my sign. I finally came to the conclusion that I felt embarrassed for Mr. Black. I had found out he wasn't unstoppable and unconquerable.

I tucked myself into bed knowing that things were going to be all right between Mr. Black and myself if I could face the fact that he *was* human. That's if he could face the fact that I knew that now too.

Chapter Eleven

The backpack I had the first time was packed and ready to go when Mr. Black arrived the next morning. I heard him pull up and was in the SUV almost before the tires stopped moving. I was ready to get out of there and start back into training. The sooner we got this done the sooner we could go out on jobs again.

I had gotten myself motivated for a long car ride again and had brought books this time. We drove to the office and when we got parked in the garage I asked him, "Should I wait in here?"

"Nope, we're flying this time," he answered.

I grabbed my stuff and we trooped up to Suite 73. Gabriella was at her post. She looked a bit dressed up; I figured she must have known Mr. Black was going to be in today.

"Good morning, Mr. Black. Good morning, Ms. Grey." she said as we walked in.

"Good morning, Gabriella." I replied and Mr. Black nodded in her direction as we passed. We went straight to Mr. White's office to find him alone in the office. I had expected to see Mr. Brown this morning too. Mr. Black had said we were flying.

"Here," Mr. White said and handed Mr. Black a satellite phone and a few other electronic devices. "Keep this at the cabin so you can report your progress."

Mr. Black handed me one of the small electronic devices and said, "Put this in your pack." I did as I was told and then had to hurry to catch up with the two men before they entered the elevator.

Mr. White pressed the down button, but I had expected him to push up to take us to the helipad. We came out at the lobby and I followed them to the car garage. Mr. White took the front passenger seat of the SUV, so I was left in the back with the gear. Mr. Black handed me the rest of the electronic devices along with the satellite phone, except a small box with a screen of some kind and said, "Put one in each bag and the phone in my pack." There were only three duffle-type bags besides Mr. Black's backpack and mine but we were on the road before I finished stowing the gadgets. I had an idea of what they were, tracking devices of some kind, but why would we need them was my question.

Mr. Black drove us to an unknown airfield some distance from the city. We unloaded the backpacks and duffel bags. Mr. White carried a duffel bag and Mr. Black and I each carried a bag and our backpacks. To where, I still didn't know. We walked across the blacktop toward a small airplane and I assumed we would be using it instead of the helicopter. I was confused, but I was just along for the ride so I didn't say anything or ask any questions. I had found it better to keep my mouth shut and wait to see what was going to happen next. Usually I could figure out what was going on without too much surprise at the last minute, usually.

We boarded the plane and Mr. White got into the pilots' seat. This was new. Hmmm. It had never occurred to me to think he could fly. Heck, Mr. Black could probably fly too. Maybe I was going to get a flying lesson today. That would be fun. That was something I had never done but would have liked to.

We hadn't been it the air long when Mr. Black started to attach parachutes to all of our gear. He showed me what he was doing and how to do it myself. Then he asked how many times I had skydived.

"Twice," I said.

"Well, you know the principals then," he replied. "Did you receive instruction on steering or did you jump with an instructor?" he asked.

"An instructor," I said, a bit embarrassed. I had listed skydiving as one of my accomplishments, but in reality I had just been along for the ride.

Mr. Black gave me a nod and began to explain what was happening. We were going to jump and I was going to have to go solo. Exciting, but scary. Was I ever going to find my confidence again?

He continued. Mr. White would fly us over the area of the cabin and we would drop our supplies, then we would jump ourselves. He continued by showing me how to put the chute on and explained about how the little chute I held in my hand would fly up and pull open the main canopy. Ok, I thought. I'm starting to remember.

Mr. Black explained how to steer by pulling on the left or right steering line and what I should do to land safely. He put special emphasis on the avoidance of trees and other obstacles. He finished his lesson just a few minutes before we reached the jumping off point. I helped him pitch out the supplies and then he jumped. I looked to Mr. White but he was looking straight ahead not even noticing I was still there, so I jumped.

The air rushed past me and the sensation was wonderful. I could see the cabin, a small spec below. The lake was there too but it was a much larger blue mark. I kept my eyes on the lake and watched it grow. It looked almost as if it were some sort of dark blue liquid that had been spilled on a picture. Mr. Black had said we would have to open our chutes at 2000 feet so I checked my reading and we were almost there. I watched the meter until it read 2000 and I dropped the little chute I held in my hand. It whipped up above me adding to the noise.

J.C. Phelps

Then I was yanked up. I worried I might have to use the backup chute, but the main one opened. I had been gaining on Mr. Black, but now he was falling farther away from me.

Had I opened my chute too soon, I wondered. Just as the thought ran its course through my brain I saw Mr. Black's chute open. I had the steering lines in my hands now and was practicing carefully. Mr. Black had told me if I pulled on either of the lines too roughly I could put myself into a spin that I wouldn't be able to recover from.

The gentle pulling that I was doing seemed to work just fine. The ground was getting more detailed as we fell toward it. The lake and the cabin were nowmore than just spots below me. I aimed for the cabin. It's where we wanted to be. I managed to keep myself almost right over the top of it by doing large circles. But as I got closer to the ground I noticed my circles had to get smaller to stay right over the cabin area and I was afraid of putting myself into a spin like Mr. Black warned me about. I adjusted my strategy and started going from the lake to the cabin in a crisscross. If I couldn't land at the cabin, the shore of the lake would be the next best place, maybe even better. It was more open than the tree-surrounded cabin.

I decided to make the shore my landing destination. It was coming up quickly but I managed to land on my feet. The chute caught some air and started to pull me toward the lake. I resisted and was hauled off my feet. I landed face first and was being towed across the gravely beach into the water. I put my hands down in front of me and I was still being dragged. The parachute was skimming the top of the water and I was about half way to the buoy before it stopped.

Mr. Black was at the edge of the water when I finally came to a stop and he yelled across the water at me, "Bring the chute back in with you."

I thought swimming with all my clothes on was hard. It was nothing compared to hauling in a wet parachute. Fortunately I was able to stand up and dig my feet into the bottom of the lake or I might not have been able to bring in the soaked fabric.

Mr. Black waited for me with a grin on his face. I was mortified and angry. "What!" I said as I came up to him on the shore.

"Roll it up to get the water out of it. Then we'll take it to the cabin and hang it to dry." I could see the glee in his eyes and couldn't help myself. I started to laugh and so did he.

"I don't know what happened. The wind just caught it I guess," I said when we finished laughing. I rolled the water out of the chute and carried it back to the cabin where we hung it on some tree limbs to dry.

Mr. Black handed me the little black box with the screen and said, "This is a tracking unit. I'm going to show you how to find our stuff."

He turned it on while it was still in my hands and showed me how to operate it. Not only did our bags show up, so did we. Both of us still had on our

Color Me Grey

wristbands we had received for the last mission. We went in search of the closest bag and found it in no time. Then Mr. Black left me to retrieve the rest of them on my own.

I found a signal for another pack and headed in the appropriate direction. I saw the white chute before I saw the green pack and if it hadn't been for the chute I might not have found the pack. It was my backpack. I grabbed it from the side of a dried-up creek bed and hauled it back to the cabin. I took it straight to my room and headed out once more. I still had two duffel bags and Mr. Black's backpack to find.

A duffel bag was the next container I discovered. I hiked it back to the cabin too and found Mr. Black still unpacking the first bag. I set the bag down by the table and continued the search.

I had located all the signals before I began my search and had retrieved the closest first and was working my way further out. The last two signals were fairly close together and I planned on retrieving them together. I had to worm my way through some tight underbrush to get to Mr. Black's backpack. I had some trouble pulling it out of the close-knit branches and got a few scrapes but I managed to get it out. I put it on my back and continued my search for the last bag. My clothes had almost completely dried out from the swim I had taken earlier and I was beginning to warm up from the exercise I was getting.

The last bag was tangled in a tree about fifteen feet off the ground. It wouldn't have been so bad, but the tree was a tall pine tree and the branch that the chute had caught on was one of the lowest branches available. I didn't know how in the world I was going to get the darn thing down.

I unloaded the pack off my back and took a running jump at it but didn't even come close to it. I did this several times before I became winded and gave it a rest. I don't know what was going through my head. Yeah, if I keep running and jumping maybe, just maybe I'll be able to reach the sky. I looked around and found a long stick to jab at the bag. It wasn't long enough though. I stood under the bag on my tiptoes trying to swing the stick up to the bag. Then I began to run and jump with the stick. Again I couldn't get high enough. One more time I thought and I hit the bag, but the only thing that happened was that I broke my stick.

I sat down on the forest floor totally discouraged. What in the world was I going to do? I didn't want to go back without the bag. I had already made one mistake today. Of course we laughed it off, but this was such a simple task that Mr. Black had given me I *couldn't* go ask for help. I had been gone over an hour and I had to get this done. I was wasting time.

I got back up and searched around for a longer, stronger branch. No luck. Plenty of little ones lying around though. I thought about this for a while and decided I would try to lash them together somehow. I looked on the ground for some type of weed, vine or grass that I could use. Nothing that would hold. Then I got a brainstorm. I started pulling the lines loose from the chute that had brought Mr. Black's pack down safely. A little less than an hour later I had enough sticks tied together to reach the pack and about fifteen minutes later the bag dropped to the ground.

Mr. Black came out of the woods and said, "Finally." Then he picked up his backpack and started the walk back to the cabin.

"How long were you out there?" I asked.

He sidestepped the question and said, "You should have come asked me for help. I could have lifted you up instead of you destroying the chutes." The other chute had been left in the tree. I had thought he would have been impressed with my innovation and was a bit disappointed in his reaction.

When we reached the cabin he took his pack to his room and told me to unload the last of the duffel bags. I opened it and found dry goods such as, toilet paper, instant potatoes, instant milk, dried eggs. It all sounded so good. I could hardly wait to eat fake food. Mr. Black was still in his room unpacking when I finished, so I thought now would be a good time to unpack my bag too. By the time we finished with all the unpacking it was beginning to get dark.

Mr. Black sat down with a book and said that I got to cook dinner. I did just that. I found some other canned goods that had been stored or brought in one of the other packs. All in all I think I did a good job with what I had. When dinner was ready we sat at the table and Mr. Black explained to me what he expected out of me this time at the cabin. He said, "No more playing around. This time we are going to get to work."

I thought he had been rough on me last time. I wondered what was in store for me now.

"I want you proficient in all general survival techniques and some other things too," he explained.

We finished dinner and he headed for his room. Just before he shut the door he said, "You should get to bed as soon as the dishes are done. I'm going to have you up early." Then the door to his room closed.

I got right on the dishes and then went straight to bed. I didn't go to sleep though. These men changed attitudes like they were socks. I finally fell asleep hoping Mr. Black would be in a better mood in the morning.

"UP!" Mr. Black yelled in my face as he shook the bed.

I jumped out of bed and was fully dressed. I had gotten up in the middle of the night and dressed. I wanted to make sure I was prepared for whatever he had in store for me.

We started out with laps around the lake and exercises on the shore. I was prepared to go swimming at his command. But after the morning exercises he marched me back to the cabin. He had me take my chute off the tree limbs and fold it back into its pack. He demonstrated the technique first with his chute, and then he stood over me while I replicated his every move. I looked up to him and asked if I had done it right.

Color Me Grey

He said, "We'll find out soon enough." He had me go out and chop some firewood and before long he came out and told me I could come back in. Mr. Black had fixed us sandwiches for lunch. We ate at the table and then he hustled me out the door. Both of us had our packs on our backs and we both carried a pack away from the cabin.

We hiked away from the cabin at a brisk pace for several hours and finally came to rest at the top of a peak. We were at the top of a sheer cliff. I don't know how high we were, but looking down made me dizzy. The view was sensational. The mountains in the foreground and trees were all staring up at us on this glorious peak. We stood for a moment taking it all in and he said in a quiet voice, "I love this place." I didn't know if he meant that particular peak or the mountains themselves. Which ever it was I was hard pressed not to agree with him.

We stood enjoying the view for a moment that didn't last long enough for me. Then Mr. Black retrieved the two packs that we carried up. One of them was the chute I had packed earlier. He attached them together and threw them off the cliff. We watched as they fell. My chute didn't open.

I was a bit discouraged and disgusted. I looked to Mr. Black.

"Parachute packing is an art that you *will* learn." We turned back to the barely visible packs just as they hit the ground.

"Ready?" he asked a moment later with desire in his eyes. He didn't even wait for a reply before he took off top speed toward the cliff. He plunged over the side and I ran to watch. Immediately he let go of the mini chute that would pull his ripcord.

"Hell, yeah I'm ready," I said to nobody and followed his lead. Watching the two packs fall to the ground so far below us could have made me think twice about jumping, but I didn't let it. I made sure to push off from the cliff. I didn't want to hit the side of it. As I fell, I took it all in. This was different than skydiving. Not totally different, but a different rush. We were much closer to the ground for one thing. I saw Mr. Black touch down at the bottom of the cliff and I tried to land close by.

Actually, I didn't do all that bad, compared to yesterday. And I had loved it. I wanted to go again. I collected my chute and started folding it back the way I was shown. Mr. Black came up to me and said, "Wait. Watch me again." He folded up his chute and then stood over me and watched my every move.

"You'll get it, but I want to watch you re-pack every time for a while." He said. His mood had lightened. I think the jump was just what he needed.

"Are we headed back up?" I asked eagerly.

"Not today. We have other things to do yet," he replied looking up the face of the cliff.

Each of us carried two packs as we jogged back to the cabin, which was actually not that far away. All this time a huge, gorgeous cliff was in our backyard and I didn't even know about it. When we reached the cabin we dropped off the chutes and trooped back to the shore of the lake. Mr. Black proceeded to kick my butt in hand-to-hand combat maneuvers. This lasted into the evening and by the time we got back to the cabin I was famished and worn out. But it soon became apparent I was going to have to be the cook this time around. I guess it was only fair because the first time we were up here Mr. Black did the cooking.

I looked through the cupboards and was able to come up with a different menu than last night. As I was cooking dinner, Mr. Black proceeded to take all of the chutes out of their packs and lay them out on the floor. I knew what was coming after dinner. I packed and re-packed the chutes until I could hardly keep my eyes open. Mr. Black must have picked up on it because he announced that it was time for bed when I finished packing the chutes one last time.

We got an early start on our morning exercises and headed back up to the top of the peak. Once again we watched the two packs fall, but the chute opened this time, then we jumped. When we reached the bottom Mr. Black had me pack his chute and watched me pack my own once again. His attitude before a jump was one of seriousness, but after a jump he was almost like a little boy that had gotten exactly what he had asked for at Christmas time. We hiked to the top of the peak three times before it was getting too late to do it again.

This behavior of morning exercises and then jumping into the late afternoon continued for several days. I managed to keep a bit of variety in our diets even though we were eating the same thing over and over.

After we had gotten into a routine, Mr. Black changed it on me. I had gotten out of bed early and was making a quick breakfast for us when he came out of his room. He went straight to the living room and moved a rug away from the edge of the couch. Under it was a trap door leading to who knows what. He opened the door and disappeared into the open hole. I heard him rummaging through things and before long up came some ropes and other equipment. Then Mr. Black lifted himself back up into the living room, replaced the door and the rug and started to arrange and check the ropes.

I announced breakfast was ready and set our plates on the table. He stopped what he was doing to join me. We ate in silence. I knew the equipment was for rock climbing and figured I must be good enough at BASE-jumping to move on. When we finished breakfast Mr. Black put on his chute and grabbed some of the gear still lying on the living room floor. I grabbed my chute and the rest of the gear and followed him out the door.

Soon we were at the face of the cliff that we had been jumping off for close to a week now. He explained the fundamentals of rock climbing and I didn't interrupt him. BASE jumping and skydiving had been fairly new to me, but rock climbing had been a passion of mine. I hadn't been rock climbing for close to a year now but I hadn't forgotten a single thing. He finished by asking if I understood everything and I nodded, ready to get to the top of the cliff and jump back down.

Color Me Grey

90

Mr. Black and I both put on our harnesses and started up the side of the cliff. It was a challenge to find footholds and hand holds because the cliff was almost smooth. It had been climbed before because there were places to attach our ropes as we moved higher. We made good time for the size of the cliff. In less than two hours we reached the top. Because we had put on our chutes earlier that day I assumed we would be jumping again, but Mr. Black changed some of the rigging around and we repelled back down the cliff. We repeated this three more times and didn't get to jump until the last climb. I guess it was more of a treat to go jumping now.

We fell into a new routine of either hiking the mountain or climbing the cliff's face and only jumped about once a day. I continued to cook for us, but had run out of menu options. I had put everything together with everything else at one time or another and I was getting tired of the same ol' stuff. I had made bread from scratch and even a pie or two, but what I really missed was meat.

Mr. Black and I had fell into the habit of talking when it was necessary but a few days after I had eaten about all I could eat of dried potatoes and canned meat I said, "Do you think you could go catch us a squirrel or something for tomorrow?"

"I was wondering how long it would take you," he replied.

"What do you mean?" I asked.

"I've been suffering waiting for you to ask for fresh meat," he answered.

"Well, if you wanted it too, why didn't you just go get us some?" I asked a bit peeved.

"Because I'm not the one who's going to get it," he said. "Get your backpack ready for a week or so away. He went to his room and shut the door. I heard him talking in there and figured he must be using the satellite phone. His voice faded after about two minutes but he didn't reappear. I did the nightly cleanup and headed to my room to pack for a week. I packed clean, dry clothes and made sure the knife he had given me was in my pack and a few other essentials. I would ask him in the morning what he thought I should bring with us.

The next morning I didn't get a chance to ask if I brought enough of the right stuff. He had me out of bed around 3:30 or 4:00 AM, I'm not exactly sure. It was still dark and remained dark for close to two hours after we headed out of the cabin.

We hiked for most of the day. Never once did we stop to eat. Every once in a while I took my canteen of water and took a sip, but that was the only refreshment I got. Close to dusk we stopped and Mr. Black said, "This is one of the best times to hunt. What do you want to try for?"

"I don't know," I said. "What do you think I should try for?"

"You've got to learn to make your own decisions," was his reply.

"Fine," I said. "I just don't know what kind of animals I would find out here."

J.C. Phelps

"Lots of things. Deer, rabbit, elk, and maybe an occasional bear," he said. "I don't think I want to hunt bear right now," I said. "Maybe a deer or rabbit I guess."

"With rabbits it's best to set traps. With deer it's best to shoot them. We don't have any traps or any guns so this will be done by hand," he said.

"Can I make a trap?" I asked.

He smiled and said, "It usually takes people a day or two of sitting out here before they ask that question. Yes, you can make a trap. I will get you started, but you're going to make it yourself."

We gathered up enough twigs and natural twine that I could make two or three traps. At least that's what Mr. Black said. Then we sat down and he began to tell me how to put it together. After he got me started he went in search of firewood. He wasn't gone long and I hadn't gotten anything to stay together so he said he would teach me to build a fire. It was just like I had joined the Boy Scouts.

We got the fire started and I was wondering what we were going to do for dinner that night. Mr. Black pulled a few tid bits out of his pack but didn't offer me any. I knew that meant I should have packed my own. Figures. I was going to starve unless I learned how to catch something. I worked on the trap for the rest of the evening before I laid out my bedroll and fell asleep.

Mr. Black started on traps of his own the next morning while I was still trying to figure mine out. I took the opportunity to glance his direction once in a while to get pointers. I tried to be sneaky about it so he wouldn't think I wasn't doing it on my own. In between stolen glances I tried to put my trap together. Mr. Black had three traps of his own done before I had gotten anything to stay together. He went off to set his traps and I managed to get one put together.

After it was together I went in search of a place to set it. I thought I might get lucky while I was trying to make the other two traps. I found a spot that looked good. I actually saw what looked like rabbit droppings nearby. Being pretty proud of myself I went back to camp to work on my other traps.

"Where have you been?" Mr. Black asked when I got back.

"I got a trap made so I thought I'd set it up," I replied.

"Good thinking. It might take you a while to make another," he replied. "I'll be back later." Then he walked off into the trees.

Mr. Black didn't come back to camp until late in the evening. I had finished another trap right after dark and had begun on another one while I waited for him to return. I had also lit the fire.

Mr. Black came to the fire's side and began to skin a rabbit. My mouth watered as I watched him. I knew I wasn't going to get any of it though. I continued to fashion my trap while the aroma of cooked rabbit hovered over my head. One thing I had never had to do was go without food for any length of time. This was going to be hard if I didn't have anything in my trap in the morning.

Color Me Grey

I did complete the other trap before I went to sleep that night. I was tempted to wait up until I thought Mr. Black was asleep and then go pick through his leftovers burning on the fire, but thought better of it.

At the break of dawn I jumped up and gathered together my other two traps. I ran to check on the one I had set the day before. It was sitting there just like I had put it. I walked around and found a couple places to put the other two traps. Then I went in search of Mr. Black's traps. Maybe if I found them, I could get some ideas on how he set them up and if there was a rabbit in one of them, maybe I could snatch it before he knew about it.

I searched for a good part of the day and didn't find anything. I was headed back toward camp when I spotted some raspberry bushes. I walked up to them and started to pick through them. I got into the bushes and almost stepped on one of Mr. Black's traps. He had baited it with raspberries. Cheater, I thought.

I picked a whole bunch of raspberries and ended up eating most of them but I did carry some back to my first trap. I thought this would probably be the best one because of the droppings I had noticed before. Then I headed back to camp.

Mr. Black had already eaten. I could smell something had been cooked recently. I looked for him and found him not too far from camp burying something.

"What are you doing?" I asked.

"I'm burying the food I didn't eat and won't eat," he said.

"Why?" I asked, thinking he was probably afraid that I might eat some of it.

"You don't want unwelcome guests. I'll be relocating tomorrow too," he said.

Well, at least he had a good reason.

Mr. Black and I sat around for a little while and then he started to talk to me about hunting and staying down wind, that kind of thing. He told me what rabbits like to eat, what deer like to eat and what kinds of places they like to hang out at. He told me I should familiarize myself with my surroundings to see if there were the proper types of food available and even water. Later into the evening right before dark, he went to check his traps and I thought I might do the same.

When I got to my first trap I noticed it was different. I walked up to it with my hopes high but the closer I got the lower my hopes became. When I reached the trap I noticed it was turned over and the raspberries were gone. I must not have set it up right. I didn't understand it though because I had checked Mr. Black's trap when I had finally found it and made sure my trap was set up exactly like his. Oh, well, I thought. I'll just have to try again. I checked my other two traps before I went back to camp but I found nothing in them either.

It was fully dark by the time I reached camp again. Mr. Black was sitting in front of the fire watching the flames dance.

"So?" he said when I got back.

"Nothing," I replied.

J.C. Phelps

"Maybe you should try for something else," he said.

"Maybe," I said.

We both sat enjoying the light of the fire and the mood was good even though I was starving. Mr. Black and I talked about hunting and he told me all about how to track an animal through the forest. He explained all kinds of hunting strategies to me. After the talk of hunting and tracking subsided, I asked Mr. Black about himself and he started to tell me. I was shocked. I had thought a question about his personal self would have been blown off. He must have been in a talkative mood. We exchanged small bits of information throughout the evening. I found out he had been born and raised in Colorado Springs, Colorado. He was thirty-two years old and had served in the Navy. He told me a few stories of his childhood and I didn't have any to compare with them so I got brave and asked him, "What's your real name?"

He looked at me and considered a moment then said, "Quinn."

I was satisfied for a second or two but the other half of his name was not forthcoming. Was Quinn his first or last name, I wondered, so I asked him.

"Last," he said.

"What's your first name then?" I asked.

"We'll leave that for another day," he said while he stepped away from the fire to set up his bed for the evening.

As I lay in my bedroll I thought of all the information I had gained that evening. Mr. Black, Quinn, had given up a lot. I was glad I knew his name, at least part of it. I still didn't know if Quinn fit him though. After thinking about it for a while I decided Quinn was an okay name. I had expected a strong name and Quinn wasn't a sissy name. I imagined what his first name would be. It would have to be strong and masculine too. Jack had a strong, hard quality to it. Maybe he had a girl's name and that's why he hadn't given it to me. Maybe it was Sue. You know, a boy named Sue… Nah. I didn't think so, at least I hoped not. All this stuff about names got me to thinking about Rumpelstiltskin. About how I was like the queen and I needed to find out his name in three days. Well, not really, I guess it's nothing like that fairy tale. Then I dozed off.

Chapter Twelve

I awoke the next morning not because I was rested but because my stomach ached from lack of food. In the past three days all I had eaten was a few raspberries. The powdered food back at the cabin sounded good again. I picked myself up off the ground and put away my bedroll. What I wouldn't give to sleep on a bed again too.

Mr. Black was nowhere to be seen, so I gathered up what energy I could find and headed out to see if my traps had been successful in the night. When I reached the first one it was the same as the day before, turned over. I began to wonder if Mr. Black was messing with my traps. I don't know why he would do that though. I was just in a real bad mood this morning. I made the rounds of the other two traps and found nothing in them either. Imagine that. I tromped to the raspberry bushes intent on eating more ripe raspberries. When I got to them all the raspberries were gone and so was Mr. Black's trap.

I decided a morning stroll would be a good idea. I could check out the area and see what I could find. Mr. Black had said deer liked to hang out at the edges of meadows. They ate mostly at dawn or dusk. Before I went on my stroll I would go back to camp to see if Mr. Black was there.

When I got to camp I noticed all his gear was gone, not just him. I didn't remember seeing it before I left to check my traps either. Well, I'll just look around anyway I thought.

I walked away from camp and it was still pretty early in the morning and there was a bit of a chill in the air. My breath hung in the air in front of me as I stood there looking around trying to decide which way to go. I remembered a little meadow on the way here that we had walked through. If I could find it again I'd scope it out.

I walked for only a few minutes back the direction that we had come and found the meadow in no time. As I got closer I slowed my pace. Good thing too. Not far from the edge of the trees were some deer. There were six of them, four doe and two fawns. It was magical. I had seen deer before when we were hiking but had never noticed them before they had turned to run away. Now I was watching them and they didn't know I was here yet. I thought about how I would be able to take one of them down, but they were too beautiful to eat. I thought about becoming a vegetarian, but remembered how much I liked meat in my diet.

J.C. Phelps

I stood motionless for a long time and then one of the deer lifted its head and looked in my direction. Then it lifted its long white tail and bounded across the field in the opposite direction with the rest of the deer following her.

I walked away from the meadow with a sense of accomplishment. I had snuck up on some deer. It didn't count that it happened to be an accident. I just had to remember exactly what I had done so I could do it again. I explored for the rest of the day.

I mapped out the area even though it was in vain. Mr. Black had said we were going to move camp today, but I figured it was good practice. Earlier that day I had sat and messed around with my wristband and had found it had a compass. I imagine that I should have thought of this before. It was a GPS device after all. I used my wristband to remember landmarks. At such and such latitude and longitude I would find the meadow, then there was a small creek off in another direction. I found we were on the top of a hill that had a sharp drop in a different direction from camp. I didn't go too far out from camp but I got further out than I had when setting up my traps. I periodically returned to camp to see if Mr. Black had returned and was ready to move to another location. Each time I returned there was no change at camp.

I worked my way back to the little creek I had found. Fish wasn't my favorite, but they might be easier to catch. Never had I gone fishing before, but had been forced to watch a few shows on the television. What was with men and fishing? Anyway, the concept was simple. I would try my luck at fishing today.

While I walked to the stream I considered how I might catch a fish. I knew in normal life people used fishing poles with hooks on the ends. How could I make a fishing pole? I found several sticks on the way to the stream that I thought might get the job done. My mind kept wandering toward a picture of a small boy sitting on the edge of a river with a stick and line hanging from it, waiting for a fish to bite.

By the time I reached the creek I had an armload of sticks. I chose the one I thought might be the strongest and then pulled off one of my shoelaces. I tied it to the end of the stick and thought about what I might use for a hook. Finally the only thing I could come up with was trying to carve myself one with my knife. I got down to business and quickly found it was nearly impossible to carve a hook. I could get a toothpick type thing carved but not a hook. They kept coming out looking like miniature spears.

Spears. Then I got another idea. I wouldn't even need to carve a hook I could maybe spear myself a fish. This required me to see a fish though. I took my shoelace that was tied to the end of the stick and used it to tie my knife onto the end of the stick. Then I got up and snuck around the banks of the stream. It didn't take long before I saw a fish. I had kept low and was being quiet. I remembered seeing on a fishing show how fish can see you better from the water than you can see them. I slowed, stood my entire height and threw the

Color Me Grey

spear I had fashioned at the fish. I missed but I managed to make a big splash. This I knew had probably scared fish away for miles in each direction. I had to wade out to retrieve my spear. Thank goodness the creek wasn't more than waist deep.

As I waded through the water I tried not to kick up too much dirt. If I muddied the water I wouldn't be able to see anything. I looked into the water in search of fish to skewer once I reclaimed my spear. I saw one just as it darted under the edge of a rock. I stood still in the middle of the creek for several hours and tried my luck numerous times. My legs were getting numb and my teeth were chattering before I decided to exit the freezing water.

I took a walk up the creek to see if there was a more shallow area I could try. It wasn't long before I found a spot that only reached my knees. I trudged in and tried my luck again. This went on until it was close to getting dark. I better get something soon or I would go without dinner again tonight.

I saw a nice sized fish, aimed and threw my spear. I missed and watched the fish dart under a nearby rock. I ran to the spot where the fish was hiding and plunged my hand under the rock after him. He swam away from me but I had touched him. This was a new concept. I began slowly and methodically feeling under rocks.

About every third or fourth rock I would feel something and then see a fish dart away. I just had to be faster. I lowered my hand back into the water and started feeling around a new rock. Ah-ha! I pushed my hand up against the rock from the bottom, trying to pin the fish so I could get a grip. I got it! I actually said this out loud. It wasn't very big and I started to close my grip. As my fingers closed around my fish I felt a sharp pain in my hand. Instinctively I pulled my hand toward my body and hanging from it was a snake!

I jumped up and down and screamed, "SNAKE! SNAKE! SNAKE!" Then I shook my hand and arm violently. The snake didn't loosen its grip. Finally I calmed down enough to try and pry the snakes' fangs away from my hand. It had a hold of me right at the base of my thumb. I wondered if it was poisonous.

I couldn't get it off! I had somehow gotten myself back to shore and was standing near my spear. I reached down and picked it up and sliced the snake in two. Its head was still hanging onto my hand and there was a lot of blood. I made myself calm down and I took my finger and thumb and pushed them into either side of the snake's mouth and was able to finally get it off me. I threw it down and stomped on it a few times. Then I reached down to inspect it with my spear.

In my effort of prying I had noticed its fangs had been more to the back of its mouth and thought that was a good sign. If the fangs were in the front of the mouth it was probably poisonous, but if they were in the back of the mouth, they were meant to hold on, not to inject venom. I did a double check by physically picking it up and opening its mouth and didn't find any vampire like fangs in the front. Maybe it might not be a bad idea to take it back to camp to see if Mr.

J.C. Phelps

Black knew what kind of snake it was. Maybe he had some anti- venom in his pack.

I picked up the dead snake parts and my spear and tromped back to camp. Mr. Black was nowhere to be seen. I sat down and tried to regulate my breathing. I remembered hearing that if you got excited it would just make the venom move faster through your blood stream. I looked down at my injured thumb to see if it had turned black like the pictures I had seen of rattlesnake bites.

It wasn't black but there was a huge gash right underneath where I had cut the snake in two. I must have cut myself with the knife. It was still bleeding and all the blood when I cut the snake must have been mine. Great. Now what? Not only am I going to die of snakebite, I might actually die from blood loss too. I started to feel light headed.

"Knock it off," I told myself out loud. Quit acting like a *girl*, I thought internally. Okay, the snake had bitten me close to half an hour ago; if it had been poisonous it would probably have kicked in by now. I hoped. Now I just had to figure out what to do with my hand. It was still bleeding heavily. I sat and looked at it. I needed stitches, that was obvious. How was I going to get stitches out here though? I pushed the cut together and that helped slow the bleeding. I *had* to do something.

I rummaged through my pack and found a book that I hadn't put in there. It was titled Herbal Remedies. Mr. Black must have put that inside. I skimmed through it quickly to see if there was anything about snakebites, but there wasn't so I put it down and continued my search. I didn't find anything else that seemed of use in my pack.

The knife Mr. Black had given me was a survival knife; maybe I would find something there. I started to play with the knife and found a spot on top that unscrewed. I opened it and low and behold there was a little baggie in there with some sort of plastic line and a FISHING HOOK. No needles though. I was so furious at myself for not snooping before. I had thought curiosity would get me into trouble one day, but never thought it could have prevented disaster.

I knew I had to sew up my hand, but I wanted to wait for Mr. Black. I was hungry, and tired and I was freezing because I was still soaking wet. I tried to start the fire because it was getting close to dusk. I finally got it lit and Mr. Black still wasn't back.

I supposed I better try to sew myself up. I tied some of the fishing line to the hook and proceeded to sew. I had never liked to sew, but this was even worse. When I had first touched the sharp end of the hook to my hand I thought it would hurt too much for me to go through with it, but my wound was numb. At least it was on the outside. If I tried to go too deep it hurt like hell. I caught myself a couple of times with my other hand because I had touched a sensitive spot and it made me almost pass out. I finished sewing up the cut and tied a knot at the end of the line. I used the knife to cut the plastic line and was pretty

Color Me Grey

impressed with myself. It wasn't too straight, but the bleeding had almost
stopped and I hadn't died because of poisoning either.

It was completely dark around my campfire now. I got up and quickly
changed my clothes. They had almost dried completely except around the
seams but I didn't want to be covered in blood anymore. I looked at the snake
lying on the ground and my stomach rumbled.

"No," I said and laid out my bedroll. Then I sat down on it and waited for
Mr. Black to reappear. He had said we were going to move camp today, didn't
he? I wondered why he wasn't back. I hoped he hadn't gotten hurt. I worried
about him a bit to keep my mind off the snake that had almost killed me. Every
once in a while I was hit with a feeling of panic because I wasn't totally
convinced it hadn't been poisonous. I thought of eating it again but decided
against it, partly because I wanted to show it to Mr. Black but mostly because I
didn't want to eat snake.

I sat and looked at it for a long time then came to the conclusion that a
snake was better than bugs. I still didn't want to eat it though because I might
need to know what kind it was later.

I stared at the snake with that thought going through my head for a while
and realized I could eat the bottom part of the snake and leave the head. That
should work, I thought. I picked up the snake and my knife and went to the fire.
I cut it open and inspected the insides while I pulled them out. Yuck, I thought,
but at the same time I was enthralled. I had never seen the insides of a snake
before.

After I got the insides out I looked at it and wondered if I should skin it too.
I tried but there was hardly any meat on the thing and I pulled most of the meat
off where I had tried to get the skin away from it. I figured I would try to cook
it with the skin on. I moved some of the hot coals away from the flames of the
fire and laid the snake on them and then turned it a few times. Every once in a
while I would open it up and look inside to see if it looked cooked. Finally, I
got up enough courage to take it off the coals and try it.

It was hot and didn't taste bad. I had heard of people eating snakes before
and had always thought they were nuts. I guess if you're hungry enough you'll
eat anything. I had heard that saying before too and had never really believed it
until now.

The snake had been a little snake that I wouldn't have probably even
noticed if it had been in the grass next to me. I didn't get much meat because it
was mostly bones. But it was enough to calm my stomach a bit.

After I was finished picking on the snake I threw the carcass into the fire
and wondered after Mr. Black again. I had had a full day and was extremely
tired. I decided I would lie down on the bedroll while I waited for Mr. Black to
come back to camp.

I woke up some time later, the fire had died down and there were all kinds
of noises around me. I sat up and looked around for Mr. Black's body laying

close by in his bedroll. Nope, just me here. I pulled the blanket of the bedroll up over my head and listened with my eyes wide open. I hadn't hid under the covers since I was a little girl. I turned over making sure my head didn't exit the blankets and noticed a light coming from somewhere. It was my wristband. That little thing came in handy.

I began messing around with it and then all of a sudden there was a little blip on the screen. It was fairly close and it had to be Mr. Black. I pulled the covers down away from my face. I thought about getting up to find him but if he was that close he was probably spying on me. The nerve. He left me out here all alone and I could have died. Instead of getting up to search him out I got up and stoked the fire. Then I got out the book he had left for me and began to read.

I found several things I could do to make sure my wound didn't get infected, if I could find the plants I needed. I had begun to get tired again so I lay back down and went back to sleep.

I awoke the next morning to a severe pain in my hand and arm. I looked at my cut and it was red and getting puffy. I better get something on this, I thought as I headed out to find the plants I needed. As it turned out there were some plants sitting in a bunch not far from camp, picked and laid out nicely so I would find them. I compared them to the pictures in the book and found them to be what I needed. I said to the surrounding trees, "Thank you." Then I picked them up and carried them back into camp. I read about the plants and what I needed to do with them. Mr. Black had picked the combination that just needed to be ground up with some water to make a paste. I walked to the creek and found a nice flat rock, one with a bit of a dip in the center and one I thought I could use to grind the plants up with. I filled my canteen and brought it all back to camp. I took the flat rock and began to grind some of the plants together. Then I switched to grinding the plants on the rock with the dip in the center because it was probably the juices from the plant that I needed most. I didn't use all the plants because I might have to make some more and it was easier than hunting down the plants for myself. I eventually added a bit of water to make it all stick together. Then I applied it generously to my hand. I took a clean sock and wrapped it around the wound to make sure the poultice I had applied would remain where it was supposed to.

After I got myself all doctored up I thought I might check my traps. I hadn't done that for a day. The sun hadn't been up too long and I walked quietly and carefully in hopes I might see some wildlife. What I would do if I saw some wildlife was a different subject I didn't have any idea about. I had brought my makeshift spear with me, just in case.

As I neared my trap that had been turned over more than once, I found the source of the vandalism. There was a beautiful buck standing near it eating on the bush that I had placed the trap beside. Of course the trap was turned over again. I stood and watched the buck for a little while and then got an idea. I

Color Me Grey

threw my spear at him and embedded it in the ground at his feet. He dashed away with his white tail flashing behind him. I was going to have to practice my throw. I went to the trap and removed it from its spot and carried it with me to check the other two. They were untouched so I left them where I had found them.

Mr. Black had been following me around. I had secretly checked my GPS occasionally throughout the morning and his blip was never too far away. I never did see him or hear him though. I looked down at the wristband again to check his location and he was further away. It looked as if he wasn't close enough to see me this time. Maybe he went to check his traps.

I had planned my day by the time I reached camp again. I was going to go fishing and while I waited for a bite, I would practice my spear throwing. I reached the creek and checked for Mr. Black but his blip still wasn't in the immediate area. I strung out the plastic line and the hook was still tied to one end of it. I started lifting rocks around the waters edge and digging in with another rock to look for worms. I finally found one and put it on the hook. Then I gauged the depth of the water and tied a small twig to the line at the depth I wanted the worm. Finally I was able to throw the line in the water. It would have been easier to hand fish, but I didn't want to take the chance of getting another snake. Besides that, I didn't want to wash off the medicine I had applied earlier. I sat and watched for a bit but decided I better start on my practicing.

It was hard to throw with a sock on my hand, but I got used to it. Sporadically I checked the line and made sure my worm was still there. Then I would go back to my spear throwing routine. I had improved considerably before I went to check my line again. I was at least making it to the target. I didn't always stick the knife into it though.

I had tied the line to a stump at the edge of the creek so I wouldn't lose it if a fish did try to eat the worm. I went to check the status and the stick was gone. I pulled on the line excitedly. Maybe I had a fish. Sure enough, I had a fish on there. It yanked back on the string and hurt my hands. Now I understood why people used the reel with the fishing rod. If they got a big fish it wouldn't cut their hands to reel him in. I pulled on the line some more and the fish pulled back on it. I struggled with him for a while getting a huge rush out of the ordeal. If I had known catching a fish was so exciting I would have taken it up years ago.

I pictured myself on a fishing show and the head fisherman guy was giving me instruction, "Tire him out. You don't want the line to break," my imaginary friend said. Finally, I got tired of listening to him and started pulling the fish in for real. When I got him to shore I jumped into the water to grab him up. I didn't want the line to break now, mostly because this was my first fish, but also because I didn't dare lose my fishing hook. It was the only one I had and it came in handy for other things.

J.C. Phelps

I reached down and grabbed him by the openings in his gills. I knew some fish you picked up by their bottom lips but some of them had teeth and I didn't know what kind this was. When I got it out of the water I guessed it must be a trout. I brought it up on the shore and retrieved my spear. I used the knife end to open the fish up and remove his insides. Then I trooped back to camp to eat my catch.

I got the fire going again and cooked the fish just like I had the snake. It took a little longer than the snake but then again it was much larger than the snake. My first fish was nice-sized. The size you would take a picture of if it were regular life.

While it cooked on the fire I continued to practice throwing. I didn't think I would be good enough by dusk tonight, but I had to try. My plan was to go back to the meadow and wait for the deer to show. Then I would attack. I wanted to get down off this hill and back to the cabin. For some reason, I knew we wouldn't go back until I bagged us enough meat to last a while.

I glanced at my wristband while retrieving my spear and noticed Mr. Black was close again. I considered going out to find him but I didn't want to try to find him if I was empty-handed. I went back to the fish and turned it one more time. Then while it finished cooking I ground up some more of the plants to make more salve to put on my hand. It was feeling better since this morning but I was pretty sure going in the water after the fish had probably washed off most of the previous application. I wanted to put on a dry sock too. I got all that done and then pulled the fish off the coals and picked at the meat through the bones. I picked them clean and threw the remains in the fire. Then I went back to throwing my spear.

My arm started to feel tired after a while so I stopped and started reading the book Mr. Black had left for me. I learned a lot in the short break I took from my throwing practice. I got up off the ground, the fire had burned itself out and it was getting close to when I needed to get to the meadow. As I was walking away from camp I checked for Mr. Black and he was out there close by still.

I reached the meadow and the deer were already grazing. I didn't want to spook them so I made sure I was downwind before I even reached them and then slowly crept up on them. I checked again and Mr. Black was some distance away now. He must not have followed me.

I circled around the deer quietly and slowly. I got as close as I could without scaring them off and threw my spear and missed. The deer scattered and I cussed. I went in search of my homemade spear to wait to see if they would come back before dark. I didn't have long to wait, for dark, not the deer. They never did show back up. I was thinking of heading back to camp but thought I might try to track down Mr. Black instead.

I did some backtracking to get closer to his signal. It had strayed from its stationary position near my camp. I passed through my camp noticing that nothing had changed. The fire was dead and my belongings didn't look to have been moved.

I got a bit closer to his signal but decided against going all the way to his camp this early in the evening because he might be paying attention to my signal on his wristband. I didn't want to give myself away. I went back to my camp but didn't light the fire. I checked periodically on Mr. Black's signal and it stayed put. I sat for a good two hours before I couldn't stand it anymore. The wait was driving me bonkers. I went to see if the buck had returned to the scene of the crime. It was completely dark with the moon behind clouds. I was able to remain quiet as long as I took my time. Normally it took me about fifteen minutes to get to the spot where I had placed my first trap, but I was going on about forty-five minutes. My eyes were adjusted to the light or lack of and I could see reasonably well. I was coming up on the spot where I had seen the large buck before. I stopped to check the wind and realized that I had better circle around to come upon the spot downwind.

I did just that and next thing I knew, I saw the monster right in front of me! He couldn't have been more than seven or eight feet away. I immediately launched my spear and it hit its mark. Well, not quite. I had been aiming for the heart and I got the deer in the neck. It bounded off and I raced after him. Soon he was out of sight. Shit. I thought. Now if I didn't find him, I lost my knife. I had to find him because I couldn't be out here without that knife. I didn't realize until it disappeared with the buck that I used the knife for so much.

I got to the spot where I had last seen the deer and searched around for clues. I was lucky and found some blood in the low light. Then I got a bit luckier as the night went on. It had been over an hour since I had stuck the buck and the moon finally started to shine. The clouds had blown away to hinder someone else, thank goodness. I was able to follow the blood trail much better with the moonlight. I made much better time but it had been so long that the deer could have made it to either coast by now. I still had hope though. I kept finding the blood trail so I continued to follow it. Soon I saw the buck lying on the ground breathing hard. He wasn't all the way down yet. I walked around him and saw the spear had been broken off but the part with my shoelace and knife were still embedded in his neck. Man, I had gotten *so* lucky.

I tried to approach the deer and he tried to get up. I backed up because Mr. Black had told me they could kill a person if they kicked them in the right spot. I waited a bit longer and he finally put his head down. Poor thing, I thought. I killed Bambi's dad. I felt a lump in my throat and had to remind myself I was still kind of hungry and I wanted to get back to the cabin. Besides I hadn't even cried for the *man* I had killed! I will admit though, the deer hadn't posed a threat to me and was much more attractive. Callous thoughts, but that's what was bouncing around in my skull at the time.

The deer kept his head down at my second approach and when I got to him he was still breathing so I finished the job. There was no recovery for him even if I did want to change my mind. I had found out the hard way just how sharp my knife was and the repeated throwing it at trees and into the ground must not have dulled its edge at all. I proceeded to gut the deer. Man, it stunk! I stuck it out though. I gagged when I had to stick my hands inside and found the deer felt hot. It had never occurred to me I would experience all these different sensations while cleaning out my buck.

When I finished emptying the unnecessary parts out on the ground I tried to pick him up on my shoulders to haul him back to camp. I got him up there, but figured it would be easier to drag him. I made good time back to camp. When I got there I sat and rested for a while and admired my kill. I was proud, I wanted to show it off. I decided I would try to haul it into Mr. Black's camp and surprise the hell out of him.

I started to drag the deer again, but soon I was too close to his signal. I didn't want to alert him to my presence before I was on top of him. I let go of the buck's antlers and closed in on Mr. Black's signal in a circling motion. Finally, I saw the embers of a fire and a shape inside a bedroll. I carefully and quietly went back for my buck. This time I hoisted it on my shoulders and trudged as quietly as I could toward Mr. Black.

I walked right into his camp and he didn't hear me. I got right next to him and his hand shot out of his bedroll and knocked me to my feet. The buck fell down on top of me and I was pinned.

"What the hell!" Mr. Black hollered in the moonlight. I don't think he could see me under the buck.

I laughed and he said, "Shit. What the hell is this?" His voice had changed from surprised and pissed to disbelief and awe.

"This is my ticket back to the cabin," I replied.

"Damn right," he said. "I thought you were just hiking around. I had no idea you were going to try for a deer or I would have kept watching you tonight."

"Sorry you missed it," I said.

"Well, we might as well get started back down. It'll be light in about an hour and a half anyway," he said as he started to pack his stuff up. "You can leave him here and pack yourself up. I'll meet you at your camp and then you will have to carry him back down to the cabin."

I hurried back to my camp and packed up my stuff and was about to nod off when Mr. Black came toward me and dropped the buck at my side. I had the pack on and it was hard to get the deer up over it. Finally, Mr. Black lifted the deer onto my shoulders and we commenced the trek back down the hill. It took most of the rest of the day to get back to the cabin but we started early enough that we had enough light to butcher the deer outside before Mr. Black took it inside and down the trap door. Turns out there was a large room down there that held a little bit of everything, including, a walk-in freezer. It also turns out the freezer was fully stocked!

Color Me Grey

Chapter Thirteen

That night Mr. Black cooked dinner for me. We had a roast we had cut from my deer. I thoroughly enjoyed it too. He even did the dishes while I showered. Even though I had missed the niceties of the hot shower and a bed with a mattress, I was glad Mr. Black had forced me to be on my own out there. I know I really wasn't alone and I knew that then too, but I think if I had to be alone in a situation like that, I could do it now. It would still be daunting, but I could do it.

I had no trouble falling asleep that night. It could have had something to do with the fact I had a full stomach and hadn't slept since yesterday, but I think it had more to do with the feeling of satisfaction I had.

Mr. Black let me sleep in the next morning. I didn't sleep in too late though. I was still up not long after the sun was. The morning still had that new feeling to it. He was sitting at the table sipping a cup of hot coffee. Can you believe it, I hadn't thought of coffee once while away. I poured myself a cup and said, "Why did you let me sleep so late?"

"You deserve it," was his response.

I agreed with him but it wasn't like him. I did say though, "I am pretty proud of that buck."

"I think you got lucky, but you did carry it all the way back here without a complaint," he said.

"Of course I didn't complain. I didn't even notice it was all that heavy until we started hauling it down to the freezer," I said. "I understand I *needed* to learn what I did up there but it still is frustrating to know all this time there was meat in the freezer," I said with a smile. If I had been told I probably wouldn't have been as motivated to get meat of my own.

"Getting you back to show you the freezer was the highlight of my week," he said, smiling that wonderful smile of his. There was something about this man I liked. I think it was his no-nonsense attitude and the surprise of getting a smile out of him. Just getting him to smile was an accomplishment in itself and I had accomplished that too, more than a dozen times now that we had been up here again.

"What are we going to do today?" I asked.

"I think we both deserve a jump today, if you're up to it," he said.

"I was hoping you'd suggest that," I said. I sat for little bit longer and then started to get my chute ready. Mr. Black sat a while longer after I was ready, then we headed up to the cliff. We had brought our climbing gear too and climbed the cliff instead of hiking to the top. Our jump went great and we both were exhilarated when we reached the foot of the cliff. We went to the lake after that and practiced our hand-to-hand skills. I was quicker than he was, but I had always been quick. If he managed to get his hands on me though I was hurting before I could get away. He could still take me once in a while but I could take him now too and did more often. We spent the rest of the day beating on each other. That evening it had reverted back to me being the cook so I made fresh bread and we had roast sandwiches. It was a great change to have one more ingredient to cook with.

The next morning Mr. Black let me sleep in again. It was strange not having him in my face before the break of dawn. I walked out of my room to find him sitting at the table again with his morning coffee.

"Why did you let me sleep longer again?" I asked with a little apprehension.

"You get up early enough on your own. If I had any other new recruit up here, they wouldn't get up until I yelled at them. You're receiving the respect you've earned," he said. "Just don't take advantage of it or I'll have to start working again," he smiled at me.

I had seen him in this good mood before but never for more than half a day and now he'd been like this for two days straight. I wasn't sure about this. Don't get me wrong, I enjoyed it, but it was different.

"What's on the agenda for today then?" I asked.

"Now, we can have some fun. I figure if they want us back they can come get us. We're on vacation now." He put his hands behind his head and said, "I thought we might take in some scuba diving today. There's this great place I want to show you."

"Sounds good to me," I said as I was pouring myself a cup of coffee. I cooked some powdered eggs for breakfast and made some toast to go with them. They still weren't like fresh eggs, but if you ate them fast enough it was hard to tell the difference.

After we ate I cleaned up the plates and the rest of the kitchen. Mr. Black had retreated to the place under the trap door that he called the cellar. It was not quite what I would call a cellar though. I had never heard of a cellar containing climbing equipment, scuba gear or a walk in freezer.

He came back up with the diving equipment. I wondered about the air tanks. Had they been refilled since we used them last? I asked Mr. Black about this and he said as soon as we were told we were to come back up here, everything was replenished.

"We usually have someone come check things out at least once a month," he explained. "This place doesn't sit dormant long."

We suited up before we went to the lake. Out of the blue during the small hike Mr. Black said, "Since we are on vacation now, you can call me Adam if I can call you Alex or Lexi." He raised his eyebrows into a question.

"Sure," I said. "This is going to take some getting used to. Adam Quinn," I tested it out. Not bad but he was still Mr. Black to me.

When we reached the lake Mr. Black asked me if I was claustrophobic. I said, "No."

He replied, "Good. We're going cave diving."

Whoa, this guy did it all. What a life I was leading and I think I was getting paid for this too.

I followed him to the bottom of the lake and he led me straight to the opening of a cave. The current was strong and the water temperature coming from the cave was ice cold. I assumed this was a huge natural spring of some kind. We swam inside and it was amazing. I had done a little research on caves and had been spelunking, or cave crawling, twice. It had been hard work but the rewards were spectacular views and formations.

This cave was different than the other cave I had been in. It was larger for one thing. There were tight spots we had to navigate through but they were large enough that we could pull ourselves along and not touch the ceiling with our backs. Some of the spots had been small enough that we had to take off our tanks and pass them ahead of us, but none of them required us squishing ourselves flat to get through.

We swam along and Mr. Black pointed things out to me with his light here and there. It seemed to go on forever. We stayed close to the ceiling of the cave because there was a rope to follow. Every once in a while we would come to a split in the rope with one leading into the darkness ahead, still strung out on the ceiling, but there would be another rope snaking off a different direction or down to the darkness below. At one of these spots I shined my light down the rope and the light ran out before the rope did. I wondered what was down there.

We had been swimming for I don't know how long but finally Mr. Black and I surfaced into a huge room. When my head broke the surface of the water all I could hear were the echoes of us swimming around in the cave. I couldn't see the other side of the water. We were in an underground lake. This just got better and better.

"This is huge," I whispered.

"Just wait," Mr. Black said looking back at me.

We swam on ahead and I moved my light back and forth to catch a glimpse of an end to the lake. Before long I was able to see rocks jutting out of the water. Some of them seemed to go on forever above me and below while some of them barely broke the surface. Then I saw the wall of the room. It was covered with a beautiful ribbon-like formation. They were larger than any I had ever seen but they still looked just as fragile.

J.C. Phelps

We finally reached what could be called the shore of the lake. It was more like a lip of rock covering the surface of the lake that continued on underneath it. We climbed out and moved in a bit to find a place to sit so we could take off our fins.

Mr. Black said, "So, what do you think?"

I was literally dumbfounded by the sound of his voice reverberating off the walls back at me. Finally it subsided and I replied, "Remarkable, mind-blowing." Then I sat back and listened to my own voice talk to me from the darkness.

"We didn't bring the necessary equipment this time but we'll get back up in here and I'll show you where it comes out," he said. "Maybe tomorrow," he added.

"This is spectacular," was all that I could say as I shined the light in every direction trying to take it all in.

We walked around for a little while. The lip that covered the lake was smooth and continued on for quite a distance. Here and there I would see what looked like a gigantic stalagmite coming up from the ground. Then when we reached the edge of the lip the ground got much more uneven. Now I understood what he'd been talking about when he said we hadn't brought along the right equipment. We couldn't navigate the cave without proper footwear and ropes and not risk serious injury.

Once we reached the point at which we could go no further Mr. Black said, "We better get back. It's getting late."

"We just got here," I said.

"It'll be just about dark when we get out if we leave now," he replied.

"That can't be," I said.

"The swim to this room takes about three hours and we've been in this room a long time too," he replied.

I was stunned. Once we were inside the cave, time had ceased to exist for me.

"I must have been really involved," I said out loud. I surprised myself with my voice. That comment had meant to be an inner thought.

"That happens to the best of us," Mr. Black said as he headed back for the water.

I followed, and after we had both put our fins on we dropped back into the water. We swam to the back wall and plunged beneath the surface. We made pretty good time, I thought. I started to notice how long it took to get through the tight spots and was convinced Mr. Black must have been right.

When we reached the surface of the above-ground lake it was dark. I noticed something very large and black on the shore. My eyes adjusted to the dim light and I realized it was the company helicopter.

"Hell." Mr. Black said and I could tell that his vacation ended at that very moment, which meant mine did too.

Color Me Grey

"Well, Mr. Black," I said, "It's back to work."

We swam reluctantly back to shore and slowly walked back to the cabin. The light from the windows looked cheery but I had a bad feeling in the pit of my stomach. At first I thought it was nervousness about maybe going out on another job. Then we walked inside and I saw the faces of the two men in the room.

Mr. White was at the table with Mr. Brown. The smile that Mr. Brown usually carried around on his face wasn't there and Mr. White was frowning.

"Get dressed," Mr. White ordered to us.

We complied and each went to our rooms. I quickly changed out of my wetsuit and then packed quickly. When I came back out Mr. Black was still in his room and the other two men were still at the table. They had made coffee so I helped myself. The mood at the table was dangerous. I wanted to ask questions but I didn't dare.

Mr. Black was still in his room when I got half way through my cup of coffee. I had been cold from the swim and the hot liquid hit the spot. The three of us had been sitting in silence and then Mr. White broke it by saying, "You must have been to the caves." He turned in my direction. "So, what'd you think?"

"I loved it," I answered. His forehead had worry lines but the rest of his expression had softened. When we had first walked into the cabin his look had been one of anger and now it seemed to be one of concern and relief.

He asked me a few more questions about what Mr. Black and I had been doing up here. I told him about the camping trip and my buck. This made him raise his eyebrows.

"A buck?" he asked. I could tell he was skeptical so I offered to prove it to him. I had left the head and skin hanging out back. Mr. Black had told me I should save it when I had asked where I should take it to get rid of it. Now I understood why. He knew I would need to show it to people for them to believe it.

Mr. White and I went outside with a flashlight and I brought him to the deerskin. He swung the flashlight up and down the skin and then looked at me.

"This is yours?" he asked.

"Yep," I said with pride.

He examined it closer and then asked me for the details of the hunt. I gave him the brief version. I wanted to get back inside and hear why they had come up here. They surely had a *reason*. Something was going on, I could tell by the looks they had given us when we had come in from outside.

"Shouldn't we get back inside?" I asked.

"Sure," he said and we began to walk back to the front of the cabin.

When we walked in Mr. Black was sitting at the table with the same look the other two men were carrying around. He walked up to me and put his hand

J.C. Phelps

on my shoulder. What was this? Did someone die? I felt a streak of panic rise from my stomach to my throat with the last thought.

"What?" I said with an urgent tone.

"I've got to go. Mr. White will stay here with you," Mr. Black said.

"What's going on?" I asked Mr. White.

"Nothing that we can't handle. Mr. Black is needed on a job and you and I are going to stay here for a few days," he replied.

I looked at Mr. Brown and he was standing sober-faced and ready to get going. Then I looked at Mr. Black. He had a look of concern on his face and it was directed toward me. I didn't get this. Why were they all looking at me like I had some terrible disease and I would die at any moment. I knew I would get a straight answer from Mr. Black so I said, "What's going on, Mr. Black?"

"Mr. White will fill you in after we leave," he replied, then he walked for the door. Right before he walked out the door he added with a look at Mr. White, "Watch yourself."

"What was that about?" I asked Mr. White.

He avoided the question and said, "So, have you learned a lot up here?"

"What is going on?" I asked again.

"Have you had dinner?" he asked me.

I was getting angry. I wanted to know what was going on. Why hadn't I been invited along? Why didn't Mr. Black push to have me along like he did the last time? Why was I left here with Mr. White? That thought made me nervous. As I was thinking these thoughts I heard the chopper fly over us and into the distance.

"No. I haven't had dinner," I replied sharply.

"I'll make us something," he said as he went to work in the kitchen. It was apparent I wasn't going to get anything out of him. It could be some sort of top-secret mission they were on, I guess. That didn't explain the looks of concern though. I don't know why I'm even getting bent out of shape, I told myself as I sat at the table. I've been left out of the loop more often than I've been included. I couldn't shake the feeling it had something to do with me though.

Mr. White was cooking something on the stove when I turned to him and asked, "Why are you avoiding my questions and not telling me anything?"

"I'm not prepared to answer your questions at the moment," he replied.

"What do you mean, you're not *prepared,*" I said with disdain for the word.

"Just that," he replied.

That man irritated me every time I was around him. But he was so sexy. If I had met him at the Skylight or on the street, I would have done every thing in my power just to get him to notice me. But the situation I was in right now made me afraid of my feelings. This simple crush was too complicated. It was based entirely on physical attraction too. I didn't know him at all.

When Mr. Black and I resurfaced to see the helicopter my stomach had jumped at the thought and hope that it was Mr. White. Then when we stepped

Color Me Grey

110

into the cabin and I saw him, my breath had caught in my throat. Even though I knew there was something wrong I still lusted after him and my thoughts wandered into fantasy mode.

I turned to watch him at the stove. His jeans fit perfectly. His shirt was a bit too tight but that was to his credit. He had very nice arms. I had been swiveled in my chair admiring him for a while when he started to turn around. I made sure my mouth was closed and I remembered I was mad at him. I couldn't remember exactly why right off hand. I was tempted to turn around quickly so he wouldn't catch me looking but I kept my gaze straight for fear of him seeing me turn away. I put a mad look on my face and looked him straight in the eye.

"I'll tell you all about it when I receive confirmation myself" he said.

"When will that be?" I asked remembering why I was angry.

"Sometime tonight," he said and brought dinner to the table.

He had cooked some kind of concoction of venison, eggs and cheese. It looked suspect but I took a bite.

"This is good," I said. We sat in silence and ate. The worry lines still creased his forehead.

We were still eating when there was a noise out back and Mr. White jumped up. He said, "Go to your room." He waited until I got there then said, "Shut the door."

"It's probably a raccoon," I said. "There's been one hanging around and we've heard him rummaging around at night."

"Shut the door," he repeated.

"Fine," I said and did as I was told.

I heard Mr. White open the front door but then I didn't hear anything else. There were no windows in my room so I couldn't even look out to see what he was doing. I hoped it was a skunk. No I don't. I retracted my thought. If it were a skunk Mr. White would come back into the cabin and stink the whole place up.

I heard a noise in the front of the cabin and opened my door a crack. I wasn't frightened but I was cautious. Mr. White seemed too much on edge. When I looked through the crack I saw Mr. White shutting the door. I walked out of the room and said, "What was it?"

"You were right, raccoon," he replied.

"Are you always this jumpy?" I asked.

"Do you always have a bad attitude?" he asked back.

"Only when I'm frustrated,"

We both had sat back down at the table to finish our dinner and he said, "Mr. Black says that you follow orders without questions or comments. What makes you act differently around me?"

"You frustrate me," I said.

"Why do I frustrate you?" he asked.

J.C. Phelps

"Because," I said. Now that was a good answer. I knew why he frustrated me but I didn't want him to know the real reason. I tried to come up with something to add to it but I couldn't think of anything. See, I told myself, I can't even think when he's around. What the hell is wrong with me? Mr. Black is buff, sexy *and* he doesn't frustrate me. Why can't I like him instead? I didn't think Mr. Black harbored any sexual feelings for me. I don't think I could get involved with him even if he did.

Mr. White eyed me from time to time, but it felt purely sexual and I didn't want that. Eventually, I wanted a man to love me more than the rest of the world and that included himself. I didn't think Mr. White could love me at all, not to mention more than he loved himself.

I thought now would be a good time to change the subject.

"What time tonight will you receive confirmation, so you can tell me what's going on?" I asked.

"You never give up," he said while picking up our empty plates from the table. "Okay, I'll tell you what I know." He set the dirty dishes in the sink and returned to the table.

"One of our clients has been threatened. I am up here so Mr. Black can confirm the client is safe," he said.

"Is that all?" I asked.

"Until I get a report back, yes that's all." He got up and moved to the living room. "If you hurry and get the dishes done, we can play some cards."

I did the dishes and we played several card games. Then Mr. White said he was going to read and I should go to bed. I told him that I might like to read too. I didn't want to get too far away from him and the satellite phone. I wanted all the details as soon as I could get them. I still had that gnawing feeling that this had *something* to do with me.

We both picked books to read and sat on opposite sides of the couch. It wasn't long before I wasn't comprehending what I was reading. I was so tired I was just going through the motions.

I woke up when Mr. White was trying to straighten me out on the couch. I pretended like I was still asleep though, just to see what he would do. His touch was gentle and comforting. After he got me laid down he came to where my head was and lifted it so he could sit there. He put my head back down on a pillow in his lap.

Physically it was amazingly comfortable, but emotionally I was very uncomfortable. He could have woke me up and told me to go to bed or moved somewhere else after he had me situated on the couch. I decided it was okay as long as he thought I was asleep. I stayed awake for a long time after that but eventually fell back to sleep.

The phone was ringing. I sat straight up on the couch in time to see Mr. White pick the phone up from the table to answer it. He hadn't been on the couch. He must have gotten up after I fell back to sleep. It was a brief

Color Me Grey

conversation filled with yes's and no's and I see's. He put the phone back down on the table and just sat there.

I said, "Well?"

"Well," he said back to me. "The client is not safe. He's been kidnapped."

"What do we do?" I asked.

"We set up a recovery team and pull him out," he said.

"Are they on their way to pick us up then?" I asked.

"No. You and I will stay here until this is over," he replied.

"Why? Don't they need your help?" I was about to offer my help when he said, "No. You do." He looked up from the table at me.

"What do you mean?" I thought maybe he meant I was going to be training more, but something in his eyes told me that's not what he meant.

"There have been threats made against you," he said.

"Against me? Why?" For the life of me I couldn't understand why there would be a tangible threat against me.

"The recovery job that you and Mr. Black did," he explained. "The target is a high-profile terrorist. His name is Abbas Salah." He waited for some recognition from me. "Also known as 'The Lion'," he added.

"Oh," I said when it registered. He was a bad guy. His name had been in the papers and on TV for numerous atrocities. He was a real bad guy.

According to the national news, The Lion had other bad people stashed all over the world just waiting to get their orders to commit terrible crimes against humanity. I didn't understand the reasoning of this group. They didn't claim any religious affiliation or a political one either. They were evil just to be evil.

"Oh shit," I said again when it hit me that The Lion, or his followers were after ME. What had I *ever* done. Wait, never mind. I had kidnapped the leader of a wicked cult. Shit.

My heart leapt in my chest. I was sure my dad had been the *client* for that job. Mr. White had said the client had been kidnapped. I jumped to my feet and began to breathe heavier.

"Where is my dad?" I asked.

Mr. White got a stunned look. "How...what makes you think the client was your dad?"

"Don't play around with me right now. Where is my dad?" I repeated. "Is my Mom okay?" I added.

"Your Mom will be fine. She was roughed up a bit, but nothing substantial. I guess they tried to take her too, but she put up a fight and got away," he said.

"I want to help," I said.

"Absolutely not. You are in too much danger."

"I want to see my mom and make sure she's going to be okay," I said. My eyes started to burn with the expectation of tears. I fought it and was able to keep them suppressed.

J.C. Phelps

"This is about the only place you'll be safe right now. Nobody knows how to get here except my partners."

"What about the other recruits you've brought up here?" I asked.

"There have been no other recruits up here," he said.

"But you said and Mr. Black said I had gotten up here faster than any of the other recruits," I said.

"Yes. We were talking about ourselves and the other partners," he explained. "People who work *for* us don't get this kind of training."

I tried to calm myself down by taking some deep breaths. "Do you know where my father is?" I asked.

"Not yet," he said.

"How are you going to find out?" I asked.

"Your mother shot one of the men that were sent to take you all away. We have him in custody. He said the only way we'll get Admiral Stanton back is if we deliver up The Lion."

"When and where?" I asked.

"The government has him in custody and they won't give him up," he looked back to the table.

"What do you mean? They won't trade? Why not?" I asked.

"Your father is very important, but the government doesn't give in to terrorists. Not to mention they won't even claim they have The Lion," he explained.

"Well, what are we going to do?" I asked with terror in my voice.

"I'm not sure. Your father is why I'm doing what I'm doing now. He's the reason I turned out to be a good guy instead of a villain. I will figure something out."

I started pacing and we were both quiet for a long time. Finally Mr. White said, "You should get some sleep."

"You're kidding right? There's no way I could sleep," I said, still pacing.

"Then sit down. That really bothers me."

I took a seat on the couch. While I was there I was wondering what was going to happen to my father. He was the one man I truly loved. I didn't know if I could live without him. Thoughts like these and all my fond memories flooded in on me. I felt a tear hit my cheek and quickly wiped it away. I couldn't let Mr. White see me cry.

Chapter Fourteen

The sun came up and we both were still sitting around doing nothing. I stood up and asked Mr. White what he was doing about this right now. Was Mr. Black starting the search? Was he interrogating the guy that Mom shot? I received a yes to both of my questions and was told to sit down again.

"I can't just sit down. There has to be something I can do," I said.

"You can calm down and keep yourself safe," he replied.

"I'm not the one who matters," I said. "My dad is the important one!"

"You're worth more than you think," he said. "The original threat was against you and not your father. They're using Admiral Stanton to get to you."

"Because I helped to retrieve The Lion," I said.

"No, because you are the daughter of Admiral Stanton. I don't think they knew you were involved in the retrieval," he said. "Believe it or not, but you are a better bargaining chip because your dad controls the strings attached to The Lion. They know the government won't negotiate with them, but your dad might, if they had you."

"How do you know all this stuff?" I asked.

"It's my job," he said in a matter of fact tone.

I wasn't getting anywhere with this so I went to take a shower. Maybe that would make me feel better.

When I got into the bathroom I had second thoughts about getting undressed. I always had trouble showering and changing clothes in a new place. The first time I was up here it was hard, but Mr. Black was in the other room, not Mr. White. Just get over it, I told myself. I finished my shower and was brushing my hair when Mr. White knocked at the door.

"What are you doing in there?" he said.

"Brushing my hair," I said as I opened the door. I walked to my room to finish putting my hair up. I saw him watching me and it was making me uncomfortable. So I said, "Don't you need the bathroom?" He wasn't making any effort to go into the room he had just disturbed me away from.

"No. I just wanted to make sure you were still in there," he said.

"Well, I *was*," I said snottily. He went to the couch and picked up a book and sat down. I felt a bit bad for being such a jerk, but the circumstances were such that I couldn't help it. I was a nervous wreck and there wasn't anything I could do about it.

J.C. Phelps

I roamed around the cabin for a while. I thought about reading but I couldn't sit still long enough to read a whole sentence. Finally I started to bake. There were quite a few recipes I could choose from that I could substitute our dry ingredients for the wet ones, like eggs. The cupboards were stocked well with things like spices and flavorings that had a long shelf life. I made pies with the canned fruit. I made oatmeal cookies and molasses cookies. I had been at it for several hours when Mr. White came up behind me. He stood closer than he needed to and asked if he could have a cookie.

"Help yourself," I said as I took in his scent. Knock it off, I said to myself. Your dad has been kidnapped and you're smelling some guy. Well, I can't do much of anything else. I threw back at my inner voice.

He reached over and took a handful of cookies and went back to the couch and his book. I finished up my baking and cleaned up my mess and said, "I'll be back later." I headed for the door and Mr. White jumped up.

"No you don't. You don't leave this building without me."

"I'm just going for a run around the lake," I said.

"Well, I'll come with you then," he said as he opened the door for me.

I sighed and took off at a jog for the lake. He kept up with me into several laps then he fell behind and watched from the shore. Eventually he pulled up a log and sat there waiting. I continued to run. I didn't have any intention of stopping even after it started getting dark. Mr. White had stepped in my path the last couple of laps and I had just dodged him. I didn't want to have to deal with my situation. At least not the way I was being forced to deal with it. I wanted to get out there and *do* something. Just hanging out was beginning to eat away at me. If I had to stay up here it would have been better for me to have not known what was going on.

I was coming up on Mr. White again. I was prepared to dodge him but he fell into step with me instead of trying to stop me.

"We have to get back to the cabin," he said. "It's getting dark and I can't protect you out here if I can't see."

"It's not dark yet," I said even though the light was fading fast.

"This is your last lap," he told me.

"Really?" I retorted and sprinted on ahead. He stayed right behind me until we got back to the side of the lake where the path to the cabin began. Then he sprinted on ahead of me and quickly turned around. I didn't see it coming. It all happened so fast. The next thing I knew I was being carried back to the cabin over his shoulder. I don't even know how he did that.

"Put me down!" I yelled trying to wriggle from his grasp.

"Not until we're inside," he said.

I fought for a little longer but his grip was firm so I calmed down and said, "Let me down." My voice was much more even. "I'll walk."

He set me on my feet and we walked side by side to the cabin.

When we reached the cabin he went straight for the cookies.

Color Me Grey

"You're going to get fat," I said.

"You made 'em." Like it was my fault he was going to get fat.

"Did anyone call today?" I asked. He had brought the phone with him to the lake but I hadn't seen him use it.

"No. They should check in this evening," he replied. "Do you want to play cards or something?"

"I suppose." We got out the cards and sat at the table. We passed a couple of hours that way. Then Mr. White said he was done for a while. He was hungry and was going to find something to eat. He got up from the table and asked if I wanted anything. I told him no. I looked to the satellite phone that had been sitting on the table next to Mr. White. It didn't ring, no matter how hard I pushed my thoughts through the air at it.

"You should get some sleep," he said when he came back to the table. He had settled for more cookies.

"I'm not tired," I said.

"Well, I am and if you don't sleep, neither do I," he explained.

"Why? Do you think I'm going to take off?" I smiled. The thought had occurred to me, but I was too tired to go running off into the woods alone.

"Yes, actually, I do," he said.

"Oh, go get some sleep," I said tiredly. "I won't leave tonight. I promise," I said.

"Right," he said and put a cookie into his mouth. "These are really good, by the way," he added.

"Thanks," I said and I walked to the couch and sat down. I picked up a book for show, but didn't read anything.

Sometime later Mr. White came and sat on the couch next to me. "Are you ever going to turn the page?" he asked.

"When I'm done reading it," I said defensively. Just then the phone rang. He jumped up to get it.

"Yes?" he said. A pause and then, "I see." More talking on the other end, then Mr. White replied, "Rough." I was getting nothing out of this and was about to ask who it was when he said, "No problem," and disconnected.

"So?" I asked with enthusiasm.

"Nothing yet," he said.

"I can't stand this," I said.

"I know. You have got to calm down. A lot of what we do is wait," he explained.

"This is my DAD," I said. "We have to do something."

"We are," he said. "Everything we can right now," he stated.

I had gotten up and moved to the table while Mr. White was on the phone, so I returned to my position on the couch and so did Mr. White. I sat with the book in my lap for a while, then wondered if I slept if it would make it go away. I rested my head on the back of the couch and fell asleep.

J.C. Phelps

When I woke up the next day it was well into the afternoon. Mr. White was asleep on the floor in front of the couch. His hand was up on the couch so if I moved I was sure he'd feel it. I lay there for a good hour so he could get some rest too. I didn't know how long he had been asleep on the floor but I knew if I got up so would he and he could use some sleep.

Finally, I had to use the bathroom. I slowly lifted my body so I could crawl over the back of the couch and hopefully not disturb Mr. White's slumber. I had been watching him sleep and he was so peaceful looking. His features weren't as sharp while he slept. He actually looked relaxed. When he was awake he was very alert. I don't think he missed much of anything going on around him.

I rolled over the back of the couch and quietly walked to the bathroom. I locked the door in case he woke up while I was gone. I didn't want him barging in on me.

When I got out of the bathroom Mr. White was making some coffee.

"So you're awake finally," I said.

"Yep. I needed that," he had his coffee cup where the pot belonged and the machine was happily filling it for him.

I went to the cupboard and got myself a cup. I sat at the table waiting for his to get full so I could do what he was doing.

"What do you want to do today?" I asked.

"I thought we could go to the shore and practice hand-to-hand maneuvers," he replied. "My style is a bit different than Mr. Black's and I think you could benefit from it."

"Okay," I said, but I wasn't really all that okay with the idea. I would have to get close to him and then I would think about things that I shouldn't, especially with my dad being in trouble. I knew today was going to be a day of guilt for me. I just won't let him get to me, I told myself. Besides, I'm not drunk this time; maybe he won't get the best of me so quickly like he did in the parking lot of the Skylight.

We sat across the table from each other. The satellite phone was sitting beside Mr. White and that's where my eyes strayed. I just couldn't get rid of the feeling there had to be something I could do. I had been racking my brain but I hadn't come up with a solution.

"How did my dad know that the target was going to be on his yacht in that particular place and time?" I asked.

"I'm sure he had an informant of sorts," Mr. White said.

"But who? Maybe they could help," I said with hope.

"I don't know who. Admiral Stanton is the only one who knows that. It's possible that they could help but…" he left it hanging.

"Well, are you trying to find out who this person is?" I asked.

"We have no way of finding out," he replied getting a bit irritated.

"Did you have someone go through my dad's files at home and his computer?" I asked.

Color Me Grey

"Yes and there was nothing there. We are doing everything to find him Alex," he said.

Alex? He had never called me anything other than Ms. Stanton or Ms. Grey.

"Well, Malone," I threw it back at him. "I bet he has it listed somewhere. He's meticulous with that kind of thing. It might not be listed as 'The Lion informant'." I was getting irritated myself.

"Fine. Have it your way. I'll call Black and have him double check," he said after a short stare down. I liked getting my way.

He picked up the phone and punched in some numbers. After a bit of a wait he started talking to someone. The conversation lasted a few seconds. Then he turned to me and said, "Mr. Black is on his way to your parent's house right now. He'll call us back when he gets there."

Finally, I was doing something to help my father. I just hoped it wasn't a waste of time. Mr. White must have thought it was a good enough idea to actually have Mr. Black go check it out. I was pretty pleased with myself.

We both sat at the table and waited for the call back. The wait was only about half an hour but seemed like a lifetime.

Mr. White answered the phone and told Mr. Black to look through all the filing cabinets for something that seemed to be linked to The Lion in any way. Mr. White was quiet for a second then looked to me and said, "Gabriella's with him. He's just telling her what to look for." Then he looked back down at the table and said into the phone, "Okay, now I need you to get back onto the computer and start looking there." He paused. "That's fine, here you go," and he handed the phone to me. "Hello?" I said.

"Ms. Grey." it was Mr. Black. "How are things up there?" he asked.

"Nerve racking, but fine. Have you gotten anywhere yet?" I questioned him.

"Not really. The guy your mom shot doesn't speak English. Mr. Red is fluent in several different languages and until today we were trying to have him translate by phone. But he got into town a few hours ago. It's hard to intimidate a person over the phone so I think we should make progress with him now," he explained. "I'm going to look through the files. I'm going to let Gabriella get on the computer. She has more experience with them than I do. Just a sec." He must have handed the phone to Gabriella because next thing I knew she was on the line.

"Ms. Grey?" I heard her ask.

"Yes," I said.

"What am I looking for?" she asked.

"I need you to get into my dad's personal files. They are password protected so I'll walk you through it," I said.

"Okay," she replied. "Ready whenever you are."

J.C. Phelps

I told her to turn on the computer. Then I gave her my dad's password to open up the main screen. She had no problem with that. I had her bring up the files on the screen and had her read them to me. There had been a few I made her open and they turned out to be nothing. Then she found one labeled 'Friends'. I had her click on it. The computer asked for a password. I told her to use my dad's password for starting the main computer. It was denied. If only I could have been the one there, I might be able to get into it. I could usually figure out my dad's passwords but this one I had no idea about. It helped me when I was sitting in his chair, thinking about what I would put down if I were him. I closed my eyes and tried to put myself in his place. I rubbed my eyes with my free hand and told myself to think.

Soon Gabriella said, "Ms. Grey?"

"I'm still here," I replied. "Just give me a second." I needed to work on my concentration skills. Her voice brought me right back to the real world and I lost my train of thought.

"What other kinds of work does my dad have you do?" I asked Mr. White.

"All kinds of things," he said. "He's had us go overseas to retrieve people and parcels. We've been a delivery service, we've even taken high profile people off his list," he said.

This caught me off guard. They killed people for my dad? Is that what he meant by taking them off the list? I came back to my senses and said, "What kinds of things does he have you do that could use the help of informers?" I asked, trying to stay on track in my mind. "Specific jobs."

"Let me see…" He paused and then began to tell me about separate jobs that my dad could have used some outside help. None of the descriptions were helpful though and he didn't know for sure where my dad got his information for most of them.

"Okay, Gabriella? Are you still there?" I asked.

"Yep," she said.

"Okay. Let me see. That file is labeled 'Friends'." I thought on it some more. "What's another name for friend?" I said out loud. "Try acquaintance for the password."

"Okay." I heard her typing. "Not it."

"Try 'advisor'." But that didn't work either. We went through several different words and then Gabriella said, "Uh-oh. I think the computer just crashed."

"What?" I said. "What happened?"

"It just shut itself off and now I can't get it to come back on," she said.

I tried to figure out what was going on through the phone. I gave her several different things to try including totally unplugging the computer from the wall and letting it sit for a couple of minutes. She had even made sure the electricity in the house was still on. Nothing helped. The computer had shut down. I gave the phone back to Mr. White who spoke with Mr. Black for a few moments. While he was still talking to him I was in the background saying I thought we should go back and maybe I could do something with the computer.

He disconnected and said, "I've arranged for Mr. Brown to come get us. He should be here sometime this evening."

"Finally," I said. I began to pace again and kept it up until Mr. White said, "That's it. We're going to go get rid of some of your energy."

We walked to the lake where Mr. White proceeded to teach me a few new moves. They were similar to ones I already knew but he had different little tricks to add. His movements were more fluid than of any other person I had sparred with. It was like it was second nature to him to fight.

Before too long Mr. White told me, "Show me what you've got."

We circled each other a few times and I made my move. He counteracted me and had me on the ground. He stayed on top of me while he explained what I did wrong and how he knew I was going to do what I did.

"Let's go," he said as he finally got off me. Sitting over the top of me with his face close to mine, his breath hot on my neck had disoriented me. I think he knew it too. It took me a second or two to finally shake the feeling enough to get up off the ground.

"Get your mind on what you are doing, Ms. Grey," he said and lunged for me. I went low to the ground and was barely able to get out of the way.

"Good. Keep it up," he said while we began to circle each other again.

This went on for a while, then I heard the chopper in the distance. Mr. White looked to the sky and I went for him. I had him down on the ground in no time. I had him pinned with a move Mr. Black had shown me and he couldn't get away.

"What are you doing? The chopper's coming," he said, flustered.

"What was it you said to me at the Skylight? Oh, yes. I'm just taking advantage of a situation," I said in a calm cool voice as close to his neck as I could get without being obvious. I could tell I had completely caught him off guard. The closeness of me affected him the same way it had affected me every time he had gotten me down.

"Let me up," he said. "We have to get out of the way so they can land."

I got off him and he was up off the ground in a flash. I was in defense mode and jumped away from him instinctively. He grinned that devious grin of his and I couldn't help but smile myself. Then thoughts of my dad flowed over the excitement of the moment.

"Let's get back to the cabin and get things ready to close up," he said as he began to walk in that direction.

It didn't take us long to get things put away and ourselves packed. I wondered if I should leave my deer skin hanging out back and Mr. White said we should bring it home with us. He'd have it dropped off at the taxidermist so I could keep it. I wasn't all that sure I wanted to keep it, but hey, maybe I could sell it someday, or show it to my grandkids.

J.C. Phelps

As I was bringing in the deerskin, Mr. Brown walked up. He had landed the chopper and came to see if we needed any help closing up the cabin. I told him I thought we were pretty much ready. Then he commented on my buck.

"Nice buck. Mr. Black told me you had bagged yourself a big one." His infectious smile had returned to its normal position on his face.

"Thanks," I said. I still wasn't sure about him. He had a way of saying the wrong things. I waited for it to come but it didn't.

When we got inside he grabbed one of the two packs waiting to be carted off and headed back to the chopper. Mr. White grabbed the other and told me I needed to carry the deer.

We were in the air and headed home within a matter of minutes. The trip seemed to take longer than it had before but I knew it was because I was in a hurry to get there. After we reached the office we went straight to my parent's house.

I walked into Mr. Black and Gabriella looking through paperwork of my father's.

"Did you find anything?" Mr. White asked as he came through the office door.

"Nothing," Mr. Black answered.

I went straight to the computer and tried to get it to work. It wasn't off, the screen was just blank. I tried to shut it off and it wouldn't shut off so I unplugged it again. This shut it off. I plugged it back in but the start up screen didn't appear. I tried several basic commands but they wouldn't work either. Nothing was working. Then I got an idea.

I walked to my house and Mr. White was right on my heels. I got inside and went straight to my computer. I turned it on and tried to access my dad's computer from mine. I got it up. I started a simple search of the hard drive and found the file labeled 'Friends'. I hoped this was the correct file or I had just wasted a lot of everyone's time. I was just about to try to open the file when Mr. Black walked in.

"The computer screen came back on over there," he said.

"Good," I replied as I got up out of my chair. It was best to try it from the master computer. We all went back to my dad's office and I sat back down at the computer. I started putting in passwords that we had already tried. I had Mr. White writing them down as I tried them and had him cross them off one by one. I got to the last one we put in before the computer crashed and didn't use it. I tried another because I wanted to see if it had been the word that had shut off the screen or the number of try's we had done.

I typed in 'monkey' because I was pretty sure that wouldn't be the password. Nothing happened except it told me I didn't have the correct password. I tried 'mole', which was the last word we had tried before. The computer screen went blank and it looked like the computer had shut itself off. There was a faint green light coming from the monitor though, so I knew it

Color Me Grey

hadn't shut itself off, it had just gone to a blank screen. I sat and thought for a minute then figured it out. Dad had done this one other time to me. It was like a game between us. I have always tried to break into his computer and he was always trying to come up with new ways to protect it from me. He didn't always know I had broken his security though, so he would use the same method if he thought they were Alex-proofed. This must have been one of those. I will admit, it did take me a while to figure it out, but I knew how to fix the problem.

"Okay, everybody," I said to get everyone's attention. "I need you to look for a separate hard drive. It'll be a little box that I can plug into the computer."

I got up and went in search of it myself. The last time I had run into this problem, the external drive had been in his bedroom upstairs. This was the first place I looked. Again Mr. White followed me. He helped me look upstairs but we didn't find it in any of the rooms up there. I decided I'd check the living room and had no luck there either. As I walked past my dad's office I saw Gabriella, Mr. Black and Mr. Brown were all busy looking through things. I rounded up Mr. Brown to come help us look through the library.

We started by looking under all the cushions of the chairs and couch in the room. Then we moved onto the books. I knew my dad had some hollow books where he stashed things, so I went straight to them first. They all had some sort of stash, like cash or his cigarettes and lighter. He used to sneak a cigarette every once in a while, but by the look of the cigarettes in the stash box, he hadn't done that in quite a while. Then Mr. White said, "Is this what you're looking for?" He lifted up a small box that looked like the one dad had used before.

"Could be," I said. I moved over to him and took it. "Thanks," I added as I walked back toward the office.

I got it plugged in and the computer came back to life. The file opened and everyone was standing over me as I searched through it. There were lots of names, each with an address and/or phone number. Some of them had dates next to the names. I thought the dates might be the place to start. I didn't know what they stood for, but it could have been the dates my dad received information from them or dates of a job he hired out.

I found a date close to the date of my first job and the name next to the date was Abdullah Salah. Now if that wasn't a good sign I didn't know what was! There was no address but there was a contact number. I wrote it down and handed it to Mr. White.

"This should be the guy," I said.

He nodded and took the paper from me. Turning to Mr. Black he said, "I need you to take care of Ms. Grey. I'm going to have Mr. Red call this guy up." He turned to me and added, "Good job. This might be what we need to get the ball rolling. I'll back before too long." With that, he left. Mr. Brown and Gabriella went with him. Leaving just Mr. Black and myself to clean up the mess we had all made.

J.C. Phelps

Cleaning up didn't take all that long. When we finished, I told Mr. Black I'd like to go to my place to clean up. On the walk to my house I asked him how long he thought it might take to locate Abdullah Salah, the suspected informant. He said it shouldn't take too long, but he didn't know if he would be cooperative with us.

After I cleaned myself up and changed my clothes Mr. Black and I sat back and watched some TV. It was something I was able to do because my mind didn't have to work. I could just sit there and become part of another world and not have to think about anything.

Chapter Fifteen

Several days passed with Mr. Black and myself hanging out at my place. He made and received calls daily, but there had been no luck in finding my dad's informant.

I had gotten over being antsy because I had gotten things moving, but now that no progress had been made I was becoming restless again. Mr. Black and I had a meeting at the office today and I wanted to get in there and get it over with. I was hoping something had come up so we could get busy. I was pretty sure Mr. Black was tired of sleeping on my couch too. It wasn't big enough for him to stretch out on. It was a bit more comfortable than the ground up in the mountains though.

I hadn't been able to see my mother yet. They had brought her to a safe house and they didn't want anyone to know where she was. I had spoken to her on the phone and she seemed very normal for what was happening. It didn't seem to bother her she had shot someone. She did have a bit of trouble with the fact that Daddy had been kidnapped, but told me she knew I could find him and get him back. Nothing like a little pressure to make a person feel great about sitting at home doing nothing.

It was time for the meeting so we got into my Mustang. Mr. White and company had taken both vehicles the other day so it would seem that nothing had changed. Later that day he had tried to place me in a safe house but I wouldn't go. I told him if The Lion's cultists came back for me, Mr. Black and I would handle it and maybe it could help us out if we were able to capture the bad guys. After I pointed out that bit of information I didn't get much argument from Mr. White.

We pulled into the car garage and Mr. Black pointed to my very own parking spot. He told me they had set it up while he and I had been at the cabin. I guess I'm in it for the long haul now, I thought.

Mr. Black held the elevator door for me and opened the door to Suite 73 just like he had before. I noticed these things. Mr. White had done the same on some occasions but Mr. Black did it almost every time. The only time he wasn't a gentleman in this way was at the cabin. I had to fend for myself up there, most of the time. He slipped once in a while, but I didn't mind.

Gabriella looked up from her desk and said, "Nobody's here yet. I'm supposed to tell you they would be about half an hour late."

Mr. Black said he'd be back in twenty minutes and walked out the door.

"I'm sorry about Admiral Stanton," Gabriella said after I sat down in front of her desk. "He is such a nice man."

"You know my dad?" I asked.

"Not well. He's been here a couple times, but he was always so polite," she said. "I took your deer to the taxidermist yesterday. Did you really get him all by yourself?" she asked.

"Yeah," I said. "It was kind of an accident, but don't tell the guys that."

She smiled. "I won't tell. I just love the fact that a woman is right up there with these guys. Don't tell them, but none of them came back with a buck that size, not even Mr. Black."

"They've all brought back deer?" I asked.

"Yeah, it's like an initiation of sorts with them. Mr. White, Mr. Brown and Mr. Red were all here the other day and they were talking about your deer," she said. "Sometimes they forget I'm in here and I get some juicy gossip. But anyway, Mr. White was bragging you up to Mr. Red because I think Mr. Red had the biggest buck before." She got a disgusted look on her face. "I don't really like Mr. Red. He walks around thinking he's all that. I think it's because he can speak so many different languages."

"I've not met Mr. Red yet," I said with a bit of worry in my voice.

"Ah honey, don't worry. He's not all that bad; he just walks around with his nose in the air. You could knock him down a few pegs," she said. Then she added with a sly look, "I also heard Mr. Brown razzing Mr. White about how you had him down on the ground. What were you doing out there with Mr. White?" she asked.

"We were practicing hand-to-hand maneuvers and Mr. White was distracted by the chopper so I took him down," I said with a big smile on my face. I was more proud of that than the buck. "I didn't know Mr. Brown saw it." I was a bit embarrassed.

"Well, Mr. White got a bit upset with Mr. Brown after he said that," Gabriella said. "He told Mr. Brown that you two were practicing, like you said, and you weren't that kind of girl." Her smile broadened.

"Really?" I said, my face getting hot.

"Oh, look at that. You're blushing. You better try to control that because if these guys see that, they'll pick on you forever," she said.

"I know," I said. I knew I did better around them than her though. Gabriella had a way of reading me and knowing just what to say to get a reaction out of me. I suppose it was because she was a woman and could understand the things that went through my head.

We talked about other things, like how Mr. Black had actually spoken to her since he had been back. They had talked about me mostly, but he asked her about herself too. That was a good sign for her I told her and she agreed. I didn't know if they would ever hook up, but at least she was getting to talk to

Color Me Grey

126

him a bit. She told me he had seemed to open up more. She thought it might be because I had come along. She said he talked about me just like one of the other guys, but he was proud when he spoke of me. This woman was a fountain of interesting information. She did most of the talking, but that was the way I liked it anyway. I gave her a little bit of information about myself here and there, but tried to keep it limited to stuff I might not care if other people found out about.

Mr. Black finally came back and the three of us sat in silence for a while. Then I told him Gabriella had taken my buck to the taxidermist. He told me it would have to go back to the cabin because everyone else's was there. The plan was to build onto the cabin to include rooms for everyone and the skins would hang in everyone's separate room. They just hadn't gotten around to building on yet. He said it was a good thing too, because now I could have my own room.

Before long, Mr. White came in and without words Mr. Black and I followed him to his office. Mr. Black shut the door behind us and we all took seats. It was quiet for a while and the look on Mr. White's face didn't seem promising. He finally broke the silence by saying Mr. Red had gotten in touch with the informant but he wouldn't help us unless he had proof Mr. Red was who he said he was. The only proof he would accept was me.

All these different people knew me and I didn't have a clue as to who they were. I really wished I had snooped more into what my dad's job was.

"What does he want me to do?" I asked.

"He will meet only with you," Mr. White said. "But we can't do that, because I don't know if we can trust him."

"We'll just have to take the chance, won't we," I said defiantly.

"Ms. Grey might be right," Mr. Black said. "I don't want to put her in danger, but we could control the meeting. We'd have everyone posted around to make sure nothing could happen to her. We just need to choose the right place for the meeting," he said.

"I would prefer someplace public where it would be hard to spot us and hard for them to get to her," Mr. White said.

"It couldn't be a large place like a mall though," Mr. Black said.

I cut in and said, "What about the Skylight? Pretty much everyone there knows me and it's a small type of bar. The building is fairly large, but it's mostly open and the clientele doesn't change much. I could probably pick out the people who didn't belong or I could have Colin check things out before I go in."

It was quiet for a moment then Mr. Black said, "That would probably work."

"It could, but I'm not sure about putting you in that kind of danger," Mr. White said.

J.C. Phelps

"If he is my dad's informant then I should be safe right?" I asked and got an affirmative nod from Mr. White. "If he's not, then you guys will be around so I should still be safe," I said.

"Should be," Mr. White said. "Okay, I'll set up the meeting for tonight. You can use Gabriella's phone to see if you can set it up with your friend. I'll get Mr. Red on the phone and get him started on setting up the meeting with Salah."

"Should I tell him everything that's going on?" I asked. "Colin likes to know what's going on in my life."

"Don't tell him all the details, but you can tell him some of them. Just be as discreet as you can be," he said as I walked to the front office to use the phone. I looked back and he was already on his phone. I assumed he was calling Mr. Red to get the ball rolling.

I asked permission from Gabriella before I picked up her phone. Then I dialed Colin. I was glad to hear his voice. It had been a while since we last talked. I asked him how he was doing and what he had been up to. He had met a girl while I had been gone but it wasn't serious. I felt a pang of jealousy at this because Colin had always been mine even though I didn't really want him. He had had other girlfriends in the past and I never liked any of them. We did a little more catching up before I asked my favor. Finally I said, "I was wondering if you could do me a favor tonight?"

"Depends on what it is," he said. "I'm supposed to meet Olivia tonight at the Skylight." Olivia was his new girl.

"Well, all I need is for you to keep an eye out for me at the Skylight," I said.

"What do you mean?" he asked.

"I'm on this job and I'm supposed to meet a guy there. If he's who he's supposed to be then there should be no problem, but if not, there may be some other people around I would need to know of. You know everyone there and I thought you could let me know if there were a lot of different faces in the crowd before I came in."

"Yeah, I could probably do that. What kind of job is this?" he asked.

"I can't tell you any details, but I can tell you it's extremely important," I said.

"I don't mind helping you, but the guys you're working for is a different matter," he added.

"Well, this is mostly for me. It's a job I'm on, but I have personal ties to it. Does that help?" I asked.

"A little. You're going to have to tell me all about it later though. Do we have a deal?" he said.

"Sure," I said. "Thank you. I really appreciate this, Colin."

Before I hung up Mr. Black came up to me and told me he needed to pick up Colin and bring him to the office to be instructed on how to do this right. He also wanted to set him up with a wire of some kind so it wouldn't be obvious that he was communicating with anyone outside the building. I told Colin to expect Mr. Black some time soon. He wasn't too happy with being chauffeured around but finally agreed on it.

Mr. White had been in the other room talking with Mr. Red. A few minutes after I finished speaking with Colin he hung up the phone and motioned me back into his office. Mr. Black had gone to retrieve Colin so it was just Mr. White and myself after I shut the door, closing off Gabriella. Being in a room alone with Mr. White had gotten a bit easier since I had spent a few days with him at the cabin, but it was still stressing for me.

I took a seat in front of his desk and he told me what information I needed to get from, Abdullah Salah, the informant and probable relative of The Lion. It was pretty simple if he was on our side. I should have no problem getting him to come in to talk to all of us. Mr. White or Mr. Red would handle him then, but if he wouldn't cooperate I was going to have to ask the questions. I was going to have to determine for myself which side I thought he was on. Mr. White told me several things to watch for to establish whether or not I thought he was lying to me. The instruction on subtle interrogation lasted until Mr. Black returned with Colin.

They both walked into the office with sour looks on their faces. Colin came up to me and we hugged. He said, "This guy has no sense of humor. He doesn't say much either."

"He's more of an action, not words type of person," I said with a smile to Mr. Black. His expression didn't change though.

"Petty Officer DeLange," Mr. White acknowledged Colin with a nod.

"Malone," Colin said back with a bit of contempt, deliberately leaving out any title before the name. I hadn't told him Mr. White's real name, so I'm guessing Colin either finally remembered or had known all along. There must have been something that happened between these two I didn't know about. I'd have to try and weasel it out of Colin later.

The rest of the afternoon was spent schooling Colin on what he was to do inside the Skylight and getting him fitted for both audio and video devices. Then it was my turn. I wouldn't let them tape it to my chest like they had with Colin though. I watched carefully on how they put it all together and went to the bathroom to do it for myself. We did a check on both Colin's audio and mine and we were both hooked up correctly. Mr. White had pulled out a jacket for Colin to wear that had a camera in one of the buttons.

Mr. Red had set up the meeting for early evening so the bar wouldn't be too busy and the band wouldn't be playing yet. Time was closing in when Mr. White said, "Mr. Black, you will drive Petty Officer DeLange to the club. I want you in position before I send in Ms. Grey." Mr. Black nodded understanding, his cooler-than-cool look had returned. I hadn't seen that look for a while, but it was reassuring.

"How am I supposed to know who the guy is?" I butted in.

"He says he knows you and he will approach you," Mr. White said to me. "Colin, I want you to make a check into both bathrooms before you go to the main part of the bar," he continued.

"The women's too?" Colin asked.

"Yes, I want to make sure there aren't any surprises. This is for Alex's safety," Mr. White said.

"Alright," Colin said, but I could tell he was uncomfortable with the thought of having to go into the women's restroom.

Mr. Black and Colin left and Mr. White went over my role again. I just needed to go in and grab a seat at the bar and wait. After a few minutes of reviewing the plan Mr. White and I left the office to the car garage below. A dark van was parked and waiting for us. Mr. Blue was in the drivers' seat. I hadn't seen him since the day he picked me up to go train at the cabin the first time.

"Mr. Blue," I greeted him.

"Ms. Grey. How are things?" He was professional but there was a quality of familiarity to his greeting.

"Not bad," I said and got in. Mr. White sat in the back with what looked like a small television station. I saw the inside of Mr. Black's SUV on one of the screens and assumed it was Colin's video feed.

The van sped off toward the Skylight and I kept my head turned to watch the show unfolding on the screen. Mr. White had turned up the volume and Colin was talking a mile a minute. Every once in a while he'd pause to see if Mr. Black would say something but he never did. Mr. White then said into a microphone, "Mr. Black would you please tell him to quiet down?"

I heard Mr. Black's voice say, "With pleasure. Petty Officer, I have been instructed to ask you to quiet down."

"Are they listening already?" Colin asked.

"To every word," Mr. Black replied.

We pulled into the parking lot of the Skylight. There were a few cars parked outside, but it was just a fraction of what would be there in a few hours. Mr. Blue found us a spot with no trouble and I was about to get out when Mr. White stopped me.

"Wait. I'm not satisfied yet." He had been watching Colin's movie unfold. He kept his eyes on the screen and said, "Looks like everyone's in place." Then into the microphone he said, "Mr. Black, grab a seat by DeLange so we can speak."

Before a minute had passed I heard Mr. Black's voice, "In position."

"Have Colin start pointing out the regulars along with the new people," Mr. White said.

Mr. Black instructed Colin and the camera started to pan the room. He stopped at every face including the employees. Colin knew the names of most of the people in the building. If he didn't know the names, he knew the faces.

Color Me Grey

He came to Mr. Brown and I heard Mr. Black tell him to pass him up. There were two other men he stopped the camera on in different places throughout the building, but was told to by pass them as well. I assumed it was the two other partners, Mr. Red and Mr. Green. One of the men was a scrawny looking type and the other was quite handsome. I wondered which was which.

"All right, Mr. Black," Mr. White said when Colin finished scanning the room. "Have Colin watch the door and report any new customers. I will send in Ms. Grey in a few minutes." He switched off the microphone and looked to me. "Are you ready?" he asked me.

"Yep," I said straightening my shirt.

"I have something for you," he said and reached into his pocket. He pulled out a beautiful necklace with a golden angel for a charm. I was surprised. Why would he be giving me a necklace?

"Move your hair," he said and reached over to fasten the necklace around my neck. "Now, make sure you keep this outside your shirt so I can see what's going on," he added.

I felt stupid. I'm glad I didn't open my mouth. He switched on another screen and my video signal was coming through fine, I could see the back of his head in the monitor.

"Okay, it's working. Now head in and sit at the bar. We just have to wait now. If Salah doesn't show in an hour I'll have Mr. Black escort you back to the van."

I stepped out of the van and walked inside. I was nervous but I couldn't let it show. I got to the bar and took a seat. Anthony was working, yuck. He came up to me and said, "What can I get for ya, babe?"

"Just a Coke please," I said, maybe a little too nicely.

He walked away and came right back with my drink. "I haven't seen you around for a while."

"I got a new job that takes me out of town," I explained, making sure I wasn't too friendly this time. I didn't have any feelings for this guy. Not any good feelings. I didn't hate him, but I really didn't want to involve him in my life in any way.

"So, you must miss me. You haven't sat at the bar for a long time." He got a sickening grin on his face.

"Nope. Just felt like sitting at the bar tonight," I said.

"Yeah, right. That's why you haven't even gone over to see Colin yet. I know you and you want me."

How disgusting this guy was. I couldn't understand what I had ever seen in him. "Don't start with me Anthony. I'm not interested in you *at all*," I said through clenched teeth. I reached down to adjust the camera. I most definitely didn't want it falling into my shirt.

"Look, you're fidgeting," he said. "You used to do that when I would make you nervous."

J.C. Phelps

"Anthony," I said, trying to contain my voice. "Leave me alone and wait on your other customers."

"Do you want to check out the booth over there?" he asked trying to look sexy. "It's early enough I could get away for a bit."

"Yeah," I said with fake enthusiasm. "It would only take a second too." Then I gave him a vapid smile.

He expanded his grin to try to lure me away from the bar then it finally registered that I had just insulted him. The smile dropped from his face. It was priceless.

"You're a bitch," he said.

Mr. Black was right behind me and had put his hand on my shoulder. "Alex," he said in an ominous voice, "is this guy going to be a problem?" Then he shot an evil look to Anthony.

I smiled and said, "Well, Anthony? Are you going to be a problem?"

"No," Anthony was quick to answer. "I'm sorry, Lexi. I didn't know you were here with anyone." Then he was gone to harass some other poor girl at the opposite side of the bar. Some men never learn.

"I could have handled him," I said to Mr. Black "But that *was* fun," I added.

"Don't mention it," he said and walked off to stand where he could see the entire room.

The good-looking man I had seen in Colin's camera was also at the bar situated not far from me. He had been watching me since I sat at the bar. He was quite handsome and held himself above the rest of the crowd. This must be Mr. Red, I thought as I gave him a nod of acknowledgement.

He nodded back politely and gave me a smile that would have melted any woman in the room. He didn't quite have the allure of Mr. White, but he was definitely not an eyesore. I located Colin and looked for the other man that had been caught in the camera when I was in the van. I couldn't find him though.

The bar stool I had chosen gave me a good view of the door and soon I saw a man walk in that didn't look like he belonged. There was an air of familiarity to him though. He came straight to the bar and sat next to me. My stomach did a flip. Was this Abdullah Salah?

"Lexi Stanton?" he said.

"Yes," I said.

"You don't recognize me do you?" he asked.

"No, I'm sorry but I don't," I replied.

"Your father and I have been friends for a long time. I've been to your house a few times but not for years."

"Mr. Jones?" I asked surprised to remember his name. I barely remembered him, but I knew Dad had helped him out years ago with something.

"Yes," he said with a smile of relief. "Your father has always been a good friend to me and I want to help."

"What do you mean?" I asked.

"I'm Abdullah Salah. You were too young back then to know what was going on, but your Father helped me to get myself settled here in the United States," he explained.

He had a foreign look but no accent of any kind. He spoke like he had been born and raised in my neighborhood.

"Are you connected to The Lion?" I asked.

"He's my cousin," he said with a hint of revulsion in his voice. "I am glad to find you here. I was afraid my cousin had found out I had been relaying information to your father."

"Would you be willing to come into our offices and speak with my partners?" I asked.

"Will you be there?" he asked, looking around.

"If you want me there, I'll be there," I replied.

"I'm not sure I can trust anyone though and I don't know if you should either," he said.

"I know what you mean, but I'm sure these men I'm with right now are on my side, which puts them on your side too." I tried to convince him everything would be all right.

"I'm taking a big risk already, just coming here to talk to you. I think there have been people following me. I'm not sure, but it's not the first time I have been spied on by my family and their friends," he said, starting to get more and more agitated.

"It's alright," I said, trying to calm him down. "The men helping me will make sure everything will be okay."

"Can you take me to them right now?" he asked. "I would feel better if we just got this over with."

"Of course. Let's go," I said as I stood up from the barstool. We walked together down the hallway and I knew Mr. Black was directly behind us. Abdullah glanced over his shoulder and I said, "It's alright. That's Mr. Black."

The three of us stepped out the door and were walking toward the van in the lot when a white Celebrity station wagon sped up toward us. I pushed the informant at Mr. Black and then I fell to the ground. I didn't know why, but my leg wouldn't work. Mr. White jumped from the van and picked me up. He carried me back to the van where Mr. Black had already stashed Abdullah. The other two partners that had been inside with us were standing with weapons drawn, firing at the vehicle speeding away. Then they ran for their vehicle, I assumed to give chase.

"Go!" Mr. White yelled to Mr. Blue as he shut the van's sliding door. Mr. Blue took off out of the parking lot.

Abdullah Salah was in one corner of the van crying. Everything was happening so fast and blending together. I saw Mr. White and Mr. Black talking to each other and looking at me. Finally, the excitement of the moment had

J.C. Phelps

started to die down and I was able to focus much better. I had a terrible pain in my leg. I looked down at it and there was a small puddle of blood pooling on the floor of the van.

Mr. White came to my side and said, "Wait. Mr. Blue will look at it." He had Mr. Blue pull over and Mr. Black took control of the driving. Mr. White hadn't left my side and it was getting crowded in the back of the van. He instructed Salah to move to the front seat. He had to physically pick him up and put him into the passenger's seat. Then he returned to my side. By the time he had gotten the informant placed out of the way, Mr. Blue had already cut open my pants leg.

"So?" Mr. White said with concern in his voice.

"She'll be fine," Mr. Blue answered him shaking his head. "The bullet is still in her leg but it should be no problem to get it out. It didn't even come close to her artery."

Bullet? I had been shot? Wow, I thought that being shot would have been more exciting. Mr. Blue started to feel around the small hole on my calf.

"Ouch!" I said when he got closer to the wound. I felt a bit embarrassed and added, "Sorry."

"Don't be sorry," Mr. Blue said. "It's supposed to hurt. You've just been shot."

"It doesn't feel anything like I expected it would," I said.

"Where to?" Mr. Black said looking back with concern.

"To the office," Mr. Blue said. "This will be a simple removal, it's right under the skin."

Abdullah was still crying in the front of the van and it was beginning to get on my nerves. Not to mention Colin's new girlfriend's chest was larger than life on one of the screens and I could hear Colin flirting with her.

"Mr. Jones!" I yelled. "Please stop that! And turn that thing off!" I said to Mr. White.

Abdullah's sobbing ceased immediately and Mr. White jumped to shut off the equipment. We all rode in silence back to the office.

When we reached a parking spot in the garage Mr. Blue opened the sliding door and gave me a hand out of the vehicle. He started to put my arm over his shoulder but I pulled it away. I had been kicking myself all the way to the office. How could I have gotten shot? I at least could have waited until we had Dad back. But no, I have to get shot before we even know where he's being held. I was determined to walk on my own. I didn't deserve any help.

"Let me at least try," I said.

The four of us walked to the elevator inside. I hobbled and they walked. It was pretty painful, but nothing I can't handle, I told myself. I was grateful for the rest when we reached the elevator. If I didn't put any pressure on my leg it was numb, otherwise it hurt like hell. I think the endorphins had started to filter out of my system.

Color Me Grey

We reached the seventh floor and the elevator doors opened. Each man in the elevator looked to me to start the trek to the office. It had never seemed so far away before. I limped to the door and Mr. White jumped to open it for me. I could feel the hot blood running down my leg and soaking my sock.

When I got inside I noticed Gabriella must have gone home for the evening. I looked to Mr. Blue for direction. He nodded that I should go to the big office.

"Can you make it to the couch?" Mr. White asked me, the worry lines I had seen at the cabin had returned.

"Yes," I said. I was still extremely mad at myself for getting shot and wasn't going to let the pain get to me.

I made it to the couch and sat down with relief. I had worked up a sweat and Mr. Black went to the bathroom that was on the opposite side of the room and brought back a wet washcloth for my face. When he handed it to me he gripped my hand tight and gave me a nod of approval.

Mr. Blue had gone straight to one of the closets and gotten what looked like the typical doctor's bag. I hoped he knew what he was doing. I presumed he did since neither Mr. White nor Mr. Black had any objections to him taking over. Nonetheless, I was still a bit skeptical.

"Do you know what you're doing?" I asked.

"I'm a certified and licensed doctor so don't worry," he replied. That made me feel slightly better about him when he pulled out a scalpel and syringe.

He filled the syringe with a liquid and asked me if I was allergic to Novocain or any related drugs. I told him no and he stuck the needle right in my leg at the wound sight. I flinched with the pain but it was already starting to subside.

Abdullah Salah was in the corner of the room, red faced and looking like a cornered animal. Mr. White's face had worry lines throughout and he was hovering over the back of the couch. Mr. Black was sitting in a chair in front of the desk all signs of concern gone, but with a somewhat proud look on his face.

"I'm going to give this some time to kick in fully." Mr. Blue said to me. He stood up and walked to the back of the couch. He took Mr. White by the shoulders and told him to sit down and quit worrying because he knew what he was doing.

"I know that," Mr. White replied indignantly and moved to the chair next to Mr. Black.

The door to Mr. White's office had been left open and we watched Mr. Red and Mr. Green come in the door. Mr. Red wore a mad look on his face, but Mr. Green was as serene as they got. They had totally different walks. Mr. Red was cocky with his head held high and Mr. Green was like a cat slinking across the room. They seemed almost to be the opposite of each other.

"Where's Mr. Brown?" I asked no one in particular.

Mr. Red answered me in a fluid and clear voice. "He's back at the club retrieving our equipment from DeLange." Then he went straight to Salah and

J.C. Phelps

brought him to a comfortable chair. He began speaking to him quietly. Salah answered his questions with a shaky voice and frequent looks to me. I couldn't hear what exactly they were saying, but hoped they were making progress.

Mr. Blue walked back to me on the couch and knelt down to my leg. He pushed on the wound and got no response from me. Then I watched him feel over to where the bullet sat and I felt no pain there either.

"Okay," he said and reached for his scalpel. I watched him take the end of it and make an incision about half an inch wide and not at all too deep. Then he pushed the bullet out. He handed me the bullet and said,

"Good job. The bullet's in nice shape too. You should be back to normal in a couple of days." He placed the needle and syringe in a plastic bag and closed it. Then he reached over and applied something to my incision. He explained it was like super glue and would keep the cut closed. Then he applied some sort of ointment to the entrance wound.

"I can't glue the entrance wound shut because it needs to flush itself out. But in a day or so, if it looks good I might do that for you. It will minimize the scarring." Then he wrapped a bandage around my leg with instructions to change it twice a day and reapply the ointment each time.

"Now this next part is the hard part," he said. He stood up and helped me to my feet and led me to the bathroom. When we got inside he shut the door and said, "You need a tetanus shot. I could have given it to you out there, but I didn't know if you would be comfortable. I can give it to you in your arm or your butt, your choice."

"What a choice. The arm," I said pulling my shirt down over my shoulder so he could get to my arm.

"Not good enough," he said. "I need you to take your arm out of your sleeve and pull your shirt out of the way. You should be able to keep yourself covered that way still."

I did as I was instructed and he gave me the shot. It hurt almost as bad as the bullet had, almost. I still remembered the last time I had a tetanus shot and my arm had ached for a week afterwards. Something else to look forward to, I thought to myself.

"You handled that well. It's good to know blood doesn't make you pass out." I sensed a bit of humor in his words but wasn't sure because he didn't show it in his face. I had put my arm back into my shirt and was smoothing it out when he opened the door to the bathroom. All eyes in the room were on us as we walked out of the room. Mr. Blue brought his medical bag back to the closet it had originated from and I walked without a limp back to the couch.

Mr. Red was still talking to the informant and Mr. Brown was now present. He looked to me with that smile on his face again. I tried but couldn't resist smiling back at him.

Color Me Grey

I listened in on the conversation that was being held between the rest of the men. I would have been more interested in what Mr. Red and Salah were talking about but they had changed from English to some other language.

The other men were discussing the shooting and the chase. It was the general consensus that the bullet had been meant for Salah and not me, which was a relief. Then Mr. Green told them about the chase.

After a while, they had slowed to let the perpetrators think they had lost them and were able to follow them to a building not far from our office. They called in some other men that periodically worked for them to sit and wait for the people inside to make a move. The backup had orders to report in any changes and to continue to follow the men if they left the building.

Then the mood lightened and Mr. Brown said to me, "You holding up okay over there?"

"I'm fine, thank you," I replied.

He walked over to me and showed me a scar on his arm. It was barely noticeable. "See this here?" he asked. "Blue over there did a good job on this one. You probably won't even be able to see your scar without looking for it." He smiled at me some more.

Mr. Green walked up to me and said, "Since nobody is going to introduce us, I will introduce myself. I'm Mr. Green. It's nice to finally meet the prodigy girl," he said with a wink. "I hear you got yourself a hell of a buck."

"I guess," I said not sure what to think of this little man in front of me. None of these men were unattractive, but Mr. Green seemed to be hardly there. He was skinny and didn't have the muscle tone the other men had. He was wearing a long sleeved t-shirt and jeans that hung on him. He didn't look starved but he definitely didn't look buff either.

Mr. White interrupted and said, "Gabriella was to pick up the skin and bring it back this evening before she went home. I told her to put it in one of the closets." He was moving to the other side of the room. The first door he opened held my deerskin. All the men had gathered around it as Mr. White laid it out on the floor. Mr. Black came to stand next to me while the other men oohed and aahed over the dead animal.

"Good job back there," he said. "You did better than most men," he added.

"I hear women handle pain better than men," I said.

"They must," he said back with a smile.

I looked to the cluster of men in the middle of the office and Mr. Red and Salah had joined in the admiration of my kill. Salah had regained his composure and came up to me.

"Ms. Stanton, I am truly sorry for the way I acted in the van. I hope you can forgive me," he said with his head bowed.

"Not a big deal. I'm sorry I snapped at you too," I replied.

J.C. Phelps

"I hope I have been of some help to you in the search for your father. Mr. Red said he is going to help me find a place where I can be safe now that my cousin's crazy followers have found me out."

"Good," I said with genuine relief. Not so much for the man I used to know as Jones, but because I hoped he had been of some help. I wondered what he had told Mr. Red but decided to wait until they were all done playing with the dead deer before I asked any questions.

"I can't believe you took a bullet for me. I appreciate it," Salah added.

"I didn't do it on purpose," I said before I could stop myself.

Mr. Black let out his glorious laugh at my last statement. The whole room quieted at the sound. Everyone had turned and had looks of expectation. They wanted to know what was so funny that it actually got a laugh from Mr. Black.

Mr. White spoke first saying, "Mr. Red, it's time for us to get down to business. Would you please go tuck in the informant?"

Mr. Red came and collected Salah and left the room with him. The other men took seats around the room. Mr. Black gathered up the deer and put it back into the closet. Mr. Blue came to the couch and sat next to me, telling me I should keep my leg elevated. We waited for Mr. Red's return, which didn't take more than a few minutes.

Chapter Sixteen

It didn't take long at all for Mr. Red to walk back into the office. He must have stashed The Lion's cousin somewhere close by. I watched him saunter into the office and decided Gabriella had been right. He did have an air about him that screamed he thought he was better than all the rest.

After he had sat down, Mr. White asked him to fill us in on what information Abdullah Salah had given him.

Mr. Red started by telling us Salah had given him several locations we could check out. He pulled out a sheet of paper and handed it to Mr. White, explaining it was a list of these locations. He also said Mr. White would find some names on the list that might be of some help to us now and possibly in the future as well.

"Did you get the impression Salah was entirely forthcoming on this?" Mr. White asked him.

"Yes, I did. He's quite timid and I don't think he would have been able to lie efficiently," Mr. Red replied.

"Alright, everyone," Mr. White said. "You should go get some rest. I want you all back here early tomorrow morning."

We all started to say our goodnights. Mr. Blue came up to me and handed me a bottle of pills.

"These are antibiotics. Take one pill three times a day. You can start tonight before you go to bed, then I recommend taking one with every meal." He reminded me to keep off my leg as much as possible and to keep it elevated before he walked for the door.

My Mustang was still in the parking lot, but I wasn't sure I wanted to drive it home. I started to make my way to the door when Mr. White came up to me.

"You and I can start work tonight. If you feel up to it," he said with a glance at my bandaged leg.

"I'm fine," I said. I was glad to be able to do something other than wait. I hated waiting.

"Alright, let me get some things together, then we'll go to my place, he said.

His place? He had seemed professional when he said it, but my imagination started to chug along in full gear. I was a nervous wreck by the time he said, "You ready?"

J.C. Phelps

No, I'm not ready, I thought, but said, "Yep, let's go." We walked out of the office together toward the elevator. He matched my pace. I imagine he did this for the benefit of my leg. I was grateful, but didn't say anything.

Inside the elevator he pushed the button for the eighth floor. I wondered if I had misunderstood him when he said we were going to his place. Maybe he didn't mean his home, just another place he called his own.

The elevator ride was a short one since we only went up one floor. He stepped out first and automatically placed his hand in front of the doors so they wouldn't close on me. I had stopped inside the elevator and was looking around suspiciously. The doors had opened onto a small room that was painted a cream color. There was a beautiful door ahead of us. It was offset to the left of the elevator by a few feet. The door had beautiful molding around the frame and supported a small, brass peephole.

"Are you coming?" he asked in a droll voice.

"Yeah, I was just looking," I said. He smiled at me as I limped out of the elevator. With the first step I had tried to add a little extra swing to my hips, but decided against it.

Mr. White pulled his keys out of his pocket and opened the door into a huge apartment. This obviously was his home. If he just used it for another home, I couldn't even imagine what his main home would look like. My parents had a nice home and I always thought of it in terms of a mansion, even though it was actually pretty modest. With their worth, they could have had a much larger, more opulent home, but they were comfortable with what they had and I was glad to not have grown up in a museum home.

Mr. White had a similar concept to his home. It was within comparison to my parents' home. It was mostly open. We walked in and he shut the door behind me while I took it all in. I had stepped from the elevator to a cream colored carpet and then to a tiled entryway. There was a mirror to my right with a small table waiting for the keys or the mail to be set upon it. To my left was a door; I assumed it was a closet. There were three stairs leading down from the front door to the main part of the apartment. I struggled down them because there was no railing. Mr. White offered assistance, but I declined. I maybe should have taken it, but I didn't want to show any weakness. I had to lead with my injured leg because it hurt more to bend it than to put weight on it. I made it down one step at a time and it took me three times longer than it should have.

It gave me a chance to take in the sites. Mr. White had a plush dark gray carpet on the stairs and into the first room. If I had seen the carpet in a store I might have thought it would have given a room a gloomy feeling, but the feeling this room gave off was one of total comfort. The room was a recessed living room with a couch and entertainment system; which included a large screen television and a nice stereo and other electronics. It included some tasteful tables and cabinets and a couple of chairs that matched the fabric on the couch.

Color Me Grey

140

I could see into the kitchen too. It was on the other side of the living room. There were three stairs up into the kitchen area and it had a similar tile to the entryway, white with a gray marbled affect. The kitchen was a bit enclosed because the appliances need walls behind them, but there was a large island on the far end of the kitchen. The island was surrounded by high-backed barstools. The frames were metal and the backs had an intricate open design with loops and curls. The cushions were a light gray color that went well with the tile.

The apartment seemed to mainly be the two rooms. The far wall to my right had three doors. I could see into two of the rooms well enough to determine one was a bedroom and the other was a bathroom. Both were quite large. The third door was closed. Mr. White led me to that door, unlocked it and we went in.

The room looked like a spy's dream. There were TV monitors on part of one wall, with a couple computers available. It was a large area and felt cold, unlike the rest of the apartment. The room also held various other items such as filing cabinets and tables and chairs.

All the monitors and computers were turned off, so Mr. White walked to one of the computers and switched it on. He motioned me to the chair in front of it and said, "You can use this computer. I need you to track down these places and names for me." He placed the list Mr. Red had given him on the desk next to the keyboard.

"Okay," I said as I sat in the chair.

"I have access to satellite feeds all over the world and limited access to government data bases. Use what you need. Get to work and I'll go fix us something to eat," he said as he turned to go back to the kitchen.

I got to work on the places first. If I could access satellites without worrying about getting into trouble I might even be able to *see* if my dad was there. I just had to be in the right place at the right time.

Mr. White left the door open and I could hear him working in the kitchen. I hadn't even noticed I was hungry until he mentioned making us something. Now my stomach was growling.

I continued to check out all the different places while he made cooking noises in the background. I was able to figure out how to locate the position of every single person at any given place, but if they were inside buildings I wasn't able to determine whether or not one of these people was my dad.

Mr. White returned and said, "How's it going?"

"I don't know. I'm not finding anything that's helpful yet," I said, discouraged.

"Well come on out and we'll eat, maybe that will help," he said.

I stood up away from the computer screen and limped after him to the kitchen. He helped me up the stairs to the island, even after I had tried to pull away.

J.C. Phelps

"I don't want to stand around for half an hour while you try to get up the stairs," he said. "I'm hungry and I want to eat it while it's hot."

Mr. White had made us hot sandwiches with roast beef, sautéed onions and green peppers, all topped with Swiss cheese. I was about to reach for my sandwich when he reminded me of my antibiotics that Mr. Blue had given me.

I sighed and began to get off the chair.

"Where are you going?" he asked.

"I left them by the computer in the other room," I said tiredly.

"I'll get them," he said, already on his way.

During the brief moment he was away I realized I wasn't as affected by him as I had been before. Don't get me wrong, I still thought he was as sexy as they get, but I was able to control my thoughts away from the sex, for the most part. Sometimes, just a glimpse of him brought on a hot flash, but it seemed now he was becoming something more than just a face and a body. Up until today, I had never allowed myself to think of him as a person.

He returned just as I was philosophizing and wouldn't you know it, I got a hot flash. He handed me a single pill and set the bottle next to me. I swallowed it down and then reached for my food. This was better than the egg concoction he had made at the cabin and I finished it in no time. Mr. White had finished before me, but he was still sitting at the island. After I was done he took the plates and put them in the dishwasher. I waited until he finished so he could help me down the stairs again.

The dishwasher was humming me a lullaby when he came around to my side of the island. He helped me off the chair and back to my seat at the computer.

"Feel better?" he asked.

"A little," I said with a tired smile.

He reached over and brought another chair up to the desk. At first I thought he was going to sit in it next to me but he told me to put my leg up on it. Then he left the room again.

I decided I would try the people angle this time to see where it got me. I was able to find all the people on the list and print out all their information by the time he returned. He had hot coffee and a pillow to put under my leg. Then he grabbed another chair and sat beside me at the computer. I told him what I had done with the names.

"Good. I'll get them to Mr. Red first thing in the morning. How about the satellite pictures?" he said.

"I was just getting back to them," I explained. I took a sip of my coffee then pulled up the satellite on the computer. We sifted through all the sites and found nothing out of the ordinary. Mr. White went to the printer and we started reading through the people and the information that had come up for them. I also added Abdullah Salah and Abbas Salah, A.K.A., The Lion. Just for good measure.

Color Me Grey

With every name there was another location to check. Some of them were repeats of places we had already checked, so we skipped them. Abaas had a long list of locations displayed with the rest of his information. Someone had done their homework on this guy.

I put in each place systematically. The satellites would snap pictures as they passed over the coordinates. Mr. White had refilled our coffee cups twice and we still hadn't found anything. He had told me while we were searching it could take several days to locate anything that could be of help, but reassured me the other guys would help speed things along. We were looking at a small village that had come up next on The Lion's long list. We were using several different types of satellites to achieve one picture. It was complicated and time consuming. But with the different views, such as the high magnification lenses, infrared and sonic signatures we were able to see almost everything, inside and out.

In one of the buildings in this small village was a person sitting in a chair surrounded by other people. At first it didn't look suspicious, but then the pictures showed that the man in the chair was hit in the face and slumped over in the chair.

My dad! Was that my dad getting beat up? I hoped we had found him, but I didn't want it to be him in that chair.

"If that's my dad," I said with a shaky voice, but was unable to finish my sentence. I couldn't bear to watch it anymore and walked away from the screen.

Mr. White came to my side and said; "I know this has to be especially hard for you. This is what we do though." He walked me to the living room and we sat down on the couch.

"If you want out, I can do that for you, but I think you could be happy in this job. If you can cope," he said.

Tears had begun to well up in my eyes and I stopped them as soon as he spoke this last part. He was right. I couldn't be such a big baby.

"This is a special circumstance though. This is your dad, and it doesn't get much closer to home. I know you want to do all that you can to help, but I need to know if you think you can handle this. It may not have a happy ending. Are you going to be able to confine your feelings if you need to?"

We sat in silence for a short while and then I said, "I want to be a part of this. I don't know if I could stand not being a part of it."

"I understand that. I know you have the physical and intellectual ability to do almost anything this job might require of you, but do you have the emotional stability and control to deal with hard decisions?" he asked.

I took a deep breath and said, "I think I do. Dealing with my dad's kidnapping has been hard, but I think I've kept it together well enough."

"Yes, but now is when it gets rough. You might see and hear things that could be hard to contend with. I just want you to know what you're getting into."

J.C. Phelps

"This had the potential of happening before I fell into this job because of what my dad does. I guess it was just a matter of time. I'll be fine," I said straightening my back. Then I added, "I promise."

"I know you've had a lot fall in your lap these last few days. Your mother was attacked, your dad was kidnapped and you were shot. I want you to know I think you have faired better than most and I'm glad you're still interested in pursuing this with the rest of us. I had a lot of respect for Admiral Stanton before, but now that I know the kind of person you are, I have even more respect for the man. Now, with all that said," he said with a relieved look and a sigh, "we better get back to C.I.C. The rest of the guys will be here anytime. I don't want them to find us sitting here on the couch." He stood, smiled at me and offered me a hand up.

"C.I.C.?" I asked, taking his hand.

"The Central Intelligence Center." He pointed to the room that held the computers. "Sometimes we call it the war room."

We got back into the room and made our way to the computer screen that had shown potential. Mr. White told me I better put my leg up on the chair or I'd have hell to pay when Mr. Blue got here. The doorbell rang just then and Mr. White left the room.

I had my leg on the chair by the time Mr. White led all the men back to the war room. They all came together and made good time too. I was studying the screen and the figure in the chair when they walked in. Mr. White had been right about Mr. Blue. The first thing he said was, "I see you heard my instructions," and pointed at my leg.

The man in the chair hadn't moved, but the people that had been gathered around him had disbursed. It looked as if there were two of them standing guard not too far away. Mr. Red came up to the computer monitor and said, "Certainly looks like a hostage situation. This may be a break for us." He looked to me. "What did you find out on the names I gave you?"

I started to stand to get the paperwork and Mr. Blue said, "Sit. Tell one of us and we'll get what you want. You need to stay off that leg if you want it to be healed enough before we go after The Lion."

I pointed to the papers just on the other side of the desk and said, "Go after The Lion? I thought we already had him." Mr. Blue picked up the papers and handed them to Mr. Red who immediately began leafing through them.

Mr. White said, "We *retrieved* him for the government. They *have* him."

"Why do we need him if we know where my dad is?" I asked him.

"Can you be certain that is Admiral Stanton on the screen?" he asked.

"Okay, then what's the plan?" I asked.

Mr. White explained to me we would have to wait until they presented their demands in full before we could be certain on where they wanted to make the drop. We were going to avoid a trade, but it might come down to that. In the meantime, there were other methods they could use to find out if the man in the

Color Me Grey

chair was my father. They would send out an unmanned aerial vehicle, a UAV. Most importantly, we had to retrieve The Lion back to our custody. While that was underway we would find out if the man was my father. We couldn't waste time by doing one at a time, the two objectives had to be achieved as soon as possible.

I was rolled to one of the other computers so we could determine exactly where The Lion was located. According to what we found, he was still located at the small military installation where we had dropped him off. I accessed the plans for the small base and we all went to work on a plan to infiltrate and remove The Lion without alerting anyone.

It was well into the next day when we had formulated a plan that was sound. Breakfast and lunch had both been ordered in for us and Mr. Blue was very observant at my antibiotic consumption. He reminded me with every meal to take them. Then he changed the bandage for me too. If he hadn't, I may have forgotten because I was very involved in what was going on around me.

I was told I was to go on the job to retrieve The Lion. I understood why they didn't want to send me to find out the identity of the man in the satellite picture. If it was my dad I didn't know if I *could* control my emotions, especially if it was a bad scene. I made no argument against my assignment to The Lion. I wanted this to work and I didn't want to cause any trouble.

Mr. White had already set the UAV in motion. They were on their way to finding out as much information as they could for us. I guess it's a good thing to have contacts in the military.

If they were able to determine that the man in the chair was my father, then Mr. Brown was to take Mr. Green and Mr. Black a suitable distance from the location and they were to creep into the building and extract him. If they weren't able to determine that it was or wasn't my father, then the three of them would take a trip to the small village to find out.

They went to another side of the room to discuss the equipment they would need before they left. Mr. Brown was to monitor the UAV until they had positive confirmation and Mr. White and myself and Mr. Blue were to leave tomorrow morning. Mr. Red was to stay behind and hold down the fort. He was needed to keep an eye on my mom and to try to get more information from the man she had shot. He said he might take another shot at Abdullah Salah to see if he could give us more. Also, if the terrorists were to contact anyone, there would have to be someone here to take the call, so to speak.

Mr. Black gave me some pointers before I was escorted out of C.I.C. to the comfortable looking couch. Always the teacher, I thought. I hoped they would find my father out there.

Mr. Blue came up to me and said, "You need some rest before we go out. We'll be leaving in a few hours and I want your leg rested before we go."

"I am tired," I said. Mr. White walked up to me and handed me a cup of tea and told me to relax.

I didn't even finish my tea before I nodded off on the couch.

Chapter Seventeen

It was dark and quiet in the apartment when I woke up. Someone had given me a pillow and a blanket while I slept. I sat up on the couch and looked around. There were no signs of life.

The first thing that went through my mind was they had left me. I stood up and walked to the war room. The door was closed. I turned the doorknob and the door swung open. Inside it was dark, except for the light from a single lamp and the computer monitors. Mr. White and Mr. Blue were sitting at the desk with the lamp when I walked in. Abdullah Salah, my father's informant, was also sitting with them.

"I was just going to come get you up," Mr. White said. "Do you want to go over the plan again before we take off?"

"No. I think I've got it," I said. "Any word from the UAV?"

"We were unable to be sure that it was or wasn't Admiral Stanton and they left some time ago. They will contact us when they are in position. We will be leaving in about half an hour too," he said.

He handed me some clothes with instructions to change in his bathroom. I took them and went to change. I got to the bathroom and shut the door. I hadn't been in here yet and it was huge. It had a Jacuzzi bathtub and a shower with two heads. The tile was a cream color and covered the floor right on up the wall. Where the tile stopped a beautiful molding divided the walls from the ceiling. It had two sinks in a gorgeous marble topped vanity with a mirror that almost covered the entire wall. The toilet was set off to the side to allow for some extra privacy.

I proceeded to get undressed and wished I could take some time to sit in the tub. The thought to be uncomfortable changing clothes in a new place never even occurred to me. The clothes Mr. White had given me were all black and quite heavy. I found the reason for the weight when I pulled out a Kevlar vest. When I had finished dressing I checked myself out in the huge mirror. Not bad, I thought to myself. I need to do something with my hair though. It had been up in a braid like usual, but pieces were sticking out on the sides and in the braid itself. I took my hair out and re-braided it. There, now the image was complete. Ha, better than Lara Croft, I thought to myself. Except, I still don't have the accent.

J.C. Phelps

I made my way back to the war room, with only a slight limp. The rest had done wonders for my leg.

"Okay," Mr. White said looking me up and down, making my stomach do flips. "Let's get going."

The four of us went to the roof and all boarded the helicopter. It was dark outside and before we took off I asked Mr. Blue what time it was.

"9:32. That means we should reach our destination around 1:30, 2:00 in the morning."

The helicopter lifted off with Mr. White in the pilot's seat and the only conversation was Mr. Blue asking how my leg was doing periodically. It had begun to hurt like hell again, but I told him I would be fine.

We flew straight on toward the base and Mr. White radioed in for permission to land.

Mr. Blue reached back from the co-pilot's seat and handed me a pill and a canteen with instructions to take the pill. It didn't look like the huge antibiotics he had given me before.

"What is it?" I asked.

"A pain killer. Trust me, you'll need it because you can't limp around when we get there," he explained.

"It won't make me…weird, will it?" I asked.

"No, not until it starts to wear off in about eight hours. And then all that happens is you get real tired. By then we should be on our way back to the office, if not already there," he said.

I reluctantly put the pill in my mouth and washed it down.

"It should kick in soon," Mr. Blue said.

Slowly the pain subsided and I stretched my leg out, testing it. It was like I had never been shot. This is great, I thought. Maybe he'd give me more when we got back.

We received permission to land and Mr. White was allowed to set us down on the helipad with no problems. Mr. Blue remained in the cockpit as Mr. White exited. Abdullah and I jumped out the side door, heads held down. The three of us ran from the helicopter bent over until we cleared the main rotor of the helicopter.

No men met us on our way to the building like they had when we brought in The Lion. Instead the three of us marched up to the heavy gray door of the brick building unescorted.

There were two men, one on each side of the door like last time. Mr. White presented them with our papers that stated we had permission to interrogate The Lion with the assistance of his cousin. Mr. White had pulled a few strings and had been able to get us authorization to see The Lion at our convenience. The powers that be couldn't act on my father's behalf, but were glad to know we were. If they had only known what our plan was they may not have been so accommodating.

Color Me Grey

We stepped inside and I noticed a desk to my immediate left. Mr. White presented our papers to the man sitting there. While he looked them over, I looked over the building. I had memorized the plans, but the front office was smaller than I had expected. It contained two men, one desk, several monitors for the security cameras and three doors. We had just walked through the heavy gray door behind us and to my right was a bathroom door. Not far from the desk was another door that led to the holding cells and interrogation rooms that took up the majority of the building.

When the guard finished reviewing the orders, Mr. White relieved him and the other guard of their duties. I don't know why they listened to him, but they did, with sharp salutes. After the men had gone, Mr. White pointed toward the computer and then led Abdullah through the door toward the back of the building.

I was seated at the computer before the door shut behind them. I was to divert the camera's recording system while Mr. White had the two men together in the back. After I finished that job, I took out the portable hard drive I had brought along. I proceeded to download everything pertaining to The Lion.

Inside of fifteen minutes, I had finished my download and the two men were in the front office waiting for me. I turned the cameras back to record and we walked out the door.

"That didn't take long, sir," One of the guards directed at Mr. White.

"He didn't have anything to offer," he replied and the three of us marched back to the waiting chopper. We lifted off and were safely on our way home, mission accomplished.

Not until we were several miles from the installation did The Lion lift his head. Mr. White had traded him for Abdullah under the pretense we were going to free him. That way he would come with us without any trouble.

Mr. Red was on top of the building waiting for us when we landed. We all stepped out of the chopper and Mr. Red came to take custody of The Lion.

"What the hell?" Abbas, A.K.A. The Lion, screamed as Mr. Red handcuffed him.

"Relax," Mr. Red told him.

"You told me you were going to get me out of there," Abbas said with an accusatory tone to Mr. White.

"I did," Mr. White replied bluntly.

The first part of the plan had gone well and I was glad to be back so we could continue. We had a lot to accomplish yet. It was planned we would use The Lion to get my father back and hopefully have him returned to the installation before the switch off was noticed. Abdullah could maybe pull this off if the powers that be didn't want to talk with The Lion in the next few hours.

Mr. White escorted me off the elevator when we reached his floor. The other two men remained on the elevator with The Lion.

We entered the apartment and I asked Mr. White where they were taking Abbas Salah. He explained to me Suite 72 was an interrogation room and Mr. Red would begin his work there.

The war room had been locked again and Mr. White let me in. He said he'd make coffee while I examined the information on the hard drive.

I attached the external hard drive and started skimming through things. The video scenes of The Lion began with Mr. White walking him through the heavy gray door over a month ago. The Lion was quiet and calm when they placed him in his holding cell and remained that way for a couple of weeks. He didn't say a word or bat an eye.

I had slowed the video to normal speed whenever they had removed Abbas to one of the interrogation rooms, until it became apparent he wouldn't talk. This was my method for the first few weeks of his stay, then the screen went black. It startled me because for a second I thought I had maybe not gotten it all. I slowed the speed and there was audio available. It was obvious they were using unaccepted methods of interrogation by the thumps and screams present.

I had a hard time believing our country was party to this type of thing. They came and went to The Lion's cell about every fifteen minutes, making sure if he fell asleep it wasn't but for just a few minutes.

Mr. White came back in with our coffee and sat next to me. We kept skimming. The sleep deprivation went on for several days and when the tape went black we would stop to listen in. After just three of these sessions, The Lion began to sing like a songbird. He gave names and places, he admitted to atrocities of all kinds. I wondered if it all were true, some of the things he admitted affiliation to were terrible, unthinkable horrors.

Then the sessions became more subdued and he talked without *incentive*. The days became more recent and a man was introduced to The Lion as a psychiatrist. This man delved deeper into The Lion and made him bear his soul. After hearing his reasons for doing what he did, I wondered if he even possessed a soul. He had no sane reasons for anything. I had to wonder if he wasn't driven insane by the treatment he had received at the installation though.

"Can we believe all this?" I asked Mr. White.

"We are looking for specific information, it doesn't matter if it's all true or not," he answered.

"But, I'd say anything to get them to stop what they're doing!" I said, a little disgusted.

"It's just the way it is. Nobody can have that much detail about something they weren't involved with in some way. They have people sorting through it all, I'm sure," Mr. White said with no feeling in his voice.

"What are *we* looking for?" I asked.

"I imagine they will get to your father pretty soon. It would be nice if we could find something to discredit The Lion to his followers too. The government couldn't release this, but we can," he said.

Color Me Grey

"I'd think his craziness and the fact that it sounds like he gave up everyone should be enough to discredit him," I said.

"Maybe for us, it would be enough, but these people he has under his control are easier to manipulate. And once they have an idea in their heads, it's hard to get it out. What we need is something that would severely damage the reputation of The Lion," he said.

We continued with our search in the same way and got to the day my dad was abducted and slowed the video again so we could watch and hear the events. Before, there had been only a few people that had been in and out with The Lion, but on this day there was a barrage of people that came to the installation. The outside cameras captured several vehicles pulling through the main gates.

I looked at Mr. White and he wasn't surprised. He started telling me who the people were and what their role would be once they got their chance at Abbas. He was right with everyone. Some of the men went in hard with threats and blows; others were a bit subtler in their questions about where my dad could be located. In the end, Abbas couldn't tell them much. He didn't know anything about the abduction. At first he gloated and told them he better be released and returned to his country, but before long, he was blabbering on and not making much sense at all.

"Well, we've seen it all now. Let's get down to the office to see what Mr. Red and Mr. Blue have come up with," Mr. White said moving from the computer.

I followed and we went down one floor. We went to Suite 72 this time. It was a fairly large area. Upon walking in the door we were greeted with a very small room with a desk and not much else. There was a door behind the desk and Mr. White led me through it into a small hallway. To my right were five heavy doors with thin, sliding observation windows. In the middle of the hall was a door to my left. We went through that door and were confronted with two more doors directly in front of us and one on either side of us. Mr. White opened the door to my left and walked in.

It led to another small room with a two-way mirror that I could see an interrogation room with drab gray on the floor, walls and ceiling. Mr. Red and Mr. Blue were talking to each other and The Lion was slumped over in his chair. It reminded me of the man in the satellite picture. Mr. White knocked on the glass and we were motioned into the room.

I noticed when we got into the room Mr. Blue's doctor bag was sitting in the corner on the floor.

"So?" Mr. White directed to both men.

"He should come around in a few minutes." Mr. Blue said.

"I got names and places from him. Some of them are ones we didn't have before. This guy is crazy. One minute he's lucid, the next he's raving," Mr. Red said, shaking his head.

J.C. Phelps

"I gave him a sedative," Mr. Blue explained The Lion's slumped position.

Mr. Red gave me a new list of names and places to look up and said, "We've less than two hours to find something or we'll have to relinquish him." He nodded to The Lion still motionless in the chair.

Mr. White handed me the keys to his apartment and I headed back to the war room.

My leg had started to ache a little so I put it up on a chair as I began my search. We hadn't heard anything from the other men yet, so I thought I would look at the satellite picture of the man in the chair.

Nothing had changed there. The man was still in the chair and the other two men were apparently standing guard, so I went to work on the new names and places. This was a lot like data entry. I punched in the names or numbers and got a result.

I had only been at it for a few minutes when Mr. White returned.

"I got word from Mr. Black they're in position and waiting for us to tell them where everyone is located in the building. Pull up the UAV feed," he said.

I did as I was told and sure enough, there were two extra bodies right outside the building. The UAV was outfitted with several cameras so we were able to see everything in real time and because it was dark there, we were watching it all with the night vision camera. Mr. White began to describe the positions of the only other two men in the area. I saw the figures of Mr. Black and Mr. Green move around behind the building and slowly enter the room with the man in the chair. One of them went to him and lifted his head then let it fall back down on his chest. My stomach turned because it seemed as if the man might be dead. Then I saw them walk away from the building.

I looked to Mr. White with terror in my heart, making sure to keep the emotion from my face.

"Well?" I asked.

"Not him," he replied. "They're on their way back home."

I breathed a sigh of relief. I didn't know who the man was but was glad it was not my father.

"It's time to go. Did you come up with anything new?" Mr. White asked.

"No," I said.

"I think we have enough downstairs to give to his followers. You wouldn't believe how crazy he is. I don't understand how he got anyone to follow him, no matter how deprived they are. Some of the deaths in his own group were previously blamed on others but he just admitted to killing them himself. One of the men was his second in command and very well liked. Quite simply, he was the reason The Lion has supporters. No one knows he's dead either. I think it's enough to get the rest of the people to rethink why they followed him in the first place."

I was standing and ready to go. I was in a hurry to get my father back.

Color Me Grey

"I need you to stay here while the rest of us make the drop," Mr. White added, like it was no big deal.

"What? I thought I was going with you," I said a little upset.

"I need someone here to tell us what to expect. You will be following The Lion's signal. Mr. Blue gave him more than just a sedative. While he was out, he put a small transmitter under his skin. We cannot lose track of him."

"What about my father?" I asked.

"We will retrieve him."

"How do you know they will have him to trade?" I asked.

"We'll make sure everything works out right. This is the only logical way this can happen, Ms. Grey. I am not going to stand here and argue with you. You don't have the experience to go out into the field for this one. I don't want to jeopardize the Admiral's safety just to give you more experience. Do you?"

"Of course not, but…" I said and left it hanging because I couldn't think of a reason why I should be able to go.

He left me with the location of the drop and a phone number. I was given the headset he had been wearing when he spoke with Mr. Black. We tested it to make sure I could hear him and he could hear me. I was to call the phone number only if things turned bad and no body else was left to make the call. Under no circumstances was I to lose sight of The Lion.

I pulled up The Lion's signal on one computer. Then I pulled up the other UAV that Mr. White had sent to do the local surveillance on a different computer. The sun had been up for about an hour so I first looked at the site with normal vision. It was a house on a bad side of town. The house looked like it hadn't been lived in for years. The windows were boarded up and there were no signs of life anywhere except for one man on the badly weathered porch. He was standing by the front door, smoking a cigarette. Mr. White and I quickly surveyed the area so he knew the layout and then we switched to the infrared. The heat signatures came up brightly on the screen. There were three other men in the building. I assumed one of them was my father! They were all positioned toward the back of the house in one room, sitting fairly close together.

"I've got what I need. Now you need to keep an eye on things and let me know if anything changes," he said.

"Got it," I replied as he walked out to go rescue my dad. In less than fifteen minutes I heard Mr. White's voice in my headset.

"Are you still reading me?" he asked.

"Yep," I replied.

"You're going to have to learn how to talk on one of these things," he said. "Everything the same?"

"No changes," I reported.

J.C. Phelps

"Everyone has an ear piece, but only I have a microphone. I will contact you only if I need to. You are to report the position of the enemy every thirty seconds once we're on scene. Is that clear?" he asked with a military tone.

"Yes, sir," I replied.

"We should be there in about half an hour," he said and then it was quiet.

I watched the house, alternating between the infrared and normal video. Nothing changed until after Mr. White contacted me to tell me they were arriving. I watched Mr. White exit the van we had used the other night. I was surveying the entire area and saw there were three warm bodies just across the street in another run-down house. I would have reported it to Mr. White, but I also saw The Lion's signal in the same building. Ok, I know where the good guys are. I have to keep track of them. I made a mental note of the body shapes and positions.

Mr. White was escorted inside the house by the man who had been standing on the porch. I watched them walk to the back of the house. Two of the three men that had been seated stood. I assumed the one still seated was my father.

Mr. White handed one of the men something that looked like a briefcase. I couldn't hear anything, but it seemed the man was agitated.

Just about then another vehicle pulled up and three other men got out. I notified Mr. White of the situation but he didn't acknowledge. I heard one of the men say, "I don't care what you have here. You won't get Stanton until I have The Lion!" He was angry and yelling.

"I have him available." Mr. White calmly informed the man.

"I want him now, White," the man replied.

"You'll get him. My word is good. I just want you to watch that tape first," Mr. White said.

I saw the two of them go to another room in the house where the man opened the briefcase. I heard The Lion ranting and then heard him admitting proudly he had murdered several different people. The Lion went into detail about how he had killed every one of them and how the victims had reacted. It was sickening.

This took a little time and I had been surveying the area and reporting as expected. One of the three men had begun snooping around at the van, another was walking around the house and another was on his way to the house across the street. I reported every movement. I didn't get any verbal response and was afraid they weren't hearing me, so I started to give the exact positions of every person starting with the three men snooping outside. Finally I saw The Lion's signal moving inside the other house. I looked back to the infrared screen and saw one of my guys, either Mr. Blue or Mr. Red escorting The Lion away.

Mr. White then said, "Now, do you still want The Lion for the same reasons?"

"I'm going to beat him to death," the man replied softly.

Color Me Grey

"Good, as long as we're clear," Mr. White said. "When I get the Admiral safely out of here, I will call with The Lion's location."

"That doesn't work for me," the man said.

"You either give me the Admiral or I take him," then added, "*we all just want to know our positions in life.*" I assumed the last was meant for me so I gave his position first and then the other man's position again. Just then a gunshot sounded from a distance and I saw the man fall to the floor.

Mr. White walked over to him and helped him up. "That was a warning, the next time will be fatal. My man *never* misses," he emphasized. He helped the man, who was cursing, back to the room that contained my dad.

I was scanning the area and had seen the shot being fired through the infrared camera. It had come from where the Lion had been just moments ago. Then the shooter moved away quickly.

One of the men reached down and helped up my father. Mr. White turned and led them all outside. The three men that had come in another vehicle were placed at different intervals around the van and house.

"When I get the Admiral safely in the van I will hand over The Lion," Mr. White explained.

"You better not screw me, White," the man said as Mr. White helped my father into the van and drove away.

"Is my dad okay?" I said into my microphone.

"Stay focused," Mr. White's voice was firm. Then I heard my dad's voice. "What?" He said.

"I'm sorry, sir. I wasn't speaking to you," Mr. White replied.

It was quiet except for my voice reporting the positions every thirty seconds. Then I heard Mr. White tell my dad, "I need you to call in the whereabouts of The Lion to your people. Tell them to hurry or they might not get him back alive. You may want to have the local police pick them up because they have people in the area."

Then my father's voice came over the microphone. He was barking orders like he was a drill sergeant. When he was finished, Mr. White's voice came on again.

"Ms. Grey, don't lose The Lion's signal. Mr. Blue, Mr. Red, you can release the dog," then I heard him call the man at the house.

"Company's on the way," he said. I didn't know if he was warning the guy or telling him to expect The Lion. I watched The Lion walk out of the house and Mr. Blue and Mr. Red started to leave through the back door. A couple of the men had circled around the house that contained our guys and The Lion. I almost missed telling Mr. Red and Mr. Blue about the two men making their way to the back door because I was watching The Lion emerge from the front of the house. Quickly I gave the positions of the two men coming at them. They stopped in their tracks and waited for them to come. I was torn between

J.C. Phelps

watching the tension unfold at the back of the house and the violence directed toward The Lion in the front.

Slowly the two men advanced and I reported every step. Eventually the two men reached my guys. It was quick. Mr. Red and Mr. Blue had them down before they even knew what hit them. As far as I could tell it was painless, but fatal. They made a quick escape after that. I continued to report the scene until the police showed up. The Lion was beaten severely, but he wasn't dead. The men scattered, but they did manage to catch two of the three still standing along with The Lion.

Mr. White's voice came through the earpiece again telling me I could stop my reports. He told me he was taking my dad to get my mom and he was going to take them both home. He said I should wait for him there and then he would take me home to see them both.

I was grateful and exhausted. The pain killers had worn off quite some time ago and if it hadn't been for the excitement, I would have been asleep long ago.

It was about two hours before Mr. White returned to pick me up. I had fallen asleep and he woke me gently.

"Are you ready to go?"

"Yeah. Do you need anything, or can we just go?"

He shook his head no and we headed for the outside world. I shut the door to his apartment and was inside the elevator ready to get home.

"How are they?" I asked as we rode down to the garage.

"They're both just fine," he replied.

We were quiet the rest of the ride to my house. Mr. White dropped me off at my parents' door and waited until I got inside before he left.

My Mom and Dad were sitting close together on the couch watching TV; neither of them looked any different. Mom stood from the couch when I walked in and Dad looked away from the TV in my direction.

"I knew you could do it," my mom said as she walked up to me and gave me a huge hug. "I knew you wouldn't let us down."

I hugged her back, realizing how much I had missed her and Dad. The tears welled up in my eyes. I didn't need to be in control around them. They were, after all, my parents. The people I could go to if I had problems, the people I tell all my joys and sorrows to.

Mom, shhsh'd me and Dad came to our side. We all had a group hug with Mom and I crying and Dad holding us together.

"I missed you guys," I said after the extended hug. We all felt a bit uncomfortable, but I didn't care. "I didn't realize how scared I was until I saw both of you sitting there," I sniffled.

"We're all okay now," Dad said while Mom went to get her and I some tissues.

The next few days were spent at each other's sides. I think we were all just a little afraid to let a family member out of our sites. We didn't do much, just

Color Me Grey

hung out and talked. I found out Abdullah Salah, A.K.A Mr. Jones, had been an informant for my father for years. My dad had helped him find a place to live in the United States and helped him set up his own business in exchange for information.

I told them about the time I had spent at the cabin and about my buck. I was becoming more proud of that darn thing as the days passed. My mother strutted around with pride and Dad tried to talk me out of working for White & Associates. I seriously considered it for a few minutes, but told him I had never been happier in my life. I was doing things I loved and learning to love new things.

"Well, if you want to do it, then I guess you better do it," was his final comment on the subject.

We talked more about White & Associates and I learned quite a lot more about the people I was working with. My dad was full of information on all of them. Some of it he willingly gave up, other things he said he'd save for another day. I certainly didn't get any names out of him, just personality descriptions. He seemed somewhat fond of Mr. White, but tried to hide it.

A couple days into our bonding, dad began to work again. The government had let it be known The Lion was in their custody and he was to stand trial for his crimes. In which country he would stand trial first was an ongoing discussion. I didn't really care.

Things had begun to get back to normal. Mom was back to her woodworking projects and Dad was back on his computer. I had been sleeping at the main house on the couch and decided it was time for me to return to the guesthouse.

I walked home and flopped on my couch. I sat there for about an hour, just taking in the secure feeling I had when the phone rang. I jumped off the couch at the sound and realized I really didn't feel all that secure.

"Hello?" I said into the receiver.

"How are things?" It was Mr. White.

"Good," I said.

"Are you ready to come back to work?" he asked.

"Yeah," I said. "I think I am."